weep *(verb)*

1. To cry or
2. To discharge or ~~

Introduction

Behind the Weeping Walls is an interactive story with a difference because nothing here at Metamorphosis is quite what it seems and that includes both the Retreat AND you!

This is no ordinary spa break — you're not going to return home fully detoxed with glowing skin; in fact, you might not even return home at all — this is a rescue mission!

Your sister disappeared a year ago and the last known sighting was at Metamorphosis. Since then, you've been trying to discover just what is going on at this Retreat in the German forests at Bad Brocken. You have your suspicions and now it's time to face the truth. It's not going to be easy though. Finding your sister is just the start of it; convincing her to leave her new family, then extracting yourselves from their clutches is going to be much harder. You may well go behind the weeping walls, but will you ever find your way back? And just what will you have to sacrifice to do so…?

You might escape if you can piece together the clues and figure out the puzzles. To help you with that, there are record sheets on the next pages. Here, you can document all the codewords, scores, objects and hints that you collect. Well, it's the least I could do…

Metamorphosis: Daily Itinerary

Each activity or class has a different instructor every day, so each one is a different experience — some useful, some not so... With this schedule, you can make a note of the activities you've already experienced during your stay at Metamorphosis.

Class & Activity Schedule

1. Kayaking, BodyFit, Spinning, Colonic Irrigation

2. Facial, Massage, Reflexology, Acupuncture

LUNCH

3. Hypnotherapy, Hiking, Yoga

DINNER

4. Flotation Therapy, Lecture, Group Therapy

Metamorphosis

Metamorphosis Score

Whether or not the Retreat manages to transform you as it promises, depends on your METAMORPHOSIS score. You start at **zero**, and depending on if you add or subtract points, could end up with a negative or positive score. Whether that is a good or a bad thing, well, you'll just have to wait and see.

Starting Score: 0,

Final Score:

Items and Information

You will collect items and information as you go, so it makes sense to record those somewhere safe.
You wouldn't want to forget anything, now would you?

_____

_____

_____

_____

_____

_____

_____

_____

_____

_____

_____

Runestones

You will also be collecting runestones. You may see only the markings or hear only the name. Sometimes, you may get both, but you should use this list to make a note of all the stones you **collect**. And keep in mind that <u>type</u> AND <u>quantity</u> are important. For example, if you collect three Isa, no Raidho and one Sowilu runestones, your list would be marked like this:

ᛁ	✓✓✓	Isa	I
ᚱ		Raidho	R
ᛋ	✓	Sowilu	S

Some of them may prove to be highly important during your time at Metamorphosis…

Rune Symbol	✔	Rune Name	Alphabet Symbol
ᛗ		Ehwaz	E
ᚴ		Laguz	L
ᚺ		Hagalaz	H
ᚦ		Thurisaz	X
ᛞ		Dagaz	D
ᛁ		Isa	I
ᚱ		Raidho	R
ᛋ		Sowilu	S

Rune Symbol	✔	Rune Name	Alphabet Symbol
ᛘ		Mannaz	M
ᚷ		Gebo	G
ᚠ		Fehu	F
ᛟ		Othila	O
ᚢ		Uruz	U
ᚹ		Perth	P
↑		Tiwaz/Tyr	T
ᛒ		Berkana	B
ᛋ		Jera	J
ᚲ		Kauno	C K Q
ᚾ		Nauthis	N
ᛝ		Ingwuz	N
ᛉ		Algiz	Z
ᛇ		Eihwaz	Y
ᚨ		Ansuz	A
ᚹ		Wunjo	V W

The Submerged House — Floor Plan

And if you make it this far, you will definitely need to know your way around the submerged house.

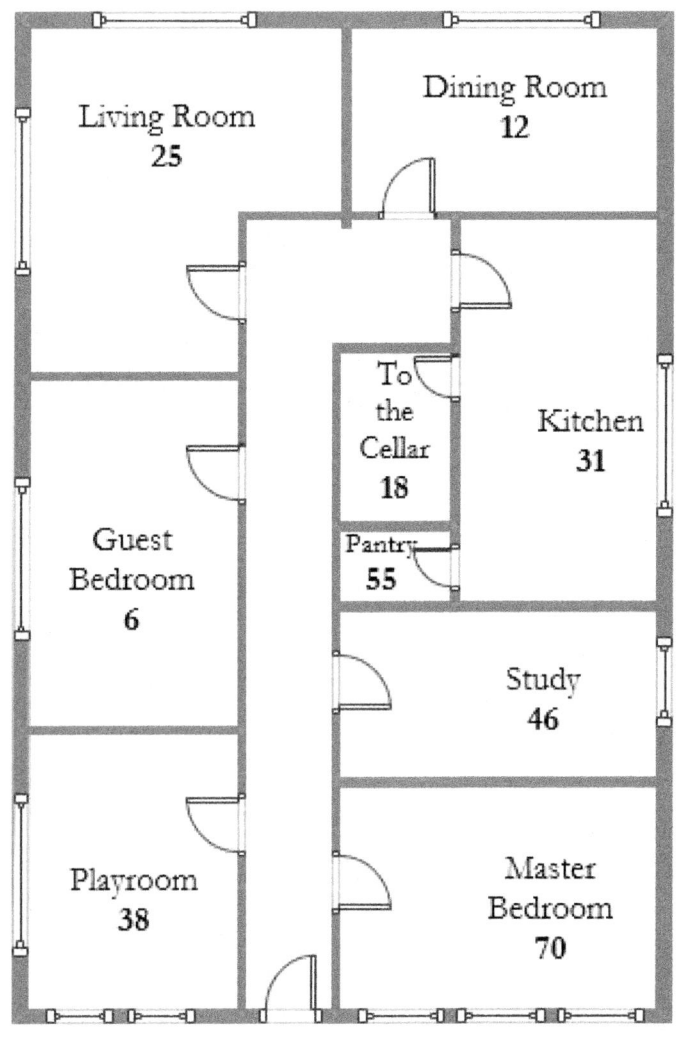

Keypad Symbols

If you do make it behind the weeping walls and beyond, you will need access to certain rooms or be able to activate devices. If you can figure out which numbers are represented by the keypad symbols, you should record them here for safekeeping.

🕷	🦅	🌳	🦋	🍄

Codewords

Finally, there are codewords for you to tick, so you can track your unique pathway throughout the entire saga.

BANDAGE	☐	SOOT	☐
BETRAYAL	☐	STROBE	☐
BLUEPRINT	☐	TEDDY BEAR	☐
BURNT FEATHERS	☐	TOXINS	☐
CHRYSALIS	☐	TRANCE	☑
FREEDOM	☐	TYR	☐
GASTROPOD	☐	ULTRAVIOLET	☐
GREY WOMAN	☐	WALPURGIS	☐
POLLUTION	☐	WITCH	☐
REVELATIONS	☐	WUNJO	☐
SCUBA GEAR	☐		

BEHIND THE WEEPING WALLS

Right then, you've collected your suitcase from the baggage carousel, gone through Customs without a hitch and now it's time to head to Metamorphosis. You've still got a long journey ahead of you, though, so while you do that, we'll find out what's going on elsewhere and catch up with you later…

Prologue

The Machinator quickly convened The Cluster.

'This latest set of experiments has yielded good results. It seems their desire to have self-control is so strong that destabilising their reality through time loops is sufficient to bring them in line. We don't need your prion to render them compliant — they'll do it themselves!'

Al-Kutbay bristled at this last comment. He was proud of that prion and still thought that it had potential, he just needed to factor in the propaganda and information flow surrounding it. How was he to know that the internet would be so influential?

'Yes, yes. We've heard it all before. "Fear is the only way. You have to make them scared, and then they'll do anything you ask of them." That sounds like you've just taken Jezebeth's idea, and we all know how *that* turned out!' He spat back at The Machinator, who fumed before making an effort to calm down.

In a conciliatory tone, The Machinator replied, 'That's a fair point, although confusing them into submission isn't quite the same as terrifying them with a mass murderer, who's Hell bent on whipping out their organs! Anyway, thanks to Jezebeth going completely off-script and amusing herself with her own tricks, lies and puppets, we'll never know.'

'I said, we shouldn't trust a demon, but did anyone listen?' a low voice floated down the table from the shadows. 'Horror will never be a long-term strategy. You have to appeal to their inherent selfishness and greed. Offer some treasure that they want and they'll salivate like dogs until they get it. You seem to think that humans are complex and deep. Have you forgotten how they behave when the latest shiny gadget is released? When will you finally accept that I'm right?'

'You'll get your turn, Cai-shen, but we have a schedule to keep to! And while we're on the subject, where is Freyja? It's her turn next!'
The Machinator looked expectantly at the others. There was an awkward pause, then with a slight clearing of the throat, Cai-shen said, 'She left.'

'Left?! What do you mean she left? We are The Cluster. She can't leave!'
There was a hint of hysteria creeping into The Machinator's voice, and the others looked nervously around. Finally, Al-Kutbay spoke up.

'We argued. She objected to my treatment of the babies in The Crucible. She said that I crossed a line. I disagreed and told her that she was being too emotional, so she left.'

'She had a point…' murmured Cai-shen and Al-Kutbay half-raised in his seat to defend himself. The Machinator held a hand up to try to restore order and said firmly, 'Enough! The experiments must be suspended until we find her, or she returns. This needs to be our priority now. Agreed?'
The rest of The Cluster nodded their heads but looked pessimistic. Where does one even begin to start searching for an aggrieved God? She could be anywhere…

PART ONE: THE RETREAT

1

Not only is your shoulder hurting from dragging the suitcase, but you're starving hungry and are starting to get the sneaking suspicion that you've taken a wrong turn. For the umpteenth time, you wish that you'd simply got a taxi from the airport and sod the cost!

But it would've been quite a cost. This holiday retreat is buried deep in the forests of Bad Brocken in central Germany and since you landed, you've spent hours on a train, then a bus and now on foot, and you're still stuck on this lonely road with dusk stealthily encroaching.

Just then though, you see a glint far ahead.

'Oh please, let this be it,' you mutter and with a sudden spurt of energy, quicken your pace towards the distant lights. Suddenly, there is a distinct rustle in the undergrowth nearby. You gasp and spin round but can see nothing lurking amid the trees. *Just a normal woodland animal,* you tell yourself. *It's not like you're in the Amazon rain forest!* With a determined sigh, you set off but a few steps later, you hear something again. A crack of dried branches underfoot and a faint snort.

The lights are closer, and you're sure that it is the Retreat, so all you have to do is stop messing about in a German forest and simply get there! You swap hands and lift the suitcase up, planning to jog from here without the noisy, rattling wheels but then it happens again. A quick crackle of feet over leaves and a deep throaty grunt. It's getting closer! With your heart beating fiercely, you search desperately and finally, you see it: A faint plume of moist breath and... 'Oh God' you whimper. The yellow eye stares right back at you, unblinking. For the longest time, you stand there frozen, watching for any hint of movement, of danger. Occasionally, the eye blinks slowly but doesn't take its gaze off you for a second. There is a sense of huge bulk to the animal, and you can just about discern a coarse grey coat, but what type of animal it is, you can't even begin to guess. However, a more pressing question is: What should you do now?

If you want to put your suitcase down and walk cautiously into the forest to investigate, turn to **158**. However, if you'd rather carry on towards the Retreat, even though that means turning your back on the creature, turn to **97**.

2

You watch as the others reach into their pockets. You see clumps of hair, toenail clippings and used tissues and they deposit these items in front of the opening. One man even urinates against the tree, which you'd think would be frowned upon, this being a sacred tree and all, but the guide smiles warmly and you hear her mutter, 'Mother Amber is grateful for your offering.'

Feeling more than a little perturbed, you and the rest of the group hike back to the Retreat without mentioning what's just happened. It's time for dinner, so turn to **56**.

3

'How long have you been here?' you shout out, as you glide towards the others.

'A couple of days now; it's wonderful,' one woman says. 'It's giving me a totally new perspective on my life. I've been so superficial, but now I'm starting to see where my old life was draining my energy.'

You smile in the hope that it disguises your cynicism — is she joking? But no, she seems to be serious, and the rest are nodding in agreement. Another one pipes up, saying, 'Me too. I'm considering never going back home. Devoting myself to Mother Amber is looking like a more solid life choice than working the rat race. It may seem strange at first,' he says directly to you, 'but I'm right. If you really examine it, you'll see how meaningless your current life is.'

After a while of them waxing lyrical about Metamorphosis, you pluck up the courage to interrupt and ask, 'Have you seen the roofs in the north of the forest? Do you know what it is?'

'Yes, it's a small village. There's a general store and a few villagers left. Apparently, they didn't like the arrival of the Retreat, but the truth can be hard for some to take.'

'People need to surrender themselves to the purity. To absorb it and become one with it. It's good that they left. Their negative energy was conflicting. Now everything is radiant.'

This is all delivered with smiles and faraway stares, which convinces you that your suspicions are accurate, but how could they have been brainwashed so quickly? They've not even been here a week yet! Suddenly, you become aware of the grey-haired woman shouting for you to return to the shore, and once you've safely deposited the life jacket and kayak, you head on back to the Retreat.

You still have enough time for another activity before lunch, so what do you fancy?

A facial	Turn to **6**
A massage	Turn to **198**
Reflexology	Turn to **67**
Acupuncture	Turn to **90**

4

There is a fluffy white towel already laid out and a disembodied voice tells you to get undressed and shower. When you arrive somewhat nervously at the tank, there is a kindly looking grey-haired woman waiting for you. If you have ticked the codeword GREY WOMAN, turn to **173**. If not, turn to **127**.

5

As you enter the room, a staff member hands you a runestone and says, '**Fehu** is represented by amber and will bring you fulfilment.' You take the stone, grab a mat and go towards the back of the room — well, you're not exactly good at yoga, so it makes sense to be discreet with your downward dog! You sit cross-legged and look around as the other people take their places. Did you do the BodyFit class this morning?

Yes   Turn to **163**
No   Turn to **54**

6

As soon as you lie on the treatment bed, you can feel your eyelids drooping. The whale noise music plays as cool fingers sweep your hair out of the way and a gentle voice says, 'You look tired. Didn't you sleep so well last night?'

You look up and see a grey-haired woman gazing down. You nod and mention the long trip and the nightmare. She sighs sympathetically and applies a hot compress over your face.

'The heat will open up your pores to help the treatment work at a deeper layer. Nightmares are a problem here. Do you want to talk about it?'

You frown underneath the steamy hot flannel as you wonder whether to trust her or not. If you have ticked the codeword GREY WOMAN since you arrived at Metamorphosis, turn to **122**; if not, turn to **185**.

7

Feeling sure that there must be a secret switch behind the gemstones, you methodically push each one. When the stone with the rune markings falls out again, you scrutinise both it and the bare stone it once occupied, but there is nothing. Absolutely nothing! You kick the hearth in frustration. What now? Time must be running out — someone is bound to catch you in here before too long. You could now try to break down the back wall (turn to **133**) or do something with the cauldron (turn to **76**).

8

After a couple more breaths of the crisp country air, she perks up and her colour returns to normal.

'Sorry about that,' she says, absent-mindedly stroking her belly. 'I'm pregnant. The morning sickness isn't nice, but it's so exciting. I was worried that I was a disappointment because I couldn't transform, but now Mother will be so proud.' You eventually utter 'Congratulations' but deep down, you feel disturbed by her words. Still, this might be a good opportunity to find out more about this mysterious Mother, but what would be a useful question to ask? If you want to know if Mother is looking forward to being a grandmother, turn to **84**, but if you'd rather know whether she and the baby will stay at the Retreat, turn to **26**.

9

She frowns, thinks for a second, then replies, 'I presume it's just a marketing slogan. You know, because caterpillars metamorphosise into butterflies.'

An old man walks in at that moment, nods and says, 'Guten Tag', which stops any further conversation. You're getting too hot now anyway, so you leave, have a quick cold shower then head to the relaxation room (turn to **27**).

10

Your eyes light up when you see her, although you are careful not to give anything away in front of the Metamorphosis lackey who's carrying the breakfast tray. The grey-haired woman says, 'You need to take normal food now to build up your strength and heal fully — no juice detox for you!' Well, you're not complaining. The tray has croissants, raspberry jam, a pot of coffee and a strange stone with a hole in the middle. Well, that's odd, but you see the grey-haired woman wink conspiratorially, so slip the stone out of sight. Make a note that you now have a **Drudenstein**. Next, the lackey goes to the bathroom to check on something. As soon as the door closes, the grey-haired woman whispers, 'You must take care of a butterfly tattoo and you must remember the word OVER — it's all important. And take this.' In the nick of time, she hands you a scrap of paper, before the lackey returns, saying that he'll bring more towels later.

It would seem that you are to remain in your room this morning to continue recuperating, but now that you're alone again, the first thing you do is examine the scrap of paper. Turn to **53**.

11

After a minute or two of an uncomfortable silence, you say, 'Hello, this is my first day here. Are you OK? You look…well, a bit sad.' As icebreakers go, it's not great, but she does attempt a weak smile and replies, 'Hi, I'm Mishka. Welcome to Metamorphosis.'

The unconvincing tone is accompanied by a solitary tear that trickles down her cheek. You reach over, grip her hand and whisper, 'Tell me what's wrong. I know something is up here and maybe I can help.'

'No one can help me, but you can help yourself by getting out and don't let them take any part of you.'

'What? What do you mean by that?'

'They harvest whatever energy or matter they can get from people — sweat, emotions, …even faeces. It all goes to Mother Amber.'

You attempt to say 'what' again, but you're just too confused by all of this. Faeces? How does anyone use faeces? Unfortunately, this pause has given Mishka time to think and now she starts to rise from the table saying, 'I shouldn't have said that. Forget everything I

said. And here…' she hands you a beautiful topaz with a strange marking on it. 'It's **Eihwaz**, the rune that represents Yggdrasil. It's no use to me. Not now.'

At this moment, a harassed looking waiter materialises at your table, and Mishka uses the diversion to leave. Once the waiter has gone to fetch your dinner, you place the rune into a pocket. Make a note that you have met **Mishka**. and while you're at it, **subtract 2** from your METAMORPHOSIS score. Now that's all done, you can enjoy dinner — here comes the waiter again. Are you on the normal diet (turn to **70**) or the juice diet (turn to **118**)?

12

You hobble down the serene corridors into the spa and a young woman greets you with a smile. When you tell her that you'd like the colonic irrigation, she beams like it's the best news she's ever heard.

'Oh, what a great decision. Many people take a few days to buck up the courage, but it's such a deep cleanse and a perfect way to start your transformation.' Once you've changed into a surgical gown, you enter the treatment room and lie on the bed as directed. A different woman is waiting for you and she attempts a smile, but it wouldn't fool anyone — she's hunched over and looks like she's got the weight of the world on her shoulders. As she talks through the procedure, you can hear the sadness in her voice, and suspect it's not necessarily because she's spending the day sluicing out intestines!

The next forty-five minutes are not exactly pleasant, but it's not as awful as you thought it might be. Every now and then, the woman even becomes slightly animated as she sees things floating down the tube and mutters, 'Yes, that's better out. These toxins are blocking your energies,' but it still sounds unconvincing, as if she's reading from a script. You are lying on your back having your abdomen massaged while the water flushes around, when the woman looks quizzically at you then almost jolts in recognition.

'You look just like your sister!'

'You know her? You've seen her?' you ask. The woman nods with a whimsical expression on her face.

'Oh yes, she's one of the Favoured Few. She went behind the wall a few weeks ago... I shouldn't have said that.' She looks back over her shoulder and winces, but then becomes professional again and pulls the tube smoothly out of your body. Despite your efforts to get her to talk about your sister, she refuses to acknowledge your questions. It would seem that this session is done. **Add 3** to your METAMORPHOSIS score. On your way out though, you notice a shallow bowl filled with stones all marked with the same

 symbol. The woman is busy tidying up for the next client, so do you call out to her and ask her about the stones (turn to **55**) or simply take one as you leave (turn to **104**)?

13

The words given by the Grey Women were hangOVER, hangMAN, hang GLIDER and hang FIRE. Even in a high stress, pressure situation, you have the mettle to come out on top. That said, actually lifting the cast-iron cauldron is another matter, but with a lot of grunting, swearing and a prolapsed disc, you manage to hang the black chalice over the hook in its rightful position. There is a satisfying click as the weight triggers the mechanism and a door in the side of the fireplace opens up. You have just enough time to smile at your success when there is a skin-crawling scurry from the depths of the cauldron and a huge spider emerges then crawls halfway up your arm. You are frozen in horror and can only stare at this monstrous arachnid. It is the size of a dinner plate and has thick furry legs and twitching fangs. Your life appears to be in imminent danger, although there is a moment when it looks at you, then at the opening, then back at you. It seems confused and this might be the only chance you have to save yourself. If you have an Algiz runestone, turn to **168**, but if you don't, turn to **143**.

14

You smile breezily and say, 'Hello, do you speak English?' The man looks slightly panicked at this and shakes his head frantically.

'English. No.' And then he points in the direction of the Retreat, 'You, *Urlaub*? Er, holiday?'
You nod, but your smile vanishes as he proceeds to mime people crying then says, 'Bad place. *Man hört immer das Weinen und…*' He's quite animated now and gestures with his hands having a huge belly. 'Many *Frauen da…Wie sagt man dazu? Schwanger*?' He looks hopefully at you, as if you might be able to translate, and he repeats the same gesture with his hands. It clicks and you shout: 'Ah, pregnant!' Unfortunately though, neither of you have the vocabulary to continue the conversation, so after a few seconds of awkward nodding and smiling, you opt for a quick 'Okay then.' But do you point at the door then wave goodbye? You could, then immediately head back to the Retreat (turn to **130**), however, if you haven't done so already and you'd like to browse around the shop before you go, turn to **105**.

15

'It's a runestone. We use them for divination and to help with our transformation. That one is **Fehu**. It represents wealth, prosperity and cattle.'
She speaks these words in a flat monotone, then blinks and continues in her normal, sad voice: 'It's linked with the stomach,' and gestures to the plastic tubes. *Oh well, that explains everything, doesn't it*, you think, but then she adds, 'You can take one, if it calls to you.' Not having much experience with shouting stones, you're not too

sure about that, but the night porter did say that runes could be important, so you put it in your pocket.

You still have enough time for another activity before lunch. Seeing as you feel a bit bloated and full after the colonic, the idea of someone massaging you is not appealing, so that leaves you with either a facial (turn to **6**), reflexology (turn to **67**) or acupuncture (turn to **90**).

16

Forty-five minutes later and you are lying drenched in sweat on the mat. Due to your prime position, you had to keep going with the endless lunges, deadlifts and squats, whereas normally, you'd have done a few, then stopped to have a long swig of water. As you lie there, the grey-haired woman approaches. She pretends she's concerned for your wellbeing, then whispers to you.

'Beware the Aufhocker! Beware the weight on your shoulders! They climb on so they can spy and kill for her, but they don't like toxins. That puts them off and they won't settle. And most important is the word GLIDER — please remember it!'

Before you can even think of replying, she has moved on. **Subtract 2** from your METAMORPHOSIS score and then clear the equipment away. If this is the first time you've noticed the large wooden wardrobe with a bird mosaic and **12 rubies**, then your curiosity is piqued, and you are tempted to take a closer look.

If you do, turn to **103**, but remember **this** section number, so you can return here after your examination.

Following a quick shower, you are now ready for the next activity. Would you like to have a facial (turn to **175**), a massage (turn to **113**), reflexology (turn to **37**) or acupuncture (turn to **85**)?

The woman is now happily paddling along, pointing out a heron's nest, so you edge your kayak closer to the grey-haired woman and ask, 'Is there a village near here? I thought I saw some buildings in the north of the forest.'

She nods and explains that there are still a few villagers and one general store, but most have left. She leans closer and says quietly, 'They went when the Retreat was set up.'

'What?' You look directly at her, but her expression tells you to ask no more. However, after a few seconds, she relents and whispers, 'You look just like your sister, and I know why you're here. The Grey Women will help and protect you, and we're not only at the Retreat, we're behind the wall too.' She then cups her hand around her mouth and whispers in your ear.

'W-w-what?' you stammer, but at that moment, the nervous woman flips her kayak over, so your instructor paddles swiftly over to retrieve her from the lake. Tick the codeword **GREY WOMAN** and **subtract 1** from your METAMORPHOSIS score. That seems to end the session, so you head silently back to the shore thinking about what she said. Although it makes no sense to you now, you have just received some very good advice.

If you find yourself in a situation where **"your life appears to be in imminent danger"**, you must **add 50** to the current section number and turn immediately to the new section.

The grey woman has her hands full with the guest, who is still spluttering, so you return to the Retreat. There is enough time for another activity before lunch, so what do you fancy?

A facial	Turn to **6**
A massage	Turn to **198**
Reflexology	Turn to **67**
Acupuncture	Turn to **90**

18

You stand up and regale the group with your story. It is designed to sound true enough so that no suspicion is raised, but far enough from the truth so that no connections can be made. With your voice breaking at just the right moment, and a tear to be wiped from your cheek, it is an acting *tour de force*. As you gracefully accept the sympathies and utterances of support, you can just see, with your height advantage, a small red light blinking in the corner of the room. Is that a camera recording the session, you wonder? There's no way that you can investigate it, but if it is a camera, then you're glad that you lied through your teeth. Thankfully, the session is now over — **subtract 1** from your METAMORPHOSIS score — so you head to your room. Before you fall asleep though, there is one crucial question: Did you acquire a Drudenstein today? If you have at least one, turn to **124**, but if you don't have any, turn to **59**.

You're right, she does want to talk about this. She drapes a warm towel over your bare shoulders, sighs again, then says, 'Oh, the entrance that takes you behind the wall is beautiful, I've heard. That's why you must have transformed, so that you're worthy to go through. There's an arch of aquamarine, although I've heard you must be careful of...'

Before she can finish that sentence though, Belinda winces and cowers. It's as if something has sunk its claws into her neck...

The massage finishes then, and she hands you a  runestone saying '**Nauthis** is for patience.' Next, she shoves the oily, damp towels into some plastic cylinders and sends them away through the pneumatic tubing. Maybe it's an efficient laundry system...

Add 1 to your METAMORPHOSIS score, put the runestone in your pocket, then make a note that you have met **Belinda**.

You could now go to the sauna (turn to **114**) or to the quiet relaxation room for a lie down (turn to **77**). However, if neither of those options appeal, you can simply head to the dining room — it is nearly lunchtime after all (turn to **92**).

20

Just before you turn the light out and brace yourself for another night ruined by nightmares, you wonder if there is anything that could stop them. If you heard about a drawing that might give you a good sleep, then you should remember that a number was associated with it. **Multiply** this section number by the shape's number, then turn to the new section.

For example, if someone recommended that you draw a 9-sided shape in your bedroom, you would turn to 180 (20 x 9 = 180).

If not, you will have to simply grit your teeth and get through it. Turn to **152**.

21

You groggily get out of bed, grope around in your discarded clothes and eventually find the strange stone with a hole in the middle. You place it underneath the pillow and are unconscious almost instantly.

You wake after a solid 9 hours of deep, uninterrupted sleep and if it wasn't for the throbbing ache in your buttock, you'd be leaping out of bed to face the day. You gingerly walk around the bedroom to test the extent of your injury. Not bad, but sore enough to limit your activities, which is just what you didn't need at this crucial point. Damn that boar! At that moment, the door opens and a grey-haired woman enters. She is carrying a tray, and it would seem that Metamorphosis will continue the special treatment. Have you ticked the codeword GREY WOMAN? If you have, turn to **180** but if not, turn to **68**.

22

Once your life jacket has been checked, you're directed to an orange kayak. It's a snug fit but also a relief to take the weight off your ankle. Gripping the paddle, you push off from the bank. There are three other guests and the young man from Metamorphosis in your group, and you all set off across the smooth surface of the lake. The man is nattering on about the beauty of nature and how it restores your energy, but it's important that 'we give some of ourselves back,' so you steer your kayak towards the guests instead.

By the way, did you choose the room that overlooks the forest (turn to **128**) or this lake (turn to **51**)?

23

The young woman who enters looks both nervous and sad. She brings a tray with delicious smelling food and nods subserviently, asking if there's anything else you need. However, when you say no and dismiss her, she hesitates then recites, 'The grey-haired woman told me to tell you that toxins like nicotine or caffeine stop the Aufhocker from getting on your shoulders, but above all, you should remember the word MAN.'

You stare dumbfounded, a small piece of bruschetta clenched between your teeth, but before you can say 'What?', she has gone. Nevertheless, the good news is that the Metamorphosis staff think your injury isn't as dramatic as they first thought, so with the instruction to 'take it easy', they are leaving you to your own devices. If you were able to work out the room number in the grey woman's clue, you should sneak there now, but if you couldn't work it out, you can either have a facial (turn to **45**) or reflexology (turn to **121**).

24

The spartan room contains a chaise-longue and an armchair in which a grey-haired woman sits. She smiles expectantly at you, so if you have ticked the codeword GREY WOMAN, turn immediately to **183**. If not, continue reading.

You're not sure what she's waiting for, so you simply recline onto the chaise-longue and smile back. Eventually, she holds up an amber pendant and swings the stone back and forth in the traditional manner. After a few minutes of this, you sit on the edge of the chaise-longue and say, 'I'm sorry but this isn't working, so I should just go.' The grey-haired woman smiles and points at the clock. To your shock, you realise that an hour has passed. An hour! If you had previously ticked the codeword TRANCE, you should now erase that, as the grey-haired woman has reversed the hypnotic suggestion. Not only that, but she also hands you yet another runestone with a meaningful wink. This one is **Algiz** and will protect you against evil. You get the feeling that she's trying to help you, so tick the codeword **GREY WOMAN**. Still feeling confused, you thank her and leave — time for dinner! Turn to **56**.

25

The shopkeeper tells you the price in colloquial German but sees your blank expression and points at the display on the till: €3.45. Make a note that you have bought a **large bag of chilli-flavoured nachos**. It would seem that the language barrier has definitely put paid to any further chats with the man, so you leave and head to the narrow footpath that will take you safely back to the Retreat. Turn to **130**.

26

She chews a lip as she considers your question, then says, 'Well, of course, I shall stay here. This is my home, and everyone here are my family now. The baby is pure and innocent and has only love in its heart, so it will go behind the wall to be with Mother, but I will stay here until I can transform. I'm hoping the birth will help with that. Now, it's time for the needles to come out.' So, swiftly and efficiently, she plucks the needles out of your skin and places them with a strange reverence into a thick plastic cylinder which then disappears with a whoosh up a pneumatic tube and out of the room. **Add 1** to your METAMORPHOSIS score, then get dressed and leave the treatment room.

You could now go to the sauna (turn to **114**) or to the quiet relaxation room for a lie down (turn to **77**). However, if neither of those options appeal, you can simply head to the dining room — it is nearly lunchtime after all (turn to **92**).

27

After a few minutes of lying there, you get bored, so decide to simply head to the dining room. However, as you pass by the magnificent fireplace with its arch of blue gemstones and **3 fire irons**, you hear an erratic, light tapping noise. You move closer to the hearth, closer and closer until you are perched on the edge, and still the tap-tap-tap noise continues. It sounds like tiny fingers but strangely, it seems to be coming from inside the cauldron. You are leaning over to peer inside it when you suddenly notice the huge web strung between the cauldron and the mantel. Urgh, you nearly stuck your face into it and…the thought occurs to you. Is that what the tapping is? Not tiny fingers but tiny spider feet!? You spring up, pressing your hand against the side of the fireplace for leverage and one of the mosaic gemstones becomes dislodged. *Good grief, this is a catalogue of disasters*, you think, as you catch the stone and try to wedge it back in. As you do that, you notice the marking on the other side — it's another rune, but there's no way you can keep such a valuable stone. Still, it might be useful to note *where* you found this particular one.

Once your DIY is finished and the fireplace looks intact again, you go to get your lunch. Turn to **170**.

28

You look at the options and don't feel particularly inspired by any of them. To be honest, you'd rather just sit in front of a television with a large glass of wine, but you can't lose sight of the goal here — you came all this way to rescue your sister from Mother Amber and her cult, so you can't give up now! What will you do then?

Listen to a lecture on runestones   Turn to **38**
Attend a group therapy session   Turn to **94**
Spend an hour in a flotation tank   Turn to **186**

A short while later, you reach the lights and see a sign:

Despite being glad to finally arrive, those words fill you with foreboding. Convincing people that they need to change definitely rings alarm bells, and you wonder just how close your suspicions are to the truth. Still, if you want to find that out, you need to play the part, so you enter the quiet lobby and approach the check-in desk. The young man behind the desk has a conventional hairstyle and an emerald-green butterfly tattooed on his forearm. He looks up with a welcoming smile and says, 'Guten Abend,' before noticing your expression and switching seamlessly into English.

'Good evening, are you checking in? May I take your name?'
The formalities and paperwork are completed quickly and efficiently, then the clerk asks if you would like a room with a lakeside view or one overlooking the forest. Well, that's a surprise, normally you don't get a choice in hotels. You mention this, and the clerk smiles.

'Mother Amber bestows her blessings that your experience here is transformative. She says that your choice of room reflects the choice on your life journey.'
You smile, although it isn't convincing. You have no idea what he's talking about and, more importantly,

who Mother Amber is. However, you won't get a key unless you answer, so which room do you prefer?

With a view of the lake   Turn to **194**
Overlooking the forest   Turn to **101**

30

You sneak into the relaxation room and stride across to the fireplace with its 3 black, sturdy fire irons. However, if you've ticked the codeword TRANCE, you must immediately turn to **164**. If not, continue reading.

So far, so good. Doubts start to flicker though, as you stare at the fireplace and see no obvious entrance or door, but you're not ready to give up at the first hurdle! What will you try in order to open the Gateway?

You could try to break down the back wall with a poker (turn to **133**), change the position of the cauldron (turn to **76**) or press the aquamarine gemstones (turn to **7**).

31

The grey-haired woman bows her head respectfully, then rapidly wipes your face clean.

'Well, we're done here. You have lovely skin. Make sure you wear sunscreen though and try out the yoga session today. I think you'll find that especially…helpful.' And with that, you are efficiently bundled out of the room.

You could now go to the sauna (turn to **114**) or to the quiet relaxation room for a lie down (turn to **77**). However, if neither of those options appeal, you can simply head to the dining room — it is nearly lunchtime after all (turn to **92**).

There's no such thing as free will at Metamorphosis. Whilst they still use the tried and tested methods of love bombing, isolation and scare tactics, this cult has another trick up its sleeve with Mother Amber. All she needs is your matter and energy, and then she has control. Every time you gave up your thoughts or let them take parts of your body — yes, even the dead skin and faeces — it gave Mother Amber more and more power over you. As much as you try to step through the Gateway, you can't. Someone else is pulling your strings now, and you are helpless to stop yourself from walking away from the fireplace and sitting on a recliner. Before long, you feel a heavy weight climb onto your shoulders and perch there with long, sinewy arms wrapping around your neck. It's difficult to breathe but when you look in the mirror opposite, you can see nothing. Sharp claws start to tickle your throat…

Who knows what Mother Amber has planned for you or how long she will play with you — her latest toy — but your heroic rescue mission has definitely ended here.

You might think that this means you have a free choice of all the available activities, but that all depends on whether someone else is pulling your strings...

If you have ticked the codeword TRANCE, turn to **147**.
If you haven't, turn to **65**.

34

You glance at the available options for the afternoon activity, but you must also factor in the state of your ankle before you decide. If you twisted it last night, turn to **125**, but if it is strong and uninjured, turn to **88**.

35

You take the path through the forest and go past the wide, old tree. There are still **8 mushrooms** standing proudly around the opening, and from a cursory inspection, you can see a bird's nest, discarded cocoons and even a small lizard leg lying around the trunk. Bizarre! You arrive at the shop, but it is an old woman behind the counter today. She doesn't speak any English and simply frowns as you peruse the shelves. If you bought anything yesterday, it may be foolish to buy the same thing again, but it is your money after all, so you can spend it however you like. What's important though is that you make a note of whether you purchase a packet of cigarettes, a butterfly-style skin transfer or a bag of chilli-flavoured nachos — and this time, you have brought enough money, so if you're feeling cavalier, you could buy all three! Once that is done, you trek back to the Retreat in time for dinner. Turn to **56**.

36

The man is now happily paddling along, pointing out a heron's nest, so you edge your kayak closer to the grey-haired woman and ask, 'Is there a village near here? I saw some buildings in the north of the forest.'

She nods and explains that there are still a few villagers and one general store, but most have left. She leans closer and says quietly, 'They went when the Retreat was set up.'

'What?' You look directly at her, but her expression tells you to ask no more. However, after a few seconds, she relents and whispers, 'You look just like your sister and I know why you're here. The Grey Women will help and protect you, and we're not only at the Retreat, we're behind the wall too.' She then cups her hand around her mouth and whispers into your ear.

'W-w-what?' you stammer, but at that moment, the man flips his kayak over, so the woman paddles swiftly over to retrieve him from the lake. Tick the codeword **GREY WOMAN** and **subtract 1** from your METAMORPHOSIS score. That seems to end the session, so you head silently back to the shore thinking about what she said. Although it makes no sense to you now, you have just received some very good advice.

If you find yourself in a situation where **"your life appears to be in imminent danger"**, you must **add 50** to the current section number and turn immediately to the new section.

The grey woman has her hands full with the guest, who is still spluttering, so you return to the Retreat. There is enough time for another activity before lunch. Reflexology is off the cards today — there's no way someone is waggling your swollen ankle around, so what do you fancy?

A facial	Turn to **6**
A massage	Turn to **198**
Acupuncture	Turn to **90**

You enter the reflexology room and see the grey-haired woman sat the with hot towels and oil at the ready. She eyes you with a piercing gaze as if she is expecting something from you… If you have ticked the codeword GREY WOMAN, turn immediately to **73**. If not continue reading.

She starts the foot massage and although it is pleasant, there is a moment when a pain shoots through you, and the grey-haired woman asks worriedly, 'Have you got any problems with your shoulders? Any pressure?' When you say 'no', she looks extremely relieved. What's that all about?

Feeling like a hypochondriac, you start to ask if she can sense illnesses, but at that moment another staff member enters the room. He stomps across to a cupboard without even apologising for the intrusion. The grey-haired woman gestures to you that the session is finished, then says, 'Can I help you, Youssef?' He is now rummaging in the first aid box and mutters that he needs a plaster. You have no option but to leave them to it, but as you are going the woman hands you the now ubiquitous gift of a runestone.

'**Othila** will guide you in knowing when to withdraw,' she explains, and despite that making no sense, you pocket it with the others. It seems like she is trying to help you though, so tick the codeword **GREY WOMAN**. It's not long before lunch, although if you like, there is still time for a quick sauna (turn to **144**) or a meditative rest in the relaxation room (turn to **27**).

You take a seat at the back, so you can watch everyone else and wait for the lecture to start. If this is the first time that you've seen the strange, old wardrobe with a bird mosaic and **12 rubies**, you will be intrigued, no doubt. Quickly go to investigate it (turn to **103**) but remember this section number so you can return in time for the presentation.

A young and very earnest woman begins clicking through her PowerPoint slides, showing you the different markings. Apparently, the runes are so valuable that Odin stabbed himself in his heart then hung upside down from the Tree of Life for nine days just to understand them. She reels off the entire alphabet with each letter's runic counterpart. You manage to conceal a huge yawn, as she talks about the divination of the runes, claiming that Dagaz indicates gateways and Perth protects against spiders. With this, you hear someone gasp and mutter nervously, 'The Guardian!' It is a member of the Metamorphosis staff, who quickly exits the room, but despite that reaction, the woman continues and hands out a different rune.

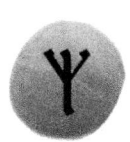

'This is **Algiz** and it protects against evil,' she announces. It is an ominous end to the lecture, but you have no qualms about pocketing the stone then heading with relief to your room.

Following a relaxing bath, you slip into bed, but as it was last night, the important question is whether you have a Drudenstein or not. If you do, turn to **161**, but if you are still lacking a stone with a hole in it, turn to **20**.

You're no botanist, but after pulling a couple of them out, you're pretty sure that the shells belonged to snails! That's a first! Either Metamorphosis is highly avant-garde or the snails have a particularly special meaning. You're about to finish the investigation when you notice a stone nestled amongst the shells. It has a single hole in the middle, and you're not sure whether it has been drilled through or if a creature from the far-distant past was responsible. It looks intriguing though, so you pluck it out of the water, drop it into your pocket, then quickly look around the room to see if anyone had witnessed your thievery. You're in luck — all the others seem to be asleep. Even the fish appear to be unfazed by it all. Make a note that you have acquired a **Drudenstein**. You leave the room, get dressed and head for the dining room. It's lunchtime and you are starving! Turn to **92**.

40

Once your dinner is served — vine-baked camembert with pepper-cranberry jelly and fennel salsa — Phillip continues.

'I don't know where the Gateway is, but I sometimes wonder if the mural is it. It's where Mother Amber lives under the lake, so maybe it's magic!' He stares with despairing hope, then starts crying again. Another staff member discreetly sidles over to your table and hooks a hand under his arm. With very little fuss, Phillip allows himself to be dragged away. **Subtract 1** from your METAMORPHOSIS score and then finish your delicious meal.

You still need to select an evening activity to keep up your ruse of being an ordinary spa guest, however, you must first turn to **140** if you have ticked the codeword TRANCE. If you haven't, turn to **28**.

41

She steps softly towards you, her eyes never leaving your face. When she's close enough to straighten your hips — an action that nearly topples you over — you whisper, 'Can you help me?' She smiles in response, says loudly, 'Make sure your knee is over your ankle,' and then, much more quietly, 'Mother Amber is not what you think she is. She is much more powerful than that, and she has acolytes too. If you get behind the Wall, you will see them, and then you will know the truth of the horrors and the sacrifice, all in the name of Freyja. And what's most important is that you don't forget the word OVER.'

You look at her with confusion and alarm, but she glides over to the next person and avoids you for the rest of the session. Nevertheless, you should **subtract 1** from your METAMORPHOSIS score. You can't get to speak to her without raising suspicion, so you leave, get a quick shower, then head to the dining room.

The place is bustling. In fact, there are only two seats free. Do you want to sit with another Retreat visitor (turn to **196**) or a Metamorphosis staff member, although she is looking rather sad (turn to **11**)?

42

You find the path that cuts through the forest and trek towards the shop. Before long, the path forks, and you see a huge, old tree at the junction. The trunk has a narrow opening cut into the bark, and you creep closer to peer into the interior of the tree — if you breathed in, you might even be able to fit… You stand up, shaking your head. What were you thinking? Squeeze into a tree? And why are there **8 mushrooms** with red and white spotted caps circling the opening? You can see a marked stone lurking under the cap of one of them, so go even closer, pick it up and pocket it. You're not sure what this is — it all looks very odd, indeed, but what's even more bizarre is the bird's nest, discarded cocoons and even a small lizard leg lying around the trunk. It's as if a strange variety of animals had gathered on this spot simply to discard parts of their bodies. There's no explanation for this, so you carry on to the shop — maybe someone there will know about this tree. However, when you arrive, it is clear from her frown that the old woman behind the counter does not speak English. You peruse the shelves, which have an eclectic mix of stock, and while you can buy whatever you like, it's important to note whether you purchase a packet of cigarettes, a butterfly-design fake tattoo or a bag of chilli-flavoured nachos. Unfortunately, you only brought a small amount of money with you, so you can afford just <u>one item</u> — record which one you buy. Once that is done, you trek back to the Retreat in time for dinner. Turn to **56**.

43

Looking over at the people supping their juices, you feel relieved with your decision. Oh sure, they're probably bursting with health and energy, but that is not enough to sustain a hamster! You're not so smug though, when your own breakfast arrives: A bowl of amaranth muesli with toasted seeds, blackberries and almond milk. Great! But at least you have coffee, which is more than those poor detoxers have. However, you make sure that you act as if you're enthusiastic about all this. After all, it's important that you raise no suspicions about the real reason you're here…

Next you go to the activities board in the lobby and look over the options for the morning. Before you make your selection though, you need to factor in whether you have a twisted ankle or not.

If you tripped over a tree root last night, turn to **60**, but if your ankle is happily free from injury, turn to **177**.

After ten minutes along the narrow road, you see a pathway cutting through the forest and take it. Surely this will lead you to the buildings. As you walk, you can feel the tension ease, and you simply enjoy your surroundings — the birdsong, the green leaves, the snakeskin…What? With an expression of both curiosity and disgust, you peer closer at the translucent, papery skin. Your astonishment grows as you realise that this reptile was huge. It could eat a whole sheep and still have room for extras! *That's not right*, you think, *snakes don't grow this big in Germany.* And then you notice the velvety white antlers discarded in the undergrowth and the scattering of grey feathers nearby and wonder what was going on here. It was as though a weird variety of animals had gathered on this spot simply to discard parts of their bodies. When you look around for more, you realise that you've reached a fork in the path: one track leads back towards the road, the other presumably to the buildings. You don't find any more animal detritus, but you're feeling unnerved, so you decide to put a spurt on and carry on with your journey.

It is a bit disappointing when you finally arrive at the small collection of houses and one store, but you might as well go in and see if you can find anything out. A bell tinkles as you enter, and the man behind the counter nods at you. Do you want to speak with him (turn to **14**) or browse around the shop (turn to **105**)?

You enter the small spa room and ease yourself into the chair with a slight wince. The man, who's about to do your facial, introduces himself as Phillip then promptly bursts into tears. Naturally, you ask what the matter is and between sobs, he tells you about the mural of the submerged house with the **5 windows** in the dining room.

'Yesterday the blue cats were there, but this morning, I saw my girlfriend. She transformed and went behind the wall when she was pregnant. I know she had the baby — a little boy — I saw her with him…' At this point, you interrupt to ask how he's seen her, and he snaps tetchily, 'Through the mural! It's how Mother watches us. Anyhow, this morning, I saw her, but she didn't have the baby and was crying. Something's happened but I can't get to them. Mother says I'm not ready to transform yet.' Phillip starts wailing now, so you pat his arm and utter sympathetic platitudes, but he suddenly throws his head back, makes a horrible choking sound and tries to grasp at something round his neck. Only as far as you can see, there's nothing there…

'Are you OK?' you ask when the episode seems to be over. Phillip shakes his head, now shocked into silence, then wipes his face and opens the door. As you hobble out, he whispers, 'Sorry, sorry. Forget I said anything.' Well, that's unlikely. Indeed, you should make a note that you have met **Phillip** and **subtract 1** from your METAMORPHOSIS score. You potter around the gardens for a while until dinner time, but now you have to decide whether you want to eat your meal in the dining room with the other guests (turn to **98**) or request room service (turn to **79**).

46

Maybe a walk in the forest will help you to think more clearly, so you go to the meeting point with a bottle of water and your hiking boots on. Have you recorded the name João since you've been at the Retreat? If you have, turn immediately to **137**, but if not, continue reading.

The guide checks her bag, adjusts her glasses, then gives everyone an **Algiz** runestone, saying, 'in case Hagalaz is in the forest.' Most of you exchange worried glances and some even start to ask, 'What is...?' but the guide dismisses the fussing with a wave of the hand and sets off. Half an hour later, you find yourself near a wide tree with a narrow opening in its trunk and you pause.

'Are these mushrooms poisonous?' you ask, pointing at the **8 red and white fungi** that circle the opening. The guide shrugs, then says, 'But the Tree of Life or Yggdrasil has many stories about it. Folklore dictates that you should give an offering to it.' There is a nervous laughter, but she gestures to the Tree and you realise that she is deadly serious. If you have ticked the codeword TRANCE, turn to **83**, but if not, turn to **2**.

47

'My sister has gone missing, and I'm sure she was here. She was...vulnerable, upset, and I don't know where she is now.'

Morris nods and says, 'Well, she wouldn't be the first person to disappear following a stay here. This place definitely needs investigating but not just for brainwashing activity. There's something strange going on here too. Have you had nightmares yet?'

Without giving you a chance to answer, she carries on.

'Something's happening to trigger it. Maybe they put drugs in the juice, or it's all a suggestion, because when I got this stone and slept with it under my pillow, the nightmares stopped. Weird, eh? And have you noticed how all the ones smiling and going on about transformations have a butterfly tattoo? Definite cult behaviour! I reckon that if you're planning to go undercover to find your sister, you need to get one too.' Finally, she pauses and takes a breath. You give her a quizzical look. 'We're in the middle of a forest! I can't get a tattoo even if I wanted to!'

'No, no, but maybe you could draw one on with a marker pen or buy a transfer design. I know it's not a brilliant solution, but it might fool them.'

At that moment, a harassed looking waiter materialises, asks for your order and politely requests that Morris vacates her seat seeing as she's finished her meal. She agrees but once the waiter has gone, returns and quickly says, 'I'm leaving tomorrow so I don't need this, but you might if the nightmares don't stop. Keep it hidden though. These lot are bound to confiscate it as contraband if they see it!' She hands you a bottle of fizzy energy drink, then dashes off. She's right about the drink though. With the amount of sugar and caffeine packed into it, the Metamorphosis folk would have a seizure if they caught you swigging it. Make a note that you have an **energy drink** and also **subtract 1** from your METAMORPHOSIS score. Now that's all done, you can enjoy dinner — here comes the waiter again. Are you on the normal diet (turn to **70**) or the juice diet (turn to **118**)?

48

You act thoroughly engrossed in wiping down the mat but out of the corner of your eye, you watch as the instructor chats with the other first-timers. They are beaming gratefully at her, seemingly pleased to have been singled out for this attention, and she is radiating so much positivity, you swear the air is crackling with it. Eventually, she gives them something — a small object, which she presses into their palms — then leaves. There's nothing else to do here, so you head to the changing room, but there is still time for another activity before lunch. What would you like to do now?

A facial	Turn to **6**
A massage	Turn to **198**
Reflexology	Turn to **67**
Acupuncture	Turn to **90**

49

Understandably, with all the other people around, she is unable to talk to you, and she doesn't want you to talk either. Even if you did want to share in this therapy session — which you most definitely don't — she refuses to give you an opportunity to speak. So instead you've heard all about Nasreen's indecision with her job and whether to take a promotion, Robin's conflict with his elderly but still domineering father, and Michelle's desire to find inner peace, whatever that meant. And then it's over. You stack your chair with the others but on your way out, the grey-haired woman pulls you over to hand you a runestone.

    '**Kauno**. The rune that represents the expulsion of darkness,' she says, loudly, then whispers, 'Put the black chalice in its rightful place. You may well *find* the Gateway, but you can't *open* it until the chalice unlocks it. And above all, remember the word MAN.'

You commit this useful, albeit confounding, advice to memory, then head with relief to your room. **Subtract 2** from your METAMORPHOSIS score. Following a relaxing bath, you slip into bed, but, as it was last night, the important question is whether you have a Drudenstein or not. If you do, turn to **161**. If you are still lacking a stone with a hole in it, turn to **20**.

50

You sneak into the dining room and stride across to the mural of the submerged house with 5 windows. This morning the woman and her blue cats have vanished, but there is a tiny yellow teddy bear nestled in the pond weed that's growing in the doorway. It's all too weird — it must be the Gateway! All you need to do now is work out how to actually pass through a solid wall…

Unfortunately, you are so caught up in your plans to break the laws of physics, you don't notice the Metamorphosis receptionist arrive. He grips your arm and escorts you out of the room, murmuring, 'We know who you are. We know who your sister is and you are not welcome here. Take the taxi and never come back!' You struggle and try to resist, but there are more people standing guard in the lobby and glaring threateningly at you. You don't stand a chance! They've even hurriedly packed up your things, so without any further ado, you are taken to the airport.

You could return later — in disguise, maybe — and at least then you might have a better idea of where to find the Gateway but for now, your rescue mission is over.

51

'How long have you been here?' you shout out, as you glide towards the others.

'A couple of days now; it's wonderful,' one woman says. 'It's giving me a totally new perspective on my life. I've been so superficial, but now I'm starting to see where my old life was draining my energy.'

You smile in the hope that it disguises your cynicism — is she joking? But no, she seems to be serious, and the rest are nodding in agreement. Another one pipes up, saying, 'Me too. I'm considering never going back home. Devoting myself to Mother Amber is looking like a more solid life choice than working the rat race. It may seem strange at first,' he says directly to you, 'but I'm right. If you really examine it, you'll see how meaningless your current life is.'

After a while of them waxing lyrical about Metamorphosis, you pluck up the courage to interrupt and ask, 'Have you seen the odd thing protruding from the lake? It looks like a spire.'

'Yes, it's a submerged village. They flooded the area a few decades ago, apparently. Taking it back the way Nature intended.'

'It's just a question of viewing your existence in a completely new way. If you want to transform, then you too can wash away all the old compulsions and be refreshed.'

This is all delivered with smiles and faraway stares, which convinces you that your suspicions are accurate, but how could they have been brainwashed so quickly? They've not even been here a week yet! Suddenly, you become aware of the grey-haired woman shouting for you to return to the shore, and once you've safely deposited the life jacket and kayak, you head on back to the Retreat.

You still have enough time for another activity before lunch. Reflexology is off the cards today — there's no way someone is waggling your swollen ankle around, so what do you fancy?

A facial   Turn to **6**
A massage   Turn to **198**
Acupuncture   Turn to **90**

52

She turns to scoop the water over the hot rocks, and you can't help but notice the huge tattoo on her back. Actually, it looks more like a branding than a tattoo — a black spiral between her shoulder blades — and you feel compelled to ask her a question. What do you enquire about?

Why the butterfly is significant   Turn to **9**
Who honours the yew tree   Turn to **69**
How she got the spiral marking   Turn to **179**

53

> The room number has three digits and is less than 200.
> Two of the digits are prime numbers.
> The sum of the first and the third digits is double the middle digit.
> All are odd numbers and none are repeated.
> The order goes from smallest to greatest.

You read it once, twice and on the third time, shake your head with barely concealed annoyance. For Heaven's sake, if she wanted you to go to this room, why didn't she just write the room number on the scrap! Why all this cloak and dagger nonsense? And what's so special about this room anyway? You're not going to find that out now though. The Metamorphosis staff are attentively seeing to your every need, so there's no opportunity for sneaking around. Instead they insist that you rest in your suite and offer you either a jigsaw or a mindful colouring book for your entertainment. You smile through gritted teeth but decide to go along with it for now. It's best to not raise any suspicions and you can always try to find the room later. So how will you fill your morning? With a 1000-piece jigsaw (turn to **156**) or some soothing colouring in (turn to **109**)?

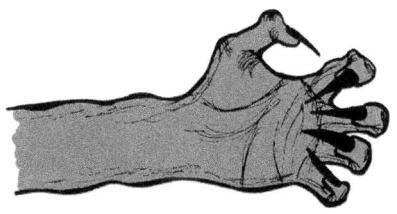

54

It seems to be a typical crowd of earnest yoga lovers and when you scan the room, you notice the huge and incongruous wardrobe at the back. It is a beautiful piece of furniture but entirely unsuited to a gym room. You go over to it , while the instructor — a grey-haired woman — is fetching her mat and chatting to some of the group. There is an image of a bird of prey on the cupboard door. Its yellow legs, fierce talons and grey feathers are designed in mosaic and surrounding this is a circle of **12 rubies**. You give the handle a little pull out of pure nosiness, but it is locked. What on earth could be inside? As captivating as it is, you have to return to your mat as the lights are dimmed and the instructor starts the session.

You go through the manoeuvres of cat/cow, cobra and forward fold, and are trembling in warrior I, when the instructor approaches you. If you have ticked the codeword GREY WOMAN, turn to **41**, and if you haven't, turn to **95**.

55

'It's a runestone. We use them for divination and to help with our transformation. That one is **Fehu**. It represents wealth, prosperity and cattle.'

She speaks these words in a flat monotone, then blinks and continues in her normal, sad voice: 'It's linked with the stomach,' and gestures to the plastic tubes. *Oh well, that explains everything, doesn't it*, you think, but then she adds, 'You can take one, if it calls to you.' Not having much experience with shouting stones, you're not too sure about that, but the night porter did say that runes could be important, so you put it in your pocket.

You still have enough time for another activity before lunch. Reflexology is off the cards today — there's no way someone is waggling your swollen ankle around and seeing as you feel a bit bloated and full after the colonic, the idea of someone massaging you is not appealing. So that leaves you with either a facial (turn to **6**) or acupuncture (turn to **90**).

56

You enter the dining room, and your hand darts to your mouth to conceal the involuntary gasp. You are fairly sure that you're not going mad, but that leaves you with the inescapable conclusion that the mural is changing. Now, there is a woman — possibly the owner of the previously huge amber eye — and she is stood in the doorway of the submerged house, holding one blue cat. Another feline is perched in one of the **5 windows** and you'd swear blind that all of them are watching you. Trying to act normal, you turn away and look for a space to sit, but what really matters is which of these codewords you have ticked so far?

| WALPURGIS | Turn to **131** |
| WITCH | Turn to **199** |

If you have *both* of them, then you must select only one, but remember that this will influence the upcoming conversation, so choose wisely. If you have *neither* codeword, then you must turn to **81**, but don't worry, you will still have company.

57

You pack a bottle of water, rub on some anti-bug lotion, then set out. The guide is a dour-faced young man called João, who leads you deep into the forest. It's a pleasant hike and not too strenuous, but then João stops in a clearing and points out the nearby trees. They are covered in white candy floss and look beautiful yet strange. He says, 'It's a spider colony and that is their web. It's made from fluffy silk so prey get tangled rather than stuck to it. And the more the prey fights to get out, the more enmeshed it becomes.' This snippet of information is delivered in a monotone, but then João continues, becoming more animated. 'That's not the spider to be careful of, though. Oh no. You really have to be scared of the Spider Guardian. It protects the entrance for the Favoured Few. It's deadly.' There's a stunned pause, in which one of the hikers pipes up and asks, 'Can I get a photo of it for Instagram?', then João, who now looks ashen with shock, shakes his head violently.

'Oh God, I shouldn't have said that. I really shouldn't have said that!' And with that outburst, he marches on. Make a note that you have met **João** and

subtract 1 from your METAMORPHOSIS score. You are about to follow him because, let's face it, there's no way you can find your own way out of this forest, but suddenly see a movement through the trees. A shuffling of coarse grey bristles as a huge animal barges through the undergrowth and yet, it just seemed to appear out of nowhere. You hadn't heard its approach at all. It freezes, as if it knows that it's been spotted, so do you want to sneak towards it to get a better look (turn to **184**) or go to the place where it seemed to materialise from (turn to **62**)? If you'd really rather not do anything to annoy this hulking great creature, then you should get a move on and catch up to your guide (turn to **139**).

58

Don't worry, there was nothing in your meal. Nothing but wholesome, fresh ingredients, just like their website claims. However, you did take advantage of the huge amount of coffee available, so tick the codeword **TOXINS**. Nevertheless, the normal food diet does not affect your METAMORPHOSIS score at all, so tally up what you have and turn to **106**.

You get undressed, climb into bed and fall asleep almost instantly. However, your dreams are anything but restful… You are running down a corridor, then burst through the door and slam it shut. The footsteps are getting closer; it's getting closer. Your feet become uncoordinated, you trip and stumble. It's getting closer. You reach the next door, it's right behind you…

You wake up in the strange dark room, heart hammering and a cold sweat pooling at your throat. Just a nightmare, you tell yourself, but when you eventually drift back to sleep, you're in the corridor again.

You wake after a solid 9 hours of fear-induced, interrupted sleep and feel like death warmed up. **Add 2** to your METAMORPHOSIS score. But there's no way you can take it easy today. You've made some progress in learning exactly what's going on here, but it's far too soon to make a move. Maybe today will bring more useful information though.

Once you've had breakfast, you see a Metamorphosis staff member by the notice board and ask if the same people run the same sessions every day. He says, 'No, we swap around to prevent stagnation of our energies and restore holistic synergy' and even though you're not entirely sure what that means, you may want to factor that into your schedule. After all, if something negative happened in an activity yesterday, maybe the same session could reverse it today… One positive is that if you twisted your ankle when you arrived at the Retreat, it is now much better. Not 100% but good enough for all the options on the itinerary. However, before you decide anything, you must first turn to **167** if you had a colonic irrigation yesterday. If, on the other hand, your bowels were not sluiced out, you should turn to **33**.

60

It was a bit swollen and discoloured when you got up this morning, so you stand on one leg to test the ankle. Whilst it can take the weight, it throbs and sends out twinges of pain, so you decide not to push your luck. One day of rest should do the trick, but it does limit your options now. What will you choose for your first activity?

Kayaking   Turn to **119**
Colonic irrigation   Turn to **12**

61

You are the last person to arrive, so have to set up at the front of the class. The class starts as you are still

attaching weights to your barbells, but the instructor, a grey-haired woman, smiles and hands you a runestone as a welcome gift.
If you have ticked the codeword GREY WOMAN, turn immediately to **16**. If not, continue reading.
Forty-five minutes later, you are lying drenched in sweat on the mat. Due to your prime position, you had to keep going with the endless lunges, deadlifts and squats, whereas normally, you'd have done a few then stopped to have a long swig of water. You listen to the excited and self-congratulatory voices around you — 'I'm totally sworn off caffeine, alcohol and sugar. Now that I got rid of these impurities, I'm not letting them back in' — and wonder why they're not in excruciating pain like you, but then see the grey-haired woman shaking her head at them. She seems like a kindred spirit, so tick the codeword **GREY WOMAN**. Eventually, you get up and clear the equipment away. If

this is the first time that you've noticed the large wooden wardrobe with a bird mosaic and **12 rubies**, then your curiosity is piqued and you are tempted to take a closer look. If you do, turn to **103**, but remember **this** section number, so you can return here after your examination.

Following a quick shower, you can now either have a facial (turn to **175**), a massage (turn to **113**), reflexology (turn to **37**) or acupuncture (turn to **85**).

62

You edge into the forest towards the place where the creature appeared, all the while on high alert for its return. You reach a forked pathway and assume this is why you didn't hear it — the cleared ground doesn't rustle when walked over — but the huge tree at the fork has caught your full attention. You don't know what type it is, only that its trunk is as broad as a car and there is a narrow opening with **8 red and white spotted mushrooms** circling it. You can see a marked stone lurking under the cap of one of them. You go even closer, pick it up and pocket it. From here you can see too, that the trunk is hollow on the inside and if you breathed in, you reckon you could squeeze through the crack and go inside the tree. But surely that's not where the beast came from? Suddenly, your sleeve is grabbed, and you almost let out a scream. It's João and he whispers urgently, 'Come on. Don't go near Yggdrasil. Don't ever go near it!'

You turn to face him. *What? The tree has a name?* João is not interested in talking about this though — he's already walking away, and you have no option but to follow him and continue the hike. Turn to **139**.

63

You lean forward and quickly whisper the words that the grey woman had told you. The effect is almost comical. The spider sinks down, deflated, and you swear that it shakes its furry head. After a moment of sad contemplation, it then nimbly scurries back down and disappears into the cauldron. You hear a brief and bad-tempered stamping of its eight feet then silence. If you didn't know better, you'd say that the Spider Guardian was sulking.

Still, no time to dwell on that — you're not sure how long the Gateway stays open for, so you better get a move on. However, before you can step a toe over the threshold, you have to count up your total METAMORPHOSIS score and there is still one final score to take account of. Stay with me on this, because it may sound odd, but did you have the juice detox diet (turn to **195**) or normal food (turn to **58**)?

64

A plate appears in front of you and the waiter announces, 'Rosemary-grilled goat's cheese with apricot relish and pistachio oil' then waits, presumably for you to say something complimentary. You nod, smile enthusiastically and say 'Danke', although you have a slight niggle of alarm. Wasn't there a problem with goat's cheese — some sort of zombie brain disease — or was that all cleared up now? You're too hungry to worry about that though, so you pick up your knife and fork and tuck in. It tastes delicious and is certainly better than the foul-looking pond juices which some others are drinking. Once finished, you sip on your rich, strong coffee and mull over what the woman had blurted out. The fact that your sister had been here wasn't a surprise; she had seemed lost and was looking for some direction in life, so it would've been easy for the cult to get its claws into her. The news that she had gone was an unexpected blow though. How can you rescue her if you can't find her? And for that matter what has she gone behind? However, you're not going to give up that quickly, so you start to plan your next move — discovering where the so-called transformed people go and then sneaking in. You briefly worry what you'll do if your sister refuses to leave, but you'll cross that bridge when you reach it!

You sit back feeling pleasantly full and wonder which activity to choose this afternoon, but that depends on whether you are staying in a room overlooking the forest (turn to **116**) or the lake (turn to **34**).

65

Your options for the first activity of the day are a BodyFit class (turn to **61**), a Spinning class (turn to **107**), colonic irrigation (turn to **182**) or kayaking on the lake (turn to **78**).

66

You are no artist and the red butterfly that you draw onto your left arm looks more like a mutant tomato. Still, with your T-shirt mostly covering it, you think it might do the job. Anyone taking a casual glance should see the hint of colour and be fooled into thinking that you are one of the Favoured Few.

Tick the codeword **CHRYSALIS**, then turn to **89**. It's time to find the Gateway!

To be honest, you're a bit of a sceptic about reflexology! Still, it might be relaxing, so you settle back in the chair and watch as the smiling man strokes and presses your feet.

After a few minutes, you are in agony and flinch with every touch. The man is not smiling now but looks genuinely concerned and says, 'So much blockage here. All your energy is repressed and cannot flow. No wonder you feel exhausted and negative. See this gritty part here…' And with that, he probes the pads of your toes. It feels like they're being impaled.

'Do you suffer from congested sinuses?' You nod and wince as he continues to massage and talk.

'So many people come here with their energy blocked. I did too, but you have to give the past away. Let it go! You are safe here. Mother Amber will keep you safe and loved.' His words filter through the pain and you ask, 'Who is Mother Amber?'

There is an awkward pause, and the man brushes his hair out of his eyes with the side of his arm. The movement lifts his sleeve and you briefly see a lilac butterfly tattoo on his bicep, before he coyly says, 'She is a mother to us all. She is love.' Although you're trying to keep a neutral expression, you can't help but raise your eyebrows at that. Luckily, the man is busy wiping the oil off your feet and stuffing the used flannels into a plastic cylinder, so he doesn't notice. The cylinder then disappears into the pneumatic tubing system, and you should **add 1** to your METAMORPHOSIS score.

 Finally, he reaches into a pocket and pulls out a stone. It has a marking on it, and he explains that it is a runestone.

'**Othila**. It links with your DNA and represents your legacy.' Lovely, you think, as you take the smooth pebble and give a courteous smile, before putting your shoes on and leaving. You could now go to the sauna (turn to **114**) or to the quiet relaxation room for a lie down (turn to **77**). However, if neither of those options appeal, you can simply head to the dining room — it is nearly lunchtime after all (turn to **92**).

68

A grey-haired woman enters the room accompanied by a Metamorphosis lackey who's carrying the breakfast tray. She breezily announces, 'You need to take normal food now to build up your strength and heal fully. No juice detox for you!' Well, you're not complaining. The tray has croissants, raspberry jam and a pot of coffee. You tuck in enthusiastically, and the lackey goes to the bathroom to check on something. As soon as the door closes, the grey-haired woman whispers, 'You must take care to have a butterfly tattoo and remember the word OVER — it's all important. And take this.' In the nick of time, she hands you a scrap of paper, before the lackey returns. Although this behaviour is weird and unexpected, you sense she's trying to surreptitiously help you. Tick the codeword **GREY WOMAN**.

It would seem that you are to remain in your room this morning to continue recuperating, but now that you're alone again, the first thing you do is examine the scrap of paper. Turn to **53**.

69

With the hot steam quickly filling the room, she looks at you intently, before saying, 'Don't you mean birch tree?' You shake your head and repeat the question. Finally, she asks, 'Did a grey-haired woman tell you about that?' An old man walks in at that moment, nods and says 'Guten Tag', which stops any further conversation, but she manages to lean forward and whisper, 'Ask me later about the witch,' before dashing out. Tick the codeword **WITCH**. When you eventually leave the sauna, you feel a little light-headed, so go into the relaxation room (turn to **27**).

70

Mm, delicious. You sniff the aubergine and mozzarella croquettes with sherry-glazed vegetables, then wolf the whole lot down. As you sit there feeling pleasantly full, your eyes drift towards the mural of the submerged house with an open door and **5 windows**. With a jolt, you realise that something is different. A cat is now sat in one of the windows. A — you squint to get a better look — a blue cat! That wasn't there earlier. Surely you'd have noticed a blue cat! However, there is no time to examine it to see if the paint is still wet, as the waiter hurries you out.

Although you are now feeling tired, it's only 7PM, so you check out the itinerary and try to decide how to fill the rest of the evening. You could spend an hour or so in the flotation tank (turn to **4**) or join a group therapy session (turn to **86**). If that all sounds too intense, you could attend a lecture on Walpurgisnacht — whatever that is! — and if you fancy that, turn to **148**.

You enter the windowless room confident that you can handle this workout. You adjust the bike saddle, place your water bottle in the holder and start to warm up as the instructor enters. He is both sinewy and muscular with a body fat percentage easily in single figures, and when he smiles, you see startlingly white teeth. He shouts, 'Good morning everyone!' You reply self-consciously but can't help noticing how bouncy and cheerful the others are. They're glowing with adoration, and it's unnerving how much they're hanging on to his every word. He turns up the music, pumps his fists into the air and yells, 'Let's go!'

Half an hour later, you've had at least three dizzy spells, almost all your water has gone and your gluts have turned to jelly. At this point, he's walking around, still shouting encouraging slogans like: 'You've got this', 'Believe in yourself' and 'Change your body, change your mind!' The others are lapping this up, giving whoops of joy, and you can't help wondering how anyone reaches this level of endorphins without having a heart attack first. He's approaching you now, so you adopt a look of total concentration in the hope that he'll just go past, but no! He stands in front of your bike and holds out a gold-coloured towel. You frown in confusion — you've brought your own — then realise that most of the others also have this extra towel. That's never happened in a gym class before!

'Just matching your commitment with our love,' he says. Well, sweat is literally pouring off you, so if you take the golden towel, turn to **142**, but if you'd rather politely decline, turn to **190**.

72

You dream of endless chases around a deserted shopping mall by masked monsters wielding machetes. Each time you feel the hot thump of the blade in your back, shoulder or thigh, you wake with a gasping scream, only for the sedative to drag you back down into yet another cycle. **Add 2** to your META-MORPHOSIS score.

When the morning sun creeps around the curtain, you abandon all hope of getting any rest and sit up in bed. The move sends a sharp twinge from the wound, and you slump back down feeling utterly sorry for yourself. At that moment, the door opens and a grey-haired woman enters. She is carrying a tray, and it appears that Metamorphosis will continue the special treatment.

Have you ticked the codeword GREY WOMAN? If you have, turn to **10** but if not, turn to **115**.

73

'Oh good,' you say, flinging off your socks and settling down into the chair, 'What help can you give me?' The grey-haired woman smiles as she wraps a deliciously hot towel around each foot, then mentions, somewhat cryptically, that her colleague doing the massages today is heavily pregnant.

'Babies are a commodity here. They can fast-track the mothers behind the Wall and then to the submerged house. Only then do they realise that they are not allowed to keep the babies. Beware — the Walls weep here. Not all sacrifices are willingly made. And don't forget the word FIRE.' After a stunned moment, you are about to ask her what this Wall is, where it is and why you need to remember that word, when another staff member suddenly enters the room. He looks fed up and stomps across to a cupboard without even apologising. Despite this intrusion, you should still **subtract 1** from your Metamorphosis score.

The grey-haired woman gestures to you that the session is finished and you should get your socks and shoes back on, then says, 'Can I help you, Youssef?' He is now rummaging in the first aid box and mutters that he needs a plaster. You have no option but to leave them to it, but as you are going the woman hands you the now ubiquitous gift of a runestone.

'**Othila** will guide you in knowing when to withdraw,' she explains, and although that makes no sense, you pocket it with the others.

It will be lunch soon, although if you like, there is still time for a quick sauna (turn to **144**) or a meditative rest in the relaxation room (turn to **27**).

74

There's no such thing as free will at Metamorphosis. Whilst they still use the tried and tested methods of love bombing, isolation and scare tactics, this cult has another trick up its sleeve with Mother Amber. All she needs is your matter and energy and then she has control. Luckily, you have avoided most of this and have picked up some valuable knowledge along the way, no doubt. Their efforts have been in vain, and your brain remains resolutely unwashed! Turn to **200**.

75

Once your life jacket has been checked, you're directed to an orange kayak. It's a snug fit, and you're alarmingly close to the lake surface, but you're sure they won't let you drown if you tip over. Gripping the paddle, you push off from the bank. There are three other guests and the young man from Metamorphosis in your group, and you all set off across the smooth surface of the lake. The man is nattering on about the beauty of nature and how it restores your energy but it's important that 'we give some of ourselves back,' so you steer your kayak towards the guests instead. By the way, did you choose the room that overlooks the forest (turn to **3**) or this lake (turn to **181**)?

76

Right, so you think that the cauldron is the key to opening the Gateway, but how? It's currently sitting on some logs just minding its own business — what could you do to it? Maybe the Grey Women told you some words and instructed you to remember them? Could this be the purpose of their cryptic ramblings? In fact, that's exactly what it was and obviously, the more clue words you got from the Grey Women, the better your chances are.

All you have to do is choose a word that joins with these other words that the Grey Women told you, and this combination must make a <u>new</u> word or phrase.

For example, if a grey woman told you to remember the word TOE, you might think that you have to **tip** the cauldron, because TIP + TOE join together to make a new word.

So, which word could it be?

HANG   Turn to **13**
SHIFT   Turn to **189**
TIP   Turn to **91**

77

The relaxation room looks like it could be found in any spa on the planet with its cream walls, broad-leaved tropical plants, abstract art and sculptures. There are a few people already ensconced, so you pick a recliner furthest from the others and lie down. For a few seconds you wait for a meditative serenity to wash over you but quickly become bored and start looking around. There is a huge fireplace at the centre of the room with a mosaiced arch of blue gemstones around the opening and on a layer of suspiciously clean logs, a black cauldron proudly sits. When you peer closer, you can see hooks protruding from the roof of the firepit — so it was a working fire at some point in the past, you muse — and **3 sturdy, black fire irons** complete the scene. At the side of the room, there is a fish tank and seeing as you're now bored, you slide your flip-flops back on and head over to the aquarium. There are the usual assortment of multicoloured fish with wispy fins, but instead of gravel, there are just strange shells piled at the bottom. If you want to reach a hand into the lukewarm water to examine them closer, turn to **39**; however, if the artwork has caught your eye, and you'd like to study that, turn to **166**.

It is a beautiful, sunny morning and you're pleased with your choice. As you set off in your kayak over the glistening lake, one of the other guests asks the group leader about a steeple he saw in the middle.

'Oh yes, that is part of the submerged village. People have tried to dive to explore it, but it is strictly out-of-bounds. Only the Favoured Few are allowed and that's only when they've been through the Gateway. To anyone else, it is dangerous and forbidden.'

You catch the others nodding and muttering, 'Yes, quite right,' so it would seem that they've already been brainwashed into the whole Metamorphosis experience. You know that you should probably keep your cover going and act in the same way but decide that time is running out. You need to take a risk if you're going to make any progress, so ask, 'Where is the Gateway?'

'I've heard that the runestone Dagaz has something to do with it, but if you're Favoured, you just know.'

He looks a bit disgruntled by that — you guess he isn't Favoured yet — but he covers it well enough. The group then disperses to take in the scenery in their own time. Do you want to head closer to the shore where the forest encroaches onto the bank (turn to **165**) or break the rules and row out towards the submerged village (turn to **141**)?

79

The young man announces, 'Room service' and pushes the trolley in. He looks twitchy though and keeps glancing up at the ceiling — are there hidden cameras up there? He starts to tell you all about the food, then whispers quickly, 'The grey-haired woman says that the nurse thinks you have to persuade her to cease to exist, and it's really important to remember the word FIRE.' With a dramatic flick of the towel, he smiles and bows out of the room, leaving you with a stunned expression. What was that all about? Persuade her? Persuade who? You replay the words back but no matter how you look at it, none of it makes sense. Oh, well.

Afterwards, you decide to take a stroll, but an attentive Metamorphosis staff member suggests that you take in the lecture before returning for an early night, adding that she's sure you'll be right as rain in the morning! It seems like you don't have a choice in this, so you head off. Turn to **172**.

80

You sneak out of the Retreat and stride through the forest to the great Tree with 8 mushrooms around the opening. Where else can this opening lead to? It must be the Gateway! All you need to do is breathe in and squeeze through into the inside…

Unfortunately, you are so caught up in your plans of botanical exploration, you don't notice the Metamorphosis staff arrive even though they are stomping through the undergrowth. One of them grips your arm and starts to escort you back to the Retreat. He simply says, 'We know who you are. We know who your sister is, and you are not welcome here!' You struggle and try to resist but are surrounded by glaring and threatening people. You don't stand a chance! They've even hurriedly packed up your things, so without any further ado, you are taken to the airport.

You could return later — in disguise, maybe — and at least then you might have a better idea of where to find the Gateway, but for now, your rescue mission is over.

81

You find the nearest empty seat and nod a greeting to the man next to you. He attempts a smile but looks thoroughly miserable. You catch him peering nervously back at the mural and wonder if he's spotted the blue cats too, so you ask, 'Do you like the painting?'. Phillip looks wide-eyed and startled, before hissing, 'She's watching. That's how she watches.'

A barrage of questions go through your mind, but eventually, you simply say, 'She?'

'Mother Amber,' he whispers, 'My girlfriend and our baby went through the Gateway. I was so proud for them to be Favoured, although I wanted to be with them. But of course, that was selfish and it blocked my transformation. He wasn't my son; he was Mother Amber's. I saw my girlfriend once at the windows in the mural, but she was crying…' He bows his head down, and you can just make out his next words: '…and now I don't know where she and the baby have gone.'

The waiter arrives at your table at this point and the man shuts up. Despite this interruption you should make a note that you've met **Phillip** then brace yourself for dinner. If you are on the juice detox diet, turn to **102**, but if you are having a normal meal, turn to **40**.

You stride into the spa, and a young woman greets you with a smile. When you tell her that you'd like the colonic irrigation, she beams like it's the best news she's ever heard.

'Oh, what a great decision. Many people take a few days to buck up the courage, but it's such a deep cleanse and a perfect way to kick-start your transformation.'

Once you've changed into a surgical gown, you enter the treatment room and lie on the bed as directed. A different woman is waiting for you, and she attempts a smile but it wouldn't fool anyone — she's hunched over and looks like she's got the weight of the world on her shoulders. As she talks through the procedure, you can hear the sadness in her voice and suspect it's not necessarily because she is spending the day sluicing out intestines!

The next forty-five minutes are not exactly pleasant, but it's not as awful as you thought it might be. Every now and then, the woman even becomes slightly animated as she sees things floating down the tube and mutters, 'Yes, that's better out. Such toxins blocking your energies' but it still sounds unconvincing, as if it's an act. You are lying on your back having your abdomen massaged while the water flushes around, when the woman looks quizzically at you and almost jolts in recognition.

'You look just like your sister!'

'You know her? You've seen her?' you ask. The woman nods and a whimsical expression appears on her face.

'Oh yes, she's one of the Favoured Few. She went behind the wall a few weeks ago... I shouldn't have said that.' She looks back over her shoulder and winces, but then becomes professional again and pulls the tube smoothly out of your body. Despite your efforts to get her to talk about your sister, she refuses to acknowledge your questions. It would seem that this session is done. **Add 3** to your METAMORPHOSIS score.

On your way out though, you notice a shallow bowl  filled with stones all marked with the same symbol. The woman is busy tidying up for the next client, so do you call out and ask her about the stones (turn to **15**) or simply take one as you leave (turn to **171**)?

83

Although you don't want to, you can't stop yourself from reaching into a pocket and pulling out a used tissue. Well, you do have dreadful hay fever, so you've had a constant runny nose. You feel compelled to drop the tissue in front of the opening, then stand back and wait while the others deposit similar items. One man even urinates against the tree, which you'd think would be frowned upon, this being a sacred tree and all, but the guide smiles warmly and you hear her mutter, 'Mother Amber is grateful for your offering.' **Add 2** to your METAMORPHOSIS score.

Now feeling slightly embarrassed, you and the rest of the group hike back to the Retreat without mentioning what's just happened. It's time for dinner, so turn to **56**.

84

After your question there is a pause, then she laughs as if it's the funniest thing she's ever heard.

'No, no, she's Mother to us all and will be Mother to the baby. We all receive her love and we all share the love. Relationships like the ones between parents and child are just forms of restraint. Now it's time to finish your treatment.' So, swiftly and efficiently, she plucks the needles out of your skin and places them with a strange reverence into a thick plastic cylinder, which then disappears with a whoosh up into a pneumatic tube. **Add 1** to your METAMORPHOSIS score, then get dressed and leave.

You could now go to the sauna (turn to **114**) or to the quiet relaxation room for a lie down (turn to **77**). However, if neither of those options appeal, you can simply head to the dining room — it is nearly lunchtime after all (turn to **92**).

85

The acupuncturist is huddled over a table, staring at a journal. As the door closes, he jumps and turns around.

'Oh, hello, welcome, I'm Youssef. Please, take a seat.' He takes a rather perfunctory history from you, and although you try to engage him in conversation, his eyes keep drifting back to the journal. Eventually, he ushers you over to the table and begins to poke needles into your flesh.

Halfway through the session, you have a brain wave and without bothering to think it through, you jolt your arm. The needle in your thumb gets caught on the sheet and yanked through the flesh. It sounds worse than it is, but it is bleeding. Youssef tuts and goes to the cupboard to find a plaster. He tuts even more when he finds that the first aid box hasn't got any in it, so leaves the room to replenish the supply. In this window of opportunity, you leap off the bed, run over to the table like a manic porcupine and open the journal. A slip of paper rests between the pages.

> For the Favoured to pass through
> the Gateway, first must solve the clue
> Both an organ and a core,
> this will help you find the door
> Spell the pump on which we depend
> then add the first letter to the end

By the time Youssef returns, you are back on the bed, albeit slightly out of breath. You tell him that you want to finish this now, so with a resigned nod, he dresses your thumb, then plucks the remaining needles out. You're in such a rush to leave that you don't even notice Youssef placing the used needles in a cylindrical container, which then disappears with a whoosh into the pneumatic tube system. **Add 1** to your META-MORPHOSIS score.

You're too early for lunch, so you could kill some time by having a sauna (turn to **144**) or spending a meditative half-hour in the relaxation room (turn to **27**). Who knows, you might even solve the puzzle.

86

You pick a chair and notice that a runestone has been placed there, presumably as a welcome gift. Your neighbour tells you that it's **Ansuz**. You pocket it then smile awkwardly at the others in the group. This seemed to be a good way to reconnoitre, but now you're not so sure. It's too late to change your mind though — a staff member closes the door and takes his place on the final chair. He smiles reassuringly and introduces himself. Apparently, he had an alcohol problem but thanks to Moth…Metamorphosis, he's feeling much more in line with his true destiny. Whatever that means, but you do catch sight of a scarlet butterfly tattoo on his ankle. Next, it's the group's turn, so each person has to say why they're here and what they want to transform in their life. Suddenly, you realise that the whole group is waiting for you to speak. If you have ticked the codeword TRANCE, turn to **193** but if you haven't, turn to **18**.

87

Luckily for you, the runestone represents partnerships, and although you were at risk of being dominated, Gebo gets you back on an equal footing and keeps Mother Amber at bay. Their efforts have been in vain; your brain remains resolutely unwashed! Turn to **200**.

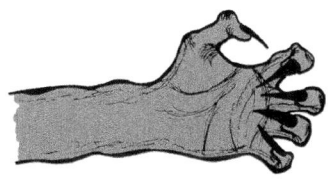

88

You look at the itinerary and with plenty of head-scratching finally make your mind up. But do you go for yoga (turn to **5**), hypnotherapy (turn to **151**) or hiking (turn to **57**)?

89

Maybe you're totally confident that you know where the Gateway is or perhaps you're just going to keep your fingers crossed and hope for the best. We'll see…

Whenever the location of the Entrance has been described, there has always been a number associated with some part of it. **Multiply that number by 10**, then turn to that section. If the section you turn to does not make sense, or if you were not so observant and have no recollection of any number, turn to **176**.

90

The acupuncturist hands you a runestone to welcome

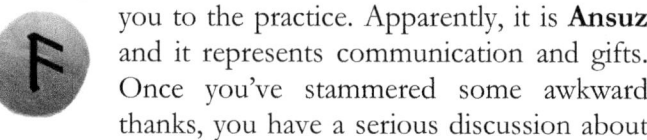 you to the practice. Apparently, it is **Ansuz** and it represents communication and gifts. Once you've stammered some awkward thanks, you have a serious discussion about your health, which includes bowel habits and sinus congestion, then lie on the treatment bed covered with a sheet. The woman smiles in a reassuring and comforting way, as she carefully places, then jabs the fine needles into your skin. It doesn't hurt; in fact, you can't really feel anything, but whenever you swallow or cough, you can see the needles in your face wobbling gently around. At this point, the woman goes across the room towards the window, opens it and takes a deep

gulp of air — she's gone quite green, which is disconcerting enough, but there may be a far more urgent consideration for you. If you had a colonic irrigation for your first session today, turn to **174**. If you did any other activity, turn to **8**.

91

Quite what you were thinking when you decided to tip the cauldron over, we will never know — a moment of madness, perhaps. With a hefty shove, the cauldron tilts, hovers precariously for a second then crashes onto its side, but disappointingly, you hear no accompanying click of a gateway opening. There's no time for you to dwell on that though. The sudden movement has disturbed the black chalice's occupant — the Spider Guardian. A huge, tarantula-like creature scurries at a lightning speed across the hearth and up your leg. It sinks thick fangs into your thigh and the fast-acting, paralysing venom courses through your bloodstream. You are aware that the Metamorphosis staff carry you out of the relaxation room, but there is nothing you can do to stop them as they toss your body into the lake. Your rescue mission has most certainly failed.

There is a pleasant smell of warm bread in the air, and your stomach rumbles as you head over to a vacant table. Looming over you is a large oil painting — a mural of an underwater scene depicting flailing pondweed and a submerged house with an open door and **5 windows**. You peer closer at the building, suddenly convinced that something will appear from within but nothing does.

'Are you on the juice detox or the normal diet?' booms a voice abruptly in your ear. You jolt and spin away from the painting to the rosy faced woman stood next to you, but before you can answer, she gasps.

'Oh, you look just like her. You must be so thrilled for her transformation. Such happy news! Are you here to join her behind…?' but before she can finish her question, another waiter pulls her sharply by the elbow. You hear him hiss, 'Was machst du?' as he hurries her away. A third Metamorphosis staff member materialises at your side and asks for your lunch option. Remember, however much you may be regretting your choice, you are committed to it, so if you are on the juice detox, turn to **145**, and if you are eating a normal diet, turn to **64**.

93

It's a bit thin, but you are literally dripping wet, so every little helps. You even use it to wipe down the bike afterwards, then copying the others, put the golden towel into a plastic cylinder which is sent off via the pneumatic tube system. **Add 2** to your META-MORPHOSIS score.

As the class leaves, the instructor rattles a bowl and tells you to take a runestone if it calls to you. It is called **Nauthis** and is represented by lapis lazuli. Naturally, everyone takes one, yourself included — who can ever resist a freebie? — but now you must decide what to do after your shower. Would you like to have a facial (turn to **175**), a massage (turn to **113**), reflexology (turn to **37**) or acupuncture (turn to **85**)?

94

You stand in the doorway having last-minute doubts but the group leader beckons you to a chair. You don't want to make a scene so you smile at the grey-haired woman and sit down. She studies your face intently, then starts to introduce herself. If you have ticked the codeword GREY WOMAN, immediately turn to **49**. If not, continue reading.

For some strange reason, she avoids you throughout the entire session. Even if you did want to share — which you most definitely don't — she refuses to give you an opportunity to speak. So instead you've heard all about Nasreen's indecision with her job and whether to take a promotion, Robin's conflict with his elderly but still domineering father, and Michelle's desire to find inner peace, whatever that meant. And then it's over. On your way out, the grey-haired woman hands you a runestone, saying pointedly, '**Kauno**. The rune that represents the expulsion of darkness. And above all, remember the word MAN.'

You pocket the stone and mull over her cryptic words. Although you don't understand what she said, you get the impression she was trying to help. Tick the codeword **GREY WOMAN**, then head with relief to your room. Following a relaxing bath, you slip into bed but again, the important question is whether you have a Drudenstein or not. If you do, turn to **161**. If you are still lacking a stone with a hole in it, turn to **20**.

95

She steps softly towards you, her eyes never leaving your face. When she's close enough to straighten your hips — an action that nearly topples you over — she whispers, 'Are you OK? Can I help you?'

You frown, confused at the question. You know that your pose is a disastrous wobble, but surely you don't need individual coaching for that! She waits, then smiles genteelly and murmurs, 'Remember that water is relaxing and will give you great insight this evening and what's important is that you don't forget the word OVER.'

You're not sure, but you think she is trying to help you — tick the codeword **GREY WOMAN**. Nevertheless, she avoids you for the rest of the session, so when it's finished, you get a quick shower, then head to the dining room.

The place is bustling. In fact, there are only two seats free. Do you want to sit with another Retreat visitor (turn to **196**) or a Metamorphosis staff member, although she is looking rather sad (turn to **11**)?

96

The shopkeeper tells you the price in mumbled German but sees your slightly panicked expression and points at the display on the till: €4.95. Make a note that you have bought a **packet of cigarettes**. It would seem that the language barrier has definitely put paid to any further chats with the man, so you leave and head to the narrow footpath that will take you safely back to the Retreat. Turn to **130**.

97

You heave up the suitcase and start running. Although your shoes pound loudly on the road, you still listen for any sign that the creature is chasing you, but the forest has become unnaturally quiet again. You can't keep up this pace, so you slow to a walk and drop the suitcase back down onto its wheels. Turn to **29**.

98

You take your place in the dining room and instantly gasp with shock when you see the mural of the submerged house. You could swear blind that the cat wasn't in it yesterday. The *blue* cat is sat in one of the **5 windows**, but that's not the worst of it. Now, there is a huge, amber eye staring out from the doorway. Are you hallucinating? Before you can examine it for wet paint, the waiter arrives with your food — a wild garlic, fennel and thyme cassoulet — and you tuck in. Between mouthfuls, you catch snippets of a nearby conversation.

'Kayaking…nearly drowned…something in the lake…pulled…sharp teeth…no, not a pike…missing now'. Before they can elaborate, another couple joins them and the conversation switches to dry body brushing and whether crystal therapy is a legitimate treatment against indigestion. This slice of freedom was nice, but don't be fooled into thinking that the Metamorphosis staff have abandoned you. One approaches and suggests you take in the lecture before having an early night, adding that she's sure you'll be right as rain in the morning! It seems like you don't have a choice in this, so you head off. Turn to **172**.

99

You set off, already feeling relieved to be away from Metamorphosis. There's only so much earnest happiness you can cope with! You take the narrow road and look for a left turning that will take you towards the buildings, however, it would be a lot quicker if you just cut the corner and went through the forest. You take a long and thoughtful deep breath. Do you really want to meet that creature again? If you choose to risk it and go through the dense forest, turn to **134**, but if you'd rather play it safe and stick to the roads, turn to **44**.

The only thing you can think of to use is toothpaste, so you sweep the bedside table clear, then squeeze the minty paste onto it in a crude pentagram shape. On the one hand, you're certain this is a sign you've gone mad, but on the other, you're getting so tired, you don't care — if you get some sleep, it'll be worth it!

To your amazement, it works like a charm. You get eight hours of deep, restful sleep, and when you wake up, feel a renewed sense of purpose albeit with a little touch of nerves. After all, it's time to make a move — if you hang around any longer, you're bound to be found out. It's now or never!

You're probably not going to return to this room, so you need to pack up all your essentials. That includes your passport, money and all the items you've collected so far at the Retreat.

Next, you know that if you do find the Gateway and make it behind the Wall, you won't have much time for artwork! From what you've seen though, the butterfly tattoo is crucial and faking it is your best bet. So if you have a butterfly transfer, turn to **136**, and if you have a marker or felt tip pen, turn to **66**. Of course, if you have *both*, you'll have to decide which one to use, but if you have neither of these, don't worry — you're sure to come up with a solution (turn to **112**).

As he unlocks your door, the night porter mumbles, 'Runestones are important here. Make sure you collect as many as you can.' You stare dumbfounded, but he starts to explain how the air conditioning works and generally acts like he hadn't said anything bizarre at all. Finally, he leaves and you close the door. You actually made it!

The room is cream with warm oak, so it has a comforting yet virtuously minimal mood to it. Yes, perfect styling for a spa retreat, and naturally, there is no television. That, and the fact you had to give up your phone at the check-in desk, is no surprise though. You knew about the mandatory digital detox rule when you signed up. "It is the most important part of your metamorphosis," the blurb had claimed. You give a slight shake of the head then continue your exploration, finding a mini bar with mineral water, smoothies and yoghurt, and a bowl of fresh fruit. You opt for a handful of cherries with the yoghurt, then go to bed.

But it is a feverish night. You dream of a heap of earthworms writhing over your body and no matter how frenziedly you push them away, they just keep wriggling across your chest, your neck, your face. Some even probe your mouth and you wake up, swiping your skin and mumbling *No, no, no.* It is a while before you eventually drift into a light sleep. **Add 1** to your METAMORPHOSIS score.

In the morning, you awake feeling haggard and try to distract yourself by flinging open the curtains to see your forest view. It is indeed an impressive sea of trees stretching as far as the eye can see, but then you notice some roofs to the north. It looks like a small village, maybe a mile or two away. You take a deep breath of the country air, then get dressed and head down to the breakfast room. A young woman with a riot of tiny cerise butterflies tattooed around her ankle smiles and asks for your room number. Once she's made a note on her clipboard, she asks, 'Have you decided to opt for the juicing detox for the duration of your stay at Metamorphosis?' Well, that leaves you lost for words, but this was on the website too, so you've had plenty of time to mull it over! What do you eventually reply?

'Yes, I'm doing the juice detox diet.'   Turn to **138**
'No, I want the normal diet please.'   Turn to **43**

102

Once your dinner is delivered — a kale, pineapple, banana, chia seeds and coconut water smoothie — Phillip continues.

'I don't know where the Gateway is but I sometimes wonder if the mural is it. It's where Mother Amber lives under the lake, so maybe it's magic!' He stares with despairing hope, then starts crying again. Another staff member discreetly sidles over to your table and hooks a hand under his arm. With very little fuss, Phillip allows himself to be dragged away. **Subtract 1** from your METAMORPHOSIS score and then finish your pleasant but unsatisfying smoothie.

You still need to select an evening activity to keep up your ruse of being an ordinary spa guest, however, you must first turn to **140** if you have ticked the codeword TRANCE. If you haven't, turn to **28**.

103

The old wardrobe is huge and made of heavy panels of varnished wood. It must be an antique and probably has some sentimental or even historical value to be here. Why else would they have such an incongruous item in this sleek, modern hall? There is an image of a bird of prey on the cupboard door. Its yellow legs, fierce talons and grey feathers are designed in mosaic and surrounding this is a circle of **12 rubies**. You give the handle a little pull out of pure nosiness but it is locked. What on earth could be inside it? Still you have no time now to explore that conundrum, especially if you don't want to raise any suspicions. Return to your previous section number.

104

With a deft sleight of hand, you take a stone, call out a breezy 'Thanks, bye,' then leave. In the corridor, you look at the stone with its strange marking. It's a runestone, you're sure, but with no internet, you have no idea which one. Still, there's no harm in keeping it, so you put it into a pocket. Make a note that you have this particularly marked runestone.

You still have enough time for another activity before lunch. Reflexology is off the cards today — there's no way someone is waggling your swollen ankle around — and since you're a bit bloated after the colonic, a massage is not appealing either. So that leaves you with either a facial (turn to **6**) or acupuncture (turn to **90**).

105

It has an eclectic mix of produce, and you wonder how weird the people who live here are, if this is what they regularly buy. You only brought a €5 note, so you can afford just one item, but of the three things that tempt you, which will you buy?

A packet of cigarettes .... Turn to **96**
A butterfly 'tattoo' skin transfer .... Turn to **178**
A bag of chilli-flavoured nachos .... Turn to **25**

If you're having second thoughts and would rather save your money, you can speak with the shopkeeper if you haven't had a conversation with him yet (turn to **14**) or simply leave the store and head back to the Retreat (turn to **130**).

106

If your final METAMORPHOSIS score is:

0 or lower	Turn to **74**
1 to 15	Turn to **126**
16 or higher	Turn to **32**

After only five minutes of high-velocity pedalling, you are already regretting this choice, but at least you don't look as fed-up as the spinning instructor. She is hunched over the handlebars and it could be sweat, but it does look like there are tears pouring down her face. Amidst the standard shouts of 'Let's do this!', 'Burn those gears!' and 'Keep going' — although that last one could've been shouted directly at you — she says, 'I hear crying behind the Walls'. Someone on a nearby bike leans back on their saddle and calls out: 'What?' It jolts the woman and she looks around alarmed before replying, 'I said, "we're trying to be kind to all."'

Later in the session, she walks around the room, unenthusiastically handing golden towels out. It's unconventional, but if you choose to take one, turn to **93**. If you decide to politely decline and stick with your own rather sodden one, turn to **154**.

'Naturally, I have answers. All my grey-haired sisters do. The nightmares come every night, so the person is frightened, tormented and exhausted. It's an excellent tactic to wear someone down and make them more susceptible, don't you think? Then they offer a safe haven and before you know it, they have you!'

Your lips move, but you can't seem to form any words. Even though, you thought it was something like this, it seems much, much worse to have it confirmed. Are you strong enough to resist or will you disappear too, like your sister? Whilst she rubs what feels like sand over your face, the grey woman says, 'First, the nightmares.

Find a Drudenstein and place it under your pillow. That will repel them.'

'A what? Repel who?' you splutter.

'A stone with a natural hole in it. And trust me, you really don't want to know who! Now go and remember the word GLIDER!'

And with a half-exfoliated face, you are pushed out of the room. What on earth was that all about? Tick the codeword **GREY WOMAN** and **subtract 2** from your METAMORPHOSIS score. You head to the nearest bathroom to wash the remaining grit off, then think about your next steps. You could now go to the sauna (turn to **114**) or to the quiet relaxation room for a lie down (turn to **77**). However, if neither of those options appeal, you can simply head to the dining room — it is nearly lunchtime after all (turn to **92**).

109

Despite having to occasionally stand up to relieve the pressure on your sore wound, you actually enjoy the colouring book. Your favourite is a picture of a large, medieval fireplace with a cauldron, spider and **3 sturdy fire irons**. It is intricately detailed and even has a symbol on one of the small aquamarine tiles in ᛗ the archway around the fire. You think it must be a rune marking but which one? You look at the clock surprised to see that it is nearly lunchtime, then hear a polite knock at the door. Before you answer it though, you tidy away all the pens and in that split-second, decide to steal the **red felt tip pen**. Well, you never know when such random objects might come in handy, do you? Once that's secreted away, you adopt an innocent expression and call out, 'Come in.' Turn to **23**.

You swivel around on shaky legs and give a thick swallow. It is huge, with coarse grey hair and twisted, gnarled tusks, and it stares at you with dark yellow eyes. It's a boar but like no boar you've ever seen. The seconds pass with you frozen in fear and the beast snorting. Its snout wrinkles up as it sniffs your scent and then it starts to paw at the ground with a cloven hoof. Your life appears to be in imminent danger, and you wonder if there's anything you can do against that size and those tusks.

Suddenly, it charges. You try to scramble away but manage only a few steps before its immense bulk knocks you clean off your feet. You land crumpled and stunned against a tree trunk and know that there is nothing you can do to save yourself. You close your eyes. Turn to **150**.

111

You bound down to the lakeside, feeling buoyed by the sound of bird song and gently lapping water. The group is already there, and you hear one of the Retreat staff members reassuring a nervous guest, saying, 'Even if you do fall in, you'll be safe. Mother Amber says the lake is the most sacred place here. Transformation can be uncomfortable or frightening, but that's just the constraints of your old life being washed away. You'll emerge reborn, I promise.' You give an involuntary eye roll but see the guest smile gratefully at him. This seems  to spur him on because he fetches some stones from his pocket and proceeds to hand them out. You examine it and he says, 'Laguz represents the lake and all its secrets.' Make a note that you have the **Laguz** runestone.

At that moment, the person in charge of the kayaks gives a quick clap to get everyone's attention, then asks, 'Who are the beginners? You will paddle close with me. If you have kayaked before, you may go further and explore, as long as you stay away from the centre of the lake.' She smiles and while you all mutter about your abilities, ties her long grey hair back. What do you plan to do now? If you say that you're a beginner and sail with the grey-haired woman, turn to **169**, but if you want to go with the others to see what you can find out, turn to **75**.

112

After being stumped for thirty seconds, you have a brainwave and start to rip up a white vest. With it cannily wrapped around your left arm, and your T-shirt obscuring most of it, you reckon you could fool any interrogators into believing that your poor butterfly tattoo has got an infection. Let's just hope that no one wants to examine it! Tick the codeword **BANDAGE**, then turn to **89**. It's time to find the Gateway!

Sat on a stool in the massage room is the most tired, most pregnant woman you've ever seen. She raises a warm smile and says 'Welcome' before lowering her voice and adding, 'Do you mind if I just do a hot stone treatment? My back is killing me!' You agree instantly, saying that she should be resting surely! She seems to appreciate your concern but replies stoically, 'If I am to transform, I have to stay strong and prove to Mother that I am worthy. I thought by getting pregnant that would be enough, but then I asked if my boyfriend could come behind the wall with me and that was that. It was my fault; I was too selfish.' By this time, you are lying face-down with a multitude of hot stones resting on your back. You can't believe what you're hearing, so you prop yourself up and say, 'But what about your baby?' One of the stones slides off, but she doesn't notice, seeing as her face is contorted with pain — is she actually in labour? Eventually, she says, 'Not mine, it's *our* baby. When it's born, it will go to be with Mother Amber, but I must stay here until I'm forgiven.'

 That brings your conversation to an end and after twenty minutes, the stones have cooled down, so you get up and get dressed. The fallen stone catches your eye. It's nestled in the crumpled sheet and has a rune marking on it. You quickly palm it then slip it into a pocket. The woman notices none of this as she is currently wracked with another contraction. You wish her all the best and slip out of the room.

It will be lunch soon, although if you like, there is still time for a quick sauna (turn to **144**) or a meditative rest in the relaxation room (turn to **27**).

You strip off, wrap yourself in a towel and enter the sauna. After a short while, you are sweating profusely and just about ready to go, when a pair enters, sits down on a lower level and starts to talk in English.

'You had a nightmare too last night?'

'Oh yes, well, I think it was a dream. I just heard things behind the walls all night. Crying, scratching, banging — you name it, I heard it. Every time I fell asleep, there was noise and it woke me up.'

'That's awful. Did you have any cheese late in the evening?'

'No, of course I didn't. I'm on the bloody juice diet, aren't I?'

As much as you want to keep listening, it's too hot and your brain feels like it's being poached. You sit up, swoop the towel back around you and leave. Whilst you're having a quick but refreshing cold shower, you notice that someone has scratched some random words into the tiles. They're small and don't make sense, but you wonder if they could be useful…

ROLL SAVE   LA SOLVER   LOVE LARS

While you ruminate on that conundrum, you can either have a quiet rest in the relaxation room (turn to **77**) or head over to the dining room for lunch (turn to **92**).

115

A grey-haired woman enters the room accompanied by a Metamorphosis lackey who's carrying the breakfast tray. She breezily announces, 'You need to take normal food now to build up your strength and heal fully — no juice detox for you!' Well, you're not complaining. The tray has croissants, raspberry jam, a pot of coffee and a strange stone with a hole in the middle. You're not sure about that but see the grey-haired woman wink conspiratorially, so you slip the stone out of sight. Make a note that you now have a **Drudenstein**. You tuck in enthusiastically and the lackey goes to the bathroom to check on something. As soon as the door closes, the grey-haired woman whispers, 'You must take care of a butterfly tattoo and you must remember the word OVER — it's all important. And take this.' In the nick of time, she hands you a scrap of paper, before the lackey returns. Although this behaviour is weird and unexpected, you sense she's trying to surreptitiously help you. Tick the codeword **GREY WOMAN**.

It would seem that you are to remain in your room this morning to continue recuperating, but now that you're alone again, the first thing you do is examine the scrap of paper. Turn to **53**.

116

An idea pops into your head, but before you go charging off, you will also need to consider your ankle. If you twisted it last night, turn to **125**, but if it is strong and uninjured, turn to **197**.

117

Did you go to the shop yesterday? If you have already been to the store, turn to **35**, but if this is your first visit, turn to **42**.

118

You curse under your breath as you look at the glass in front of you. Apparently, it is red cabbage, cucumber and blueberries and is packed full of antioxidants. You drink it down in one and contemplate throwing the glass across the room. As you sit there feeling weak and shaky, your eyes drift towards the mural of the submerged house with an open door and **5 windows**. With a jolt, you realise that something is different. A cat is now sat in one of the windows. A — you squint to get a better look — a blue cat! That wasn't there earlier, surely you'd have noticed a blue cat! However, there is no time to examine it to see if the paint is still wet, as the waiter hurries you out.

Although you are now feeling tired, it's still early, so you check out the itinerary and try to decide how to fill the rest of the evening. You could spend an hour or so in the flotation tank (turn to **4**) or join a group therapy session (turn to **86**). If that all sounds too intense, you could attend the lecture on Walpurgisnacht — whatever that is! — and if you fancy that, turn to **148**.

It's a short walk from the Retreat to the lakeside, and as you hobble gingerly along, one of the Metamorphosis staff members joins you.

'How did you hurt yourself?' he asks solicitously, nodding with exaggerated concern as you 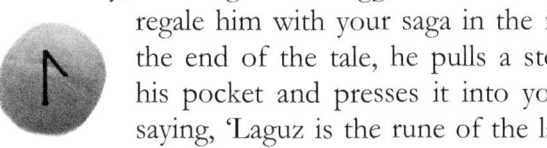 regale him with your saga in the forest. At the end of the tale, he pulls a stone from his pocket and presses it into your hands saying, 'Laguz is the rune of the lake.' You wait, expecting further words of wisdom, and you are not disappointed.

'The lake is a sacred place. Whenever I struggle with my own transformation, I go to meditate at its shores but only at dawn.'

He looks off into the distance, a peaceful smile on his face, while you stare with a fixed grin, thinking, *Metamorphosis is worse than I thought! Is my sister as brainwashed as this?*

Make a note that you have the **Laguz** runestone.

As you arrive at the row of kayaks, you suddenly remember the old man and ask, 'What does birke mean? I heard an old man say it last night, but I don't speak German.' The young man smiles again and gestures wholesomely to the forest.

'It means birch. It's a sacred tree. He was probably honouring it.'

Well, it certainly didn't sound much like he was honouring a tree, but it's best not to rock the boat — especially when you're about to get in one! And talking of which, the person in charge of the kayaks gives a quick clap to get everyone's attention, then asks, 'Who are the beginners? You will paddle close with me. If you have kayaked before, you may go further and explore, as long as you stay away from the centre of the lake.' She smiles, and while you all mutter about your abilities, ties her long grey hair back. What do you plan to do now? If you say that you're a beginner and sail with the grey-haired woman, turn to **149**, but if you want to go with the others to see what you can find out, turn to **22**.

120

You sneak into the room and stride across to the wardrobe with 12 rubies. The *locked* wardrobe. There has to be a reason why this strange, old cabinet is stood here — it must be the Gateway! All you need to do is break open the door then you can crawl through, as if to Narnia…

Unfortunately, you are so caught up in your plans of vandalism, you don't notice the Metamorphosis receptionist arrive. He grips your arm and escorts you out of the room and to the front door. Plainly not wanting to cause a scene, he simply murmurs, 'We know who you are. We know who your sister is and you are not welcome here. Take the taxi and never come back!' You struggle and try to resist, but there are more people standing guard in the lobby and glaring threateningly at you. You don't stand a chance! They've even hurriedly packed up your things, so without any further ado, you are taken to the airport.

You could return later — in disguise, maybe — and at least then you might have a better idea of where to find the Gateway but for now, your rescue mission is over.

You enter the small spa room, take off your shoes and socks then ease yourself into the chair with a slight wince. The reflexologist introduces herself as Mishka and asks how you are feeling after your accident.

'Accident!' you splutter before regaling her with your terrifying encounter. The blood drains from her face as she realises that you were gored by the boar.

'You met Hagalaz? Were you near to the tree? Is that why he attacked?'

You're annoyed by the implication that you brought this on yourself, but her reverent tone when she spoke about the tree has piqued your interest.

'Which tree? I was in the forest surrounded by thousands of trees!'

'The Tree of Life, of course. Yggdrasil. With the 8 mushrooms around the opening. It's where Hagalaz brings the offerings from the animals to be used. Skins, cocoons, feathers…even faeces. It all goes to Mother Amber.'

You attempt to say 'what', but you're just too confused by all of this. Faeces? How does anyone *use* faeces? Unfortunately, this pause has given Mishka time to think, and now she starts to press industriously over your feet, all conversation finished. Suddenly, she ducks her head down, making an agonised moaning sound and tries to grasp at something round her neck. Only as far as you can see, there's nothing there…

'Are you OK?' you ask when the episode seems to be over. Mishka shakes her head and completes the reflexology in silence. As you leave, she whispers, 'Sorry, sorry. Forget I said anything.' Well, that's unlikely. Indeed, you should note that you've met **Mishka** and also **subtract 1** from your META-

MORPHOSIS score. You potter around the garden until dinner time, but now must decide whether to eat in the dining room with the other guests (turn to **98**) or request room service (turn to **79**).

122

'Yes, I would like to know what's causing the nightmares. The other woman, the other one with grey hair said you could help me.'

She smiles at your words and starts to rub a lotion — orange and macadamia oil — into your skin with firm strokes.

'Indeed we will. The nightmares come every night, so the person is frightened, tormented and exhausted. It's an excellent tactic to wear someone down and make them more susceptible, don't you think? Then they offer a safe haven and before you know it, they have you!'

Your lips move, but you can't seem to form any words. Even though, you thought it was something like this, it seems much, much worse to have it confirmed. Are you strong enough to resist or will you disappear too, like your sister? Whilst she rubs what feels like sand over your face, the grey woman says, 'First, the nightmares. Find a Drudenstein and place it under your pillow. That will repel them.'

'A what? Repel who?' you splutter.

'A stone with a natural hole in it. And trust me — you really don't want to know who! Now go but remember the word GLIDER!'

And with a half-exfoliated face, you are pushed out of the room. What on earth was that all about? **Subtract 2** from your METAMORPHOSIS score. You head to the nearest bathroom to wash off the remaining grit, then think about your next steps.

You could now go to the sauna (turn to **114**) or to the quiet relaxation room for a lie down (turn to **77**). However, if neither of those options appeal, you could simply head to the dining room — it is nearly lunchtime after all (turn to **92**).

123

Once your dinner is delivered — a kale, pineapple, banana, chia seeds and coconut water smoothie — Flora continues.

'I've heard these zombies talk endlessly about going behind the wall. If your sister is anywhere she's there, but I haven't found the entrance yet. Have you?'

You shake your head. Suspicions, yes, but no definite answer yet. The nurse looks disappointed but says, 'Well, I think that the old, locked wardrobe, the huge hollow tree or the medieval fireplace could be likely locations, but I need to do more research. The thing is that I'm sure they're onto me. I've got to be careful. I'll go now. Enjoy your juice.'

Flora leaves you supping the pleasant but unsatisfying drink and wondering if you have gone totally insane. That conversation can't have made sense, could it? **Subtract 2** from your METAMORPHOSIS score.

You still need to select an evening activity to keep up your ruse of being an ordinary spa guest, however, you must first turn to **140** if you have ticked the codeword TRANCE. If you haven't, turn to **28**.

You place the strange stone underneath the pillow, get undressed and climb into bed.

After a solid nine hours of deep sleep, you wake up and leap out of bed ready to face the day. You've made some progress in learning exactly what's going on here, but it's far too soon to make a move. Maybe today will bring more useful information…

Once you've had breakfast, you see a Metamorphosis staff member writing on the notice board and ask if the same people run the same sessions every day. He says, 'No, we swap around to prevent stagnation of our energies and restore holistic synergy' and even though you're not entirely sure what that means, you may want to factor that into your schedule. After all, if something negative happened in an activity yesterday, maybe the same session could reverse it today… He then turns to speak to another guest, and you notice he's left a red marker pen on the shelf. In an impulsive moment, you steal the pen with one swift, cunning move. Well, you never know when it might come in handy — better to be prepared and all that! Make a note that you have a **red marker pen**.

Another positive is that if you twisted your ankle when you arrived at the Retreat, it is now much better. Not 100% but good enough for all the options on the itinerary. But before you decide, you must first turn to **167** if you had a colonic irrigation yesterday. If, on the other hand, your bowels were not sluiced out, you should turn to **33**.

125

You give your foot a tentative wiggle — no shooting pains but it still aches — so you decide to take it easy and not do anything too strenuous. That leaves either yoga (turn to **5**) or hypnotherapy (turn to **151**).

126

There's no such thing as free will at Metamorphosis. Whilst they still use the tried and tested methods of love bombing, isolation and scare tactics, this cult has another trick up its sleeve with Mother Amber. All she needs is your matter and energy and then she has control. Every time you gave up your thoughts or let them take parts of your body — yes, even the dead skin and faeces — it gave Mother Amber more and more power over you. It's teetering in the balance now, and you are so close to being her puppet. So close, but the game isn't over just yet. If you have the runestone Gebo, turn to **87**. If you don't, turn to **164**.

127

You smile at her and gesture to the tank, saying, 'I haven't done this before. I'm a bit anxious.' She hesitates for a second, then replies briskly, 'I'm afraid, you can't today. It's broken. Oh well, it looks like it's an early night for you then, but whatever you do, remember the word MAN.'

You start to complain, saying that she could've told you that before you got undressed, but another guest enters the changing room, and the grey-haired woman simply gives you a complicit nod. You have no idea what is going on, but you're getting the distinct impression that she's trying to help you. Tick the codeword **GREY WOMAN**.

With the flotation tank being a no-go, you head straight to your bedroom. Before you fall asleep though, there is one crucial question: Did you acquire a Drudenstein today? If you have at least one in your pocket, turn to **124**, but if you don't have any, turn to **59**.

128

'How long have you been here?' you shout out, as you glide towards the others.

'A couple of days now; it's wonderful,' one woman says. 'It's giving me a totally new perspective on my life. I've been so superficial, but now I'm starting to see where my old life was draining my energy.'

You smile in the hope that it disguises your cynicism — is she joking? But no, she seems to be serious, and the rest are nodding in agreement. Another one pipes up, saying, 'Me too. I'm considering never going back home. Devoting myself to Mother Amber is looking like a more solid life choice than working the rat race. It may seem strange at first,' he says directly to you, 'but I'm right. If you really examine it, you'll see how meaningless your current life is.'

After a while of them waxing lyrical about Metamorphosis, you pluck up the courage to interrupt and ask, 'Have you seen the roofs in the north of the forest? Do you know what it is?'

'Yes, it's a small village. There's a general store and a few villagers left. Apparently, they didn't like the arrival of the Retreat, but the truth can be hard for some to take.'

'People need to surrender themselves to the purity. To absorb it and become one with it. It's good that they left. Their negative energy was conflicting. Now everything is radiant.'

This is all delivered with smiles and faraway stares, which convinces you that your suspicions are accurate, but how could they have been brainwashed so quickly? They've not even been here a week yet! Suddenly, you become aware of the grey-haired woman shouting for you to return to the shore, and once you've safely deposited the life jacket and kayak, you head on back to the Retreat.

You still have enough time for another activity before lunch. Reflexology is off the cards today — there's no way someone is waggling your swollen ankle around, so what do you fancy?

A facial	Turn to **6**
A massage	Turn to **198**
Acupuncture	Turn to **90**

You grab a mat and sit cross-legged waiting for the yoga teacher to arrive. If this is the first time that you've noticed the large wooden wardrobe with a bird mosaic and **12 rubies**, then your curiosity is piqued, and you are tempted to take a closer look. If you do, turn to **103**, but remember **this** section number, so you can return here after your examination.

The teacher starts the session by handing out a runestone to each of you, saying, 'This is **Nauthis**. It represents the need to take time and reconsider your plans. If this stone calls to you, it means that you  must have patience.' Although it sounds like the typical Metamorphosis spiel, it is delivered with a flat, sad voice. The teacher, Kasper, has his greasy, unkempt hair tied back and picks at the cluster of eczema by his ear. He looks unwell and at the end of the session, when you are all in corpse pose, you realise that he's crying.

'I miss my family so much, but I shouldn't say that. Mother Amber is my family now, but I miss my real mother. They're always listening and people disappear for saying the wrong things. They say that people leave, but they don't leave, they just vanish.'

The other people in the room start to sit up and despite the awkwardness, some call out asking if they can help him. He seems to realise abruptly what he's just said, so shakes his head, then runs from the room.

Subtract 1 from your METAMORPHOSIS score and make a note that you have met **Kasper**. You have no option but to pack away your mat and head to the dining room. Turn to **56**.

It is quite a relaxing walk, and although you hear odd sounds from the forest, you feel confident that the wildlife will not venture onto the path. After ten minutes, you arrive at a fork. You know that the right-hand way must be correct but what catches your eye is the huge tree stood between the two paths. You're no nature expert, so you have no idea what type of tree it is, but its trunk is as broad as a car and there is a narrow opening gouged into it. You creep closer to peer into the interior of the trunk — if you breathed in, you might even be able to fit... You stand up, shaking your head. What are you thinking? Squeeze into a tree? And for that matter, what are those growing around the entrance? There are **8 mushrooms** with red and white spotted caps circling the opening and you can see a

 marked stone lurking under the cap of one of them. You go even closer, pick it up and pocket it. You're not sure what this is, but it all looks very strange, indeed.

You stand there for ages, just staring at the tree, but suddenly realise that you're cold and hungry, and the light is fading. It's time to get back to the Retreat.

You arrive in time for dinner and the place is bustling. In fact, there are only two seats free. Do you want to sit with another Retreat visitor (turn to **196**) or a Metamorphosis staff member, although she is looking rather sad (turn to **11**)?

You spot the woman from the lecture, so sit beside her and ask, 'Did you enjoy the lecture last night? I saw you taking notes.'

The woman eyes you up somewhat suspiciously, then replies, 'Anything to do with witches interests me. I'm Flora Demdike.'

She tells you she's a nurse and works in the operating theatres, but when you remark that it must be stressful and ask if that's why she came to the Retreat, she gives you a sideways glance.

'Bad Brocken was where the witches used to gather, so if someone needed witches to join them in an alliance, this is where they would come.'

All this is delivered with a straight face and when you let out a snort of laughter, just to show that you're not gullible, she simply stares steely eyed back at you. Oh. She's not joking then.

After an awkward pause, Flora says, 'You must have heard of Mother Amber by now. Take my advice and steer clear of her and the boar they call Hagalaz. There are others too, but I haven't identified them yet. In fact, you should just leave,'

'I'm here to find my sister,' you confide, 'She was here.' Flora nods but does not look confident in your chances.

Just as she's about to speak, a waiter interrupts to ask the crucial question: Are you on the juice detox (turn to **123**) or the normal diet (turn to **159**)?

She beams at you, strides over and pats you on the shoulder.

'You made a good choice and welcome to the family. Here.' You flinch thinking that she's about to hug you — a prospect that is far too sweaty and horrible to contemplate — but instead she hands you a small, flattened stone. You take it, turn it over and see the markings.

'This is Kauno. It is the rune for enlightenment and clarity. You've earned it today. You showed up and gave it your all. Keep up the good work.'

You nod and smile nervously, unsure of the correct social etiquette in this situation, but the others just beam at you. They're either delighted that you can deadlift twenty kilos or something else is going on. Maybe they've been brainwashed into being this enthusiastic... Nevertheless, you pocket the stone and head off to the changing room. Make a note that you have the **Kauno** runestone. There's time for another activity before lunch and they are at least less energetic than the BodyFit class. What would you like to do now?

A facial   Turn to **6**
A massage   Turn to **198**
Reflexology   Turn to **67**
Acupuncture   Turn to **90**

133

Did you seriously think you could break down an old stone wall with just a poker and do it without making any noise? Ridiculous! You are so caught up with your futile demolition, you don't notice the Metamorphosis staff members arrive. One wrenches the poker from your hands while the other grips your arm and starts to escort you to the front door. Plainly not wanting to cause a scene, he simply murmurs, 'We know who you are. We know who your sister is and you are not welcome here. Take the taxi and never come back!' You struggle and try to resist, but there are more people standing guard in the lobby and glaring threateningly at you. You don't stand a chance. They've even hurriedly packed up your things, so without any further ado, you are taken to the airport.

You could return later — in disguise, maybe — and at least then you might have a better idea of where to find the Gateway but for now, your rescue mission is over.

134

With each step your nerves grow, as you quickly lose your bearings. The thick green canopy is blocking most of the sunlight, and although you have a vague idea of the direction, orienteering is not one of your natural abilities. Will you ever be able to find your way out? Your panic rises and conjures up unwanted images of your lonely, lost skeleton curled up under a tree, but after twenty minutes of frantic trudging through the undergrowth, you see brickwork ahead — surely that must be the buildings! You heave a sigh of relief and are in the middle of congratulating yourself for such fine tracking skills when you hear it. That same rustling sound you heard last night, only this time, it's right behind you. Do you simply start running as fast as you can towards the buildings without looking back (turn to **192**) or slowly turn to face the beast (turn to **110**)?

135

Other than a pregnant woman who is cleaning out the rooms and stuffing used tissues into a plastic cylinder — how bizarre! Is that a new method of recycling? — you meet no one else on the corridors. Room 135 is silent but more importantly, unlocked. It's not clear why the grey woman wanted you to go here, but you immediately notice the jotter on the desk. In a heavy-handed scrawl, the words: 'Mural, wardrobe, fireplace, tree?' are written. Is this what you were supposed to find? You look around but see nothing useful, however, when you reach the bathroom, you spot the pile of wet towels for collection and a small heap of marked stones next to a toothbrush. Without any further ado, you scoop them all up, and if you want to risk snooping around the room even more, turn to **146**.

However, if you think that might be pushing your luck and want to leave the room immediately, continue reading.

You scuttle back to your own suite and once you've calmed down from the heist, examine your haul: **Kauno**, **Fehu**. **Ansuz** and **Algiz**. Make a note that you've acquired all these runestones, then secure them somewhere safer than the previous person did! Now you have to carry on as normal, so do you want to head down to the spa for a facial (turn to **45**) or reflexology (turn to **121**)?

136

You can't really follow the German instructions but using some common-sense deciphering of 'Wasser' to 'water', you get the red butterfly to stick onto your left arm. With your T-shirt mostly covering it, you reckon it just might do the job. Anyone taking a casual glance would be fooled into thinking that you are one of the Favoured Few. Tick the codeword **CHRYSALIS**, then turn to **89**. It's time to find the Gateway!

137

You ask, 'Which activity is João doing today?' and the guide glares at you then says curtly, 'He doesn't work here anymore. Some people are not able to transform, and they must find their own way in life.' She then checks her bag, adjusts her glasses, and gives everyone an **Algiz** runestone, saying, 'in case Hagalaz is in the forest.' Most of you exchange worried glances and some even start to ask, 'What is...?' but the guide dismisses the fussing with a wave of the hand and sets off. Half an hour later, you find yourself near a wide tree with a narrow opening in its trunk and you pause.

'Are these mushrooms poisonous?' you ask, pointing at the **8 red and white spotted fungi** that circle the opening. The guide shrugs, then says, 'But the Tree of Life has many stories about it. Folklore dictates that you should give an offering to it.' There is a nervous laughter, but she gestures to the Tree and you realise that she is deadly serious. If you have ticked the codeword TRANCE, turn to **83**, but if not, turn to **2**.

138

Whilst the beetroot, apple and ginger concoction is delicious, you seriously doubt that it can keep you going until lunchtime. What have you signed yourself up for? Your stomach gives an ominous growl in agreement. Still, you can suffer a few hunger pangs if it means finding your sister, and it's important to raise no suspicions about the real reason you're here…

You go to the activities board in the lobby and look over the options for the morning. Before you dive in enthusiastically though, you need to factor in whether you have a twisted ankle or not. If you tripped over a tree root last night, turn to **60**, but if your ankle is happily free from injury, turn to **177**.

139

After another hour of trooping through the forest with João barely talking and the other guests enthusiastically gushing about nature, you finally arrive back at Metamorphosis and head to the dining room.

The place is bustling. In fact, there are only two seats free. Do you want to sit with another Retreat visitor (turn to **196**) or a Metamorphosis staff member, although she is looking rather sad (turn to **11**)?

140

You study the options, but strangely, your vision seems to blur and only comes back into focus when you look at one particular activity. Yes, that's the one, you decide, feeling this perverse and irresistible pull towards the flotation tank. So that's where you head to next. Turn to **186**.

141

No one hollers at you to return, so it seems they just haven't noticed. Nearby you can see the spire of the sunken church, so you paddle closer. Suddenly, your kayak lurches up into the air as it is barged with a colossal force from below. You have a split-second to wonder if a shark or whale has hit you, before you sink under the water. Sink? Hang on. You're wearing a life jacket, aren't you? Yes, you are but that is no match for the hand that has grabbed your ankle and is pulling you down, deeper and deeper. Your life appears to be in imminent danger unless you can quickly think of something to do.

Apparently not, but you were warned that this was dangerous, so you've only got yourself to blame. With a huge exhale of air that bubbles to the surface, your lungs fill with water and you drown. The child-sized aquatic creature smirks, then dives to the bottom of the lake, dragging your corpse with it. Mother Amber will be pleased, it thinks.

142

It is soft and smells of flowery-scented fabric softener, but it is quite a thin towel, so it's soon soaked with perspiration. The instructor gets back on his bike to begin the warm-down.

'You are transforming your lives!' he bellows, leaning back on his saddle to punch both fists triumphantly in the air and in doing so, his vest rises up showing a perfectly toned stomach and a blue butterfly tattoo. However, you're simply relieved that you survived. With dangerously wobbly legs, you wipe down the bike then copying the others, put the golden towel into a plastic cylinder which is sent off via the pneumatic tube system. Is that a fast-track to the laundry, you wonder, giving a final grimace-like smile to the instructor, then staggering out. **Add 2** to your METAMORPHOSIS score.

The next available activities are all thankfully much less strenuous than that, but what would you like to have now?

A facial	Turn to **6**
A massage	Turn to **198**
Reflexology	Turn to **67**
Acupuncture	Turn to **90**

143

After a few seconds of you and the Spider Guardian staring at each other, the huge, tarantula-like creature decides to make a move. It runs at a lightning speed and sinks its thick fangs into your neck. The venom is fast acting and paralysing. You are aware that the Metamorphosis staff carry you out of the relaxation room, but there is nothing you can do to stop them as they toss your body into the lake. Your rescue mission has most certainly failed.

144

It's not that warm in the sauna, but at least, it's fairly empty. Apart from you, there are two men who are moaning about how tired they are. You try to relax despite the noise and hear them say, 'It's getting to the point where I don't want to sleep. The nightmares are so bad!'

'I know what you mean. I heard that drawing a pentagram in your room stops it.'

'A five-pointed star? What? It's devil worship, is it? Who told you that nonsense?'

'One of the instructors, a grey-haired woman. I know it sounds daft, but I'm going to try it tonight.'
After that, they leave and you are finally alone, but unless the sauna heats up, there's no point staying here. Just then, a woman enters and although it's too dark to see her clearly, you can tell that she's disgruntled about the temperature too. Do you offer to ladle some water over the coals (turn to **187**) or would you prefer to ask her to do it before she gets settled (turn to **52**)?

145

A tall glass of green pond water is placed in front of you. Apparently, it is kale, celery and hibiscus and should stimulate your kidneys to work more efficiently, although you have the sneaking suspicion that your kidneys are going to pack their bags and go home if you keep drinking this. You sigh resignedly and sip it, then mull over what the woman had blurted out. The fact that your sister had been here wasn't a surprise; she'd felt lost and was looking for a direction in life, so it would've been easy for the cult to get its claws into her. The news that she had gone was an unexpected blow though. How can you rescue her if you can't find her? And for that matter what has she gone behind? However, you're not going to give up that quickly, so you start to plan your next move — discovering where the so-called transformed people go and then sneaking in. You briefly worry what you'll do if your sister refuses to leave, but you shake that thought away. You'll cross that bridge when you reach it!

You finish the juice and wipe green water off your mouth. Time to distract yourself with something this afternoon, but what will you choose? Your answer to that, however, depends on whether you are staying in a room overlooking the forest (turn to **116**) or the lake (turn to **34**).

146

Keeping an ear out for any approaching footsteps, you quickly search room 135 and find a miniature **bottle of vodka** hidden in the safe. That might come in handy, so you stuff it in a pocket and leave. However, a Metamorphosis staff member is waiting in the corridor.

'I was looking for you! What are you doing?' You make a weak excuse about sharing herbal remedies with another guest, but they are not convinced and march you back to the suite, insisting that you 'recuperate in the hammock'. It's boring but what can you do? At least, they didn't find your haul of runestones — in one fell swoop, you've acquired **Kauno**, **Fehu**, **Ansuz** and **Algiz**. Soon it's dinner time and luckily, they give you a choice about where to eat. Do you want to go to the dining room with the other guests (turn to **98**) or request room service (turn to **79**)?

147

Although you read all the options on the itinerary and know that you can choose any of them, you are strangely compelled to pick one particular activity. Try as you might, there is no way you can resist this force. Turn to **182**.

148

If you took the BodyFit or yoga class today and have already examined the wardrobe, continue reading. However, if you haven't yet seen this exquisite piece of furniture with a bird mosaic and **12 rubies**, you should first turn to **103** but remember **this section number** so that you can return here afterwards.

You pick a seat and notice that a runestone has been placed there, presumably as a welcome gift. Your neighbour tells you is **Laguz**, so you pocket it, but any further conversation is prevented because the lecturer is ready to start. He's assuming an academic air with his wire-framed glasses and tweed jacket but spoils the effect by fumbling around with the projector. Eventually though, you learn that the night of the 30th of April is when Saint Walpurga, who battled against pestilence and witches, is celebrated with bonfires. Apparently, the witches met on the nearby hill called Brocken to conjure up the evil spirits. Well, this is all very interesting, but what's really got your attention is the serious young woman in the first row. She is attentively taking notes but also sneaking furtive looks around the room. Tick the codeword **WALPURGIS**. When the lecture ends and the smattering of applause dies out, the lights go on. Although you're curious about the serious woman, the crowd quickly disperses, and you are left with no option but to head to your bedroom. Before you fall asleep though, there is one crucial question: Did you acquire a Drudenstein today? If you have at least one in your pocket, turn to **124**, but if you don't have any, turn to **59**.

149

Once your life jacket has been checked, you're directed to an orange kayak. It's a snug fit, but also a relief to take the weight off your ankle. Gripping the paddle, you push off from the bank. There is only one other beginner — a man in his fifties who immediately starts babbling about drowning — and you all set off across the smooth surface of the lake. The grey-haired woman is telling you about the wildlife in and around the water, and to your relief, is not going on about 'transforming your life'. It's all quite relaxing and your mind wanders. By the way, did you choose the room that overlooks the forest (turn to **36**) or this lake (turn to **188**)?

Cautiously, you open your eyes. The beast is still there, flanks heaving with exertion and drool oozing off its tusks, but it seems to have lost interest in you. It's looking past you into the forest. And then you hear it too. A voice and it's getting closer.

'Hagalaz, no! Leave.' The woman says again and again, and eventually, the boar gives an irritated snort and walks away. She crouches down at your side, winces and says, 'Oh, you're hurt.' You shake your head and reassure her that you're just a bit winded when you suddenly feel the pain in your buttocks. Twisting round to look, you see the blood — it gorged you! Tears and nausea well up, and the woman pats you on the arm.

'It'll be alright. It looks worse than it is. Let's get you back to the Retreat and cleaned up.' Of course, you realise, she's a Metamorphosis staff member with shiny blonde hair and a small, pink butterfly tattoo inked on the inside of her wrist. She leads you slowly out of the forest and back to your room.

You are nursed like royalty with first-rate medical care. The wound has been disinfected, stitched and dressed, and you've even had a tetanus shot. Finally, the staff members gather up all the bloody swabs and used needles, place them carefully into a plastic cylinder then leave. **Add 4** to your METAMORPHOSIS score. You have been given strict instructions to rest and the mild sedative should ensure that you do, but before you drift off to sleep, you should consider something. Did you acquire a Drudenstein today? If you have at least one, turn to **21**, but if you don't have any, turn to **72**.

You decide to play it safe and tell the hypnotherapist that you're trying to eat healthier. She nods sagely and declares that it is a worthwhile step in your transformation. At this point, she presses a runestone into your hands insisting that, '**Kauno** is the beacon of truth', whilst staring directly at you. This lasts about twenty seconds, which may not sound long, but it is. You imagine that she wants to appear intense  but seeing as you're staring at her nostrils, it's just plain awkward. Eventually, she stops and holds up an amber pendant, swinging it back and forth in the traditional manner.

'Listen to my voice. You're feeling sleepy. Very sleepy.' You inwardly sigh at this — what a hack! — and then she is busying around the room, presumably getting it ready for the next client. You look at the clock and realise that an hour has passed. An hour! She sees your confusion and smiles.

'You may feel a little disorientated for a while. That happens when someone is as susceptible as you are.' Susceptible! What's that supposed to mean? But there is no time for any questions; your session is over. Tick the codeword **TRANCE** and **add 3** to your METAMORPHOSIS score.

It's time now to go to the dining room and the place is bustling. In fact, there are only two seats free. Do you want to sit with another Retreat visitor (turn to **196**) or a Metamorphosis staff member, although she is looking rather sad (turn to **11**)?

You spend the night tossing and turning, desperate to sleep but frightened to do so. Because whenever you do manage to drift off, a thick bristly arm reaches out from under the bed and wraps its sinewy fingers around your ankle. One time, you swear you can feel a tongue…

Add 3 to your METAMORPHOSIS score.

When morning finally arrives, you could cry. How are you supposed to do this heroic rescue when you are so utterly exhausted? And yet, that is exactly what you must do. After all, it's time to make a move — if you hang around any longer, you're bound to be found out. It's now or never!

You're probably not going to return to this room, so you need to pack up all your essentials. That includes your passport, money and all the items you've collected so far at the Retreat.

Next, you know that if you do find the Gateway and make it behind the Wall, you won't have much time for artwork! From what you've seen though, the butterfly tattoo is crucial and faking it is your best bet. So if you have a butterfly transfer, turn to **136**, and if you have a marker pen or felt tip pens, turn to **66**. Of course, if you have *both*, you'll have to decide which one to use, but if you have neither of these, don't worry — you're sure to come up with a solution (turn to **112**).

153

The woman is now happily paddling along, pointing out burrows and a wasp nest, so you edge your kayak closer to the grey-haired woman and ask, 'Is there something underneath the lake? I thought I saw a spire poking up through the surface.'

She nods and explains that the region was flooded a few decades ago and the old village submerged. When the water level sinks, the old church spire can be seen. She leans closer and says quietly, 'And that's not the only thing down there. People disappear. Something takes them. Takes them under the lake.'

'What?' You look directly at her, but her expression tells you to ask no more. However, after a few seconds, she relents and whispers, 'You look just like your sister, and I know why you're here. The Grey Women will help and protect you, and we're not only at the Retreat, we're behind the wall too.' She then cups her hand around her mouth and whispers in your ear.

'W-w-what?' you stammer, but at that moment, the woman flips her kayak over, so your instructor paddles swiftly over to retrieve her from the lake. Tick the codeword **GREY WOMAN** and **subtract 1** from your METAMORPHOSIS score. That seems to end the session, so you head silently back to the shore thinking about what she said. Although it makes no sense to you now, you have just received some very good advice.

If you find yourself in a situation where **"your life appears to be in imminent danger"**, you must **add 50** to the current section number and turn immediately to the new section.

The grey woman has her hands full with the guest, who is still spluttering, so you return to the Retreat. You have enough time for another activity before lunch, so what do you fancy?

A facial	Turn to **6**
A massage	Turn to **198**
Reflexology	Turn to **67**
Acupuncture	Turn to **90**

154

You wave the towel away with a genial smile that disguises the agony you're currently in. As the class leaves, the instructor rattles a bowl and tells you to take a runestone if it calls to you. It is called **Nauthis** and apparently is represented by lapis lazuli. Naturally, everyone takes one, yourself included — who can ever resist a freebie? — but now you must decide what to do after your shower. Would you like to have a facial (turn to **175**), a massage (turn to **113**), reflexology (turn to **37**) or acupuncture (turn to **85**)?

155

You're right — she does want to talk about this. She drapes a warm towel over your bare shoulders, sighs again, then says, 'Well, I have the tattoo, but that's only the first thing that shows your commitment, so I suppose, I just have to keep trying to bring in new recruits for mother and strengthen the Family. You know, make sure that she has what she needs.' Naturally, when you hear this, you have many more questions spring up in your head but before you can ask them, Belinda winces and cowers. It's as if something has sunk its claws into her neck...

The massage finishes then, and she hands you a runestone saying '**Nauthis** is for patience.' Next, she shoves the oily, damp towels into some plastic cylinders and sends them away through the pneumatic tubing. Maybe it's an efficient laundry system...

Add **1** to your METAMORPHOSIS score, put the runestone in your pocket, then make a note that you have met **Belinda**. You could now go to the sauna (turn to **114**) or to the quiet relaxation room for a lie down (turn to **77**). However, if neither of those options appeal, you can simply head to the dining room — it's nearly lunchtime after all (turn to **92**).

156

Despite having to occasionally stand up to relieve the pressure on your sore wound, you actually enjoy the jigsaw puzzle. When you finally slot in the last piece, you have a picture of a large, antique wardrobe with a mosaic of a bird of prey surrounded by **12 rubies** on the door panel. You look at the clock, surprised to see that it's nearly lunchtime, then hear a polite knock at the door. Turn to **23**.

You stick to generic topics of conversation — the weather, the journey to the Retreat, the activities you've done so far — and in doing so, make sure that you give absolutely nothing away. No one would ever suspect that you have an ulterior motive for being here. At that moment, a harassed looking waiter materialises, asks for your order and politely requests that Morris vacates her seat seeing as she's finished her meal. She agrees but once the waiter has gone, she returns and quickly says, 'I'm leaving tomorrow so I don't need it anymore, but you might if the nightmares don't stop. Keep it hidden though. These lot are bound to confiscate it as contraband if they see it!' She hands you a bottle of fizzy energy drink, then dashes off. She's right about the drink though. With the amount of sugar and caffeine packed into it, the Metamorphosis folk would have a seizure if they caught you drinking it. Make a note that you have an **energy drink**. Well, that was odd but at least now you can enjoy dinner — here comes the waiter again. Are you on the normal diet (turn to **70**) or the juice diet (turn to **118**)?

158

You step off the road and feel your feet sink into the dense layer of leaves. The yellow eye gives another blink, then starts to shuffle around. You dive towards the nearest tree, gripping its mossy trunk as you try to disappear behind it. There is a loud grunting, but you can't tell if the creature is coming to attack you or running away. Suddenly, you hear a voice shouting from the road.

'Sind Sie verrückt? Bleib aus dem Wald raus. Das ist das Reich des Wildschweins mit den bernsteinfarbenen Augen und er wird es nicht gut heißen, wenn Fremde eindringen. Er bewacht die Birke für sie. DIE BIRKE!'

You spin round and take a step towards the old man, but your foot catches on a tree root and you stumble over. There is a sharp pain in your ankle as you stand back up, wince and shout, 'I'm sorry. I don't speak German. Do you know…' But before you can ask where the Retreat is, the old man flaps his hand in annoyance and strides off down the road. Remembering the ominous creature, you peer nervously over your shoulder into the ever-darkening forest, but there is no sign of it at all. You hobble back to your suitcase — make a note that you have a **twisted ankle** — then continue your slow, painful walk towards the Retreat. Turn to **29**.

159

Once your dinner is served — vine-baked camembert with cranberry jelly and fennel salsa — Flora continues.

'I've heard these zombies talk endlessly about going behind the wall. If your sister is anywhere she's there, but I haven't found the entrance yet. Have you?'

You shake your head. Suspicions, yes, but no definite answer yet. The nurse looks disappointed but says, 'Well, I think that the old, locked wardrobe, the huge, hollow tree or the medieval fireplace could be likely locations, but I need to do more research. The thing is that I'm sure they're onto me. I've got to be careful. I'll go now. Enjoy your meal.'

Flora leaves you eating the delicious food and wondering if you have gone totally insane. That conversation can't have made sense, could it? **Subtract 2** from your METAMORPHOSIS score.

You still need to select an evening activity to keep up your ruse of being an ordinary spa guest, however, you must first turn to **140** if you have ticked the codeword TRANCE. If you haven't, turn to **28**.

160

Although the last thing you want to do is get closer to the boar, you lean towards it and clearly repeat the words that the grey woman told you.

The effect is instantaneous. The boar jerks back with a startled expression, and you could swear that it actually frowns at you, but with a final grunt, it walks away. You watch as it looks back at you warily, then disappears into the forest. Only then do you let out a long breath and lean weakly against the nearest tree trunk. When you're feeling better, you continue to the buildings. It is a small collection of houses and one store — not exactly worth what you've just been through but seeing as you're here, you might as well go in. A bell tinkles as you enter, and the man behind the counter nods at you. Do you want to speak with him (turn to **14**) or browse around the shop (turn to **105**)?

161

You slide the stone underneath your pillow and it works like a charm. You get eight solid hours of deep, restful sleep, and when you wake up, you feel a renewed sense of purpose albeit with a little touch of nerves — after all, it's time to make a move. If you hang around any longer, you're bound to be found out. It's now or never!

You're probably not going to return to this room, so you need to pack up all your essentials. That includes your passport, money and all the items you've collected so far at the Retreat.

Next, you know that if you do find the Gateway and make it behind the Wall, you won't have much time for artwork! From what you've seen though, the butterfly tattoo is crucial and faking it is your best bet. So if you have a butterfly transfer, turn to **136**, and if you have a marker pen or a felt tip pen, turn to **66**. Of course, if you have *both*, you'll have to decide which one to use, but if you have neither of these, don't worry — you're sure to come up with a solution (turn to **112**).

The large room looks mostly modern with mirrors and top-quality equipment, but there is an incongruous old wardrobe at the back. Why would they have that there? Even odder is the ornate design of a bird of prey on the door and, if you're not mistaken, there are **12 rubies** circling it. You're very tempted to see what is stored inside, but you have to get ready for the class and this could take some time… By the time you've collected the myriad of barbell weights, mat, step and dumbbells, you feel like you've already done a workout. You slump onto the mat pretending to stretch, but really you are surreptitiously listening to the nearby conversations. One group in particular has caught your attention. Like everyone else here, they are slim, smiling and brimming with vitality.

'You know, I didn't realise until I spent some time here, just how much my family was blocking my transformation,' 'Oh yes, tell me about it,' 'All that negative energy,' 'And the attitudes and the rules, it's like having a straitjacket on,' 'Totally!' You can picture the eye rolling and melodramatic grabbing of each other's arms that accompany this and then they continue.

'It was like an epiphany, I just knew what I had to do,' 'And your family will get over it, who knows maybe they'll find their way to transform too,' 'Don't be too hard on yourself though, sometimes you have to do the tough thing in order to do the right thing,' 'Yes, your family is here now.' And with that, there is a group hug and lots of tearful smiling at each other.

The instructor then enters, leaps onto the small stage at the front of the room and flicks a switch to start the music.

Forty-five minutes later and it's over. The instructor is clapping, people are high-fiving and you are staring at the array of sweaty equipment that you now have to clean and pack away. At that point, you hear the instructor yelling, 'Who's new to Metamorphosis? Is this the first day for anyone?' into her headset microphone. Do you put your hand up to let her know that you are, indeed, new here (turn to **132**) or would you rather busy yourself with disinfecting dumbbells and pretend not to have heard her (turn to **48**)?

163

You can't help but stare again at the Narnia-esque wardrobe, with its **12 rubies** circling the bird of prey. What is behind that locked door? Just as you're thinking of going across to examine it, the lights are dimmed and the instructor, a grey-haired woman, starts the session.

You go through the manoeuvres of cat/cow, cobra and forward fold, and are trembling in warrior I when the instructor approaches you. If you have ticked the codeword GREY WOMAN, turn to **41**, and if you haven't, turn to **95**.

164

You are simply unable to take charge of yourself. Someone else is now in control, and all you can do is walk away from the fireplace and sit on a recliner. Before long, you feel a heavy weight climb onto your shoulders and perch there, with long, sinewy arms wrapping around your neck. It's difficult to breathe but when you look in the mirror opposite, you can see nothing. Sharp claws start to tickle your throat... Who knows what Mother Amber has in store for you, but your heroic rescue mission has ended here.

165

You can hear the gentle rustles of birds rooting around in the undergrowth for insects to eat, but then you hear the crack of a branch as something heavy stands on it. You gasp and stare intently at the forest. For a few seconds, all is unnaturally still and then it moves. A huge grey boar. It takes a single step forward but freezes when it realises you've seen it. The beast has an old bird's nest between its jaws — what does it want with *that*? — and blinks its amber eyes slowly. From close behind, the group leader's voice cries out 'Hagalaz, go! Not here!' and the boar gives itself a shake, then casually walks away. That seems to bring the session to a close and you all disembark from your kayaks and head back to the Retreat. What would you like to have for the next activity?

A facial	Turn to **175**
A massage	Turn to **113**
Reflexology	Turn to **37**
Acupuncture	Turn to **85**

166

The paintings are all modern depictions of a tree with enormously long and wide-spread roots. You have a feeling that it has significance here — perhaps something to do with families or being grounded or making connections with the earth or... you run out of psychobabble and decide that you've had enough! You leave the room, get dressed and head for the dining room. It's lunchtime and you are starving! Turn to **92**.

167

As keen as the Metamorphosis staff are to help with your transformation, even they draw the line at *daily* colonic irrigations. This means that your options for the first activity are limited to a BodyFit class (turn to **61**), a Spinning class (turn to **107**) or kayaking on the lake (turn to **78**).

168

You pull out the stone and show the rune markings to the arachnid. The effect is instantaneous. It sinks down, dejected, and you swear that it shakes its furry head. After a moment of confused contemplation, it then nimbly scurries back down and disappears into the cauldron. You hear a brief and bad-tempered stamping of its eight feet then silence. If you didn't know better, you'd say that the Spider Guardian was sulking.

Even more inexplicable is the sudden disintegration of the Algiz runestone into a pile of fine powder that trickles between your fingers onto the hearth. Make a note that you have **lost** one Algiz runestone.

Still, no time to dwell on that — you're not sure how long the Gateway stays open for, so you better get a move on. However, before you can step a toe over the threshold, you have to count up your total METAMORPHOSIS score and there is one final score to take account of. It may sound odd, but did you have nothing but the juice detox diet (turn to **195**) or have you sampled some normal food during your time here (turn to **58**)?

169

Once your life jacket has been checked, you're directed to an orange kayak. It's a snug fit and you're worryingly close to the lake surface, but you're sure they won't let you drown if you tip over. Gripping the paddle, you push off from the bank. There is only one other beginner — the nervous woman who had been hyperventilating — and you all set off across the smooth surface of the lake. The grey-haired woman is telling you about the wildlife in and around the water, and to your relief, is not going on about 'transforming your life'. It's all quite relaxing and your mind wanders. By the way, did you choose the room that overlooks the forest (turn to **17**) or this lake (turn to **153**)?

The first thing that you notice is the mural of the submerged house with the **5 windows**. Because the blue cat has now disappeared and peering out from one of the windows is a huge, amber eye. You could almost believe that you're going mad and hallucinating, but maybe that's what they want you to think? Are they drugging you with LSD? You look again at the huge eye — is it actually staring directly at you? You shudder and turn away. No one else seems bothered by the big eye in the mural and to be honest, you're a bit scared to ask anyone about it. What if they say that there's nothing there? You sit at the nearest table with your back to it and wait for your lunch.

Either by luck or through design, the person bringing your nourishment is the same tense German waiter from yesterday. He makes a beeline for you and whispers urgently, 'If you can't find your sister behind the wall, she will have been moved down to the house under the lake.' Keeping a neutral expression, you ask from the corner of your mouth, 'So I should go directly there then? Dive down into the lake?'

'No!' he hisses, 'It's too deep and the Neckar will kill you anyway. You need diving gear and that's kept behind the Wall. But that's where the Aufhocker are and they'll kill you too!' You play with the cutlery as you process this, and although you really just want to say, 'Aufhocker? Neckar? Are you insane?' you eventually ask, 'Why are you telling me this?' To your surprise a tear wells up suddenly and he replies, 'This whole place is a mistake. I just want it all to end.' Following that he bustles away, presumably hoping that no one has realised what he's just said.

Your thoughts drift from this crucial information to what you should do this afternoon. You're tired of pretending to be a normal tourist, but have you found out all you can? On the adjacent table, you hear a couple talking about the nearby shop, so if you want to go there (turn to **117**). Otherwise, you could do a yoga session (turn to **129**), have hypnotherapy (turn to **24**) or go for a hike (turn to **46**).

171

With a deft sleight of hand, you take a stone, call out a breezy 'Thanks, bye,' then leave. In the corridor, you look at the stone with its strange marking. It's a runestone, you're sure, but with no internet, you have no idea which one. Still, there's no harm in keeping it, so you put it into a pocket. Make a note that you have this particularly marked runestone.

You still have enough time for another activity before lunch, but since you feel a bit bloated after the colonic, the idea of someone massaging you is not appealing. This leaves you with either reflexology (turn to **67**), a facial (turn to **6**) or acupuncture (turn to **90**).

You take a seat at the back, so you can observe everyone else, and wait for the lecture to start. If this is the first time you've seen the strange, old wardrobe with a bird mosaic and **12 rubies**, you will be intrigued, no doubt. Quickly go to investigate it (turn to **103**) but remember this section number so you can return in time for the presentation.

A young and very earnest woman begins clicking through her PowerPoint slides, showing you the different markings. Apparently, the runes are so valuable that Odin stabbed himself in his heart then hung upside down from the Tree of Life for nine days just to understand them. She reels off the entire alphabet with each letter's runic counterpart. You manage to conceal a huge yawn, as she talks about the runes' meanings, claiming that Dagaz indicates gateways and Perth represents hearths and spiders. With this, you hear someone gasp and mutter nervously, 'The Guardian!' It is a member of the Metamorphosis staff, who quickly exits the room, but despite that reaction, the woman continues and hands out a different rune.

'This is **Algiz** and it protects against evil,' she announces. It is an ominous end to the lecture, but you have no qualms about pocketing the stone then heading with relief to your room. Following a relaxing bath, you change the dressing, note with relief that the wound is healing well with no tusk-related infection and finally, get into bed holding the Drudenstein. Turn to **161**.

173

You give a jolt of recognition and quickly ask what help she can give you. The grey-haired woman smiles and replies, 'Talk to the nurse. The nurse with the spiral branded on her back. Ask her about the yew tree. And whatever you do, don't go in the tank. The salt solution will extract your sweat and skin oils, and it's able to harness your thoughts too. The less that Mother Amber can get her hands on, the less she's able to control you. And whatever you do, remember the word MAN.' As you process all this information, you should **subtract 1** from your METAMORPHOSIS score.

Suddenly, another guest enters the changing room, so the grey-haired woman gives you a complicit nod and you leave, heading straight to your bedroom. Before you fall asleep though, there is one crucial question: Did you acquire a Drudenstein today? If you have at least one in your pocket, turn to **124**, but if you don't have any, turn to **59**.

174

Suddenly, there is a shifting in your abdomen and an alarming sense of fullness. Fearing an impending and embarrassing accident, you leap off the table, the sheet wrapped around like a toga and needles waggling. The acupuncturist shouts something, but all that matters is that you make it to the bathroom in time. As you sit on the toilet waiting for the cramps to subside, you pull out all the needles and hold them carefully in the palm of your hand. What happens next can only be described as a comedy of errors: You flush the toilet, but when you adjust the sheet, drop all the needles down the bowl. With no other options, you fish the needles out, give them and yourself a good clean, then return to the treatment room. The woman is looking dumbfounded and simply holds out a tray for you to put the washed needles into. You mutter 'Sorry', get dressed and leave.

Your guts have settled down now, so you could go to the sauna (turn to **114**) or to the quiet relaxation room for a lie down (turn to **77**). However, if neither of those options appeal, you can simply head to the dining room — it is nearly lunchtime after all (turn to **92**).

175

You enter the small spa room and the woman holds her arms wide out to welcome you.

'What a wonderful day. And how is your transformation going? Make yourself comfortable and let me give you this.' You're quite stunned by the rapid-fire commentary but manage to both sit down and extend a hand to receive your gift. It's a runestone and this one is…

'**Fehu**! The stone of fulfilment and it's represented by amber and the cat. What a perfect combination! Mother will watch over your transformation.'

Only when she finally breathes do you get a chance to speak, so you quickly thank her and pocket the stone.

The facial continues in that vein with Cascadia — her new name now she has been reborn — talking non-stop, and you occasionally grunting in response. Once it's finished, you leap out of the chair, but just before you open the door, you notice that the bin is totally empty. That's odd. Cascadia used a ton of cotton wool balls during the treatment, so where did they go? You're about to ask her when you hear the distinct click of a container being sealed. You make a slight noise, and Cascadia jumps and turns around. 'Yes?' she asks, sounding not quite as friendly as she did a few minutes ago. You catch a glimpse of a plastic cylinder on the table, but Cascadia blocks your view and snaps, 'You should be getting on. It'll be lunch soon.' With that, you are dismissed. **Add 3** to your METAMORPHOSIS score. Cascadia is right though, it will be lunch soon, although if you like, there is still time for a quick sauna (turn to **144**) or a meditative rest in the relaxation room (turn to **27**).

176

You wander down for breakfast, hoping to have a 'Eureka' moment, but before you even reach the dining room, the Metamorphosis receptionist grips your arm and escorts you to the front door. Plainly not wanting to cause a scene, he simply murmurs, 'We know who you are. We know who your sister is and you are not welcome here. Take the taxi and never come back!' You struggle and try to resist, but there are more people standing guard in the lobby and glaring threateningly at you. You don't stand a chance! They've even hurriedly packed up your things, so without any further ado, you are taken to the airport.

You could return later — in disguise, maybe — and at least then you'll have a better idea of what to do but for now, your rescue mission is over.

177

Decisions, decisions! Today is a beautiful morning and it's day one of your furtive snooping into Metamorphosis. So what will you choose for your first activity?

BodyFit class	Turn to **162**
Spinning class	Turn to **71**
Kayaking	Turn to **111**
Colonic irrigation	Turn to **82**

178

The shopkeeper tells you the price in rapid German but sees your confused expression and points at the display on the till: €3.95. Make a note that you have bought a **butterfly 'tattoo' skin transfer**. It would seem that the language barrier has definitely put paid to any further chats with the man, so you leave and head to the narrow footpath that will take you safely back to the Retreat. Turn to **130**.

179

She doesn't seem offended by your rather personal question but simply shrugs and replies, 'Long story!'

An old man walks in at that moment, saying, 'Guten Tag', which stops any further conversation.

You're getting too hot now anyway, so you leave, have a quick cold shower, then head to the relaxation room (turn to **27**).

180

Your eyes light up when you see her, although you are careful not to give anything away in front of the Metamorphosis lackey who's carrying the breakfast tray. The grey-haired woman says, 'You need to take normal food now to build up your strength and heal fully — no juice detox for you!' Well, you're not complaining. The tray has croissants, raspberry jam and a pot of coffee. You tuck in enthusiastically, and the lackey goes to the bathroom to check on something. As soon as the door closes, the grey-haired woman whispers, 'You must take care of a butterfly tattoo and you must remember the word OVER — it's all important. And take this.' In the nick of time, she hands you a scrap of paper, before the lackey returns and informs you that he'll bring more towels when he collects the tray later.

It would seem that you are to remain in your room this morning to continue recuperating, but now that you're alone again, the first thing you do is examine the scrap of paper. Turn to **53**.

181

'How long have you been here?' you shout out, as you glide towards the others.

'A couple of days now; it's wonderful,' one woman says. 'It's giving me a totally new perspective on my life. I've been so superficial, but now I'm starting to see where my old life was draining my energy.'
You smile in the hope that it disguises your cynicism — is she joking? But no, she seems to be serious, and the rest are nodding in agreement. Another one pipes up, saying, 'Me too. I'm considering never going back home. Devoting myself to Mother Amber is looking

like a more solid life choice than working the rat race. It may seem strange at first,' he says directly to you, 'but I'm right. If you really examine it, you'll see how meaningless your current life is.'

After a while of them waxing lyrical about Metamorphosis, you pluck up the courage to interrupt and ask, 'Have you seen the odd thing protruding from the lake? It looks like a spire.'

'Yes, it's a submerged village. They flooded the area a few decades ago, apparently. Taking it back the way Nature intended.'

'It's just a question of viewing your existence in a completely new way. If you want to transform, then you too can wash away all the old compulsions and be refreshed.'

This is all delivered with smiles and faraway stares, which convinces you that your suspicions are accurate, but how could they have been brainwashed so quickly? They've not even been here a week yet! Suddenly, you become aware of the grey-haired woman shouting for you to return to the shore, and once you've safely deposited the life jacket and kayak, you head on back to the Retreat.

You still have enough time for another activity before lunch, so what do you fancy?

> A facial   Turn to **6**
> A massage   Turn to **198**
> Reflexology   Turn to **67**
> Acupuncture   Turn to **90**

182

'Wonderful!' exclaims the spa receptionist when you tell her you'd like to have a bowel cleanse. You're not sure whether to be reassured or alarmed by such enthusiasm, but you are immediately ushered through to the changing room. Soon you are lying on your side, in a surgical gown with your knees pulled up and the tube already inserted. The man in charge of the cleanse is soothing, and the whole experience is not as bad as you thought it would be. As he massages your abdomen, he talks about how Metamorphosis has transformed his life. How he was self-centred and greedy, but now he has given it all to Mother Amber and feels enlightened. He gently touches the silver butterfly tattoo on the nape of his neck and says wistfully, 'Maybe soon I can go through. Go behind the Wall and be with Mother Amber.' You nod encouragingly, and he continues, 'I want to bring the joy to you too. Let me help you get rid of all those accumulated toxins, then you can be free too.'

You try to politely object, but with a tube still in your rectum, you are quite limited in this protest. He grabs a jug of brown liquid and adds it to the inlet tube, cheerily saying, 'Coffee enemas are the gold star in clearing out heavy metals, yeast and even parasites from the intestines.'

'But I don't think I have those...' you try to point out but it's too late.

It's probably best to not go into details, but you definitely do have a very thorough bowel clear-out. **Add 4** to your METAMORPHOSIS score. Perhaps to make up for this, he presents you with a runestone, saying, '**Laguz**. It represents flow.' Is he joking? You shoot him a sharp look, but no, he doesn't seem to be mocking your recent outpouring. Despite the gift, you have persistent, painful cramps and return to your room for the rest of the morning. As lunchtime approaches, you're feeling slightly better, so would you like to squeeze in a quick sauna first (turn to **144**) or have a meditative lie down in the rest room (turn to **27**)?

183

'I think I'm getting closer to finding my sister, but can you tell me anything?' you say urgently to the grey-haired woman. She nods and replies, 'But we must keep up appearances too.'

She holds up an amber pendant and begins to swing it in the time-honoured fashion. After a few minutes, you are about to impatiently repeat your question when you notice the clock. An hour has passed! You gasp and she smiles, then says, 'Whilst the chrysalis is vital, the key to the Gateway lies with the cauldron, so remember the word OVER.' But before you can even begin to process that nugget of information, you're dismissed. You bow your head in frustration and wonder why the Grey Women have to be so cryptic.

Despite your annoyance, she has been very useful and if you had previously ticked the codeword TRANCE, you should now erase it, as the grey-haired woman has reversed the hypnotic suggestion. You should also **subtract 1** from your METAMORPHOSIS score. Not only that, but she also hands you yet another runestone. This one, you are informed, is **Algiz** and will protect you against evil. Well, that's nice, you think and although you're still feeling faintly irritated, you leave as instructed — time for dinner! Turn to **56**.

You creep forward, although you can't imagine that this beast would be scared of anything, let alone you! It's a wild boar but one of huge proportions. Its grey coat gives a ruffle as its muscles shift underneath, and you wonder whether it's preparing to charge. If it did, the sheer weight of it would surely kill you and if not, then the gnarled tusks would definitely finish the job. The dark amber eyes stare at you, but it's hard to read any mood behind it. The boar looks both thoughtful and malevolent. With a forceful huff, a plume of breath erupts from its mouth, and you finally notice the bundle of branches clenched in its jaws. That's not normal boar behaviour, surely. It looks like it's building a nest or something! Suddenly, your sleeve is grabbed, and you almost let out a scream. It's João. He tugs you back, whispering urgently, 'Come on. Don't upset Hagalaz. Don't ever upset Hagalaz!'

You turn to face him. *What? The boar has a name?* João is not interested in discussing this though. He's already returned to the rest of the group, and when you look back to the boar, it has gone. You have no option but to continue the hike. Turn to **139**.

185

Do you want to talk about it? Well, that suddenly seems to be a very loaded question. She starts to rub a lotion — orange and macadamia oil — into your skin as she waits for your answer. If you eventually say, 'The nightmare was a manifestation of my inability to surrender and let go of my blockages,' you should turn to **31**. However, if you think you can trust her, you should ask, 'What's happening to cause the nightmares then? There's something dodgy going on here, isn't there?' and turn to **108**.

186

You have a quick shower, then climb naked into the tank. It is a weird sensation to float in total darkness and silence. Your heartbeat sounds very loud, but eventually, you relax, your mind drifts, and you feel rejuvenated when you climb out after an hour. **Add 3** to your METAMORPHOSIS score. All of which you announce to the staff member in charge of the tank, but he doesn't seem interested in you. He's staring at his arm, and you realise that he's actually cut a symbol into his own skin next to a turquoise butterfly tattoo. You blurt out, 'Urgh!' and he looks up then says, 'This will help me to find the gateway and if I focus really hard, maybe I can leave my sins behind. I have to prove how committed I am to Mother Amber.' With a slightly gaping mouth, you stand there dripping onto the tiled floor. What do you say to that? Finally, you decide upon, 'Thanks for the session,' and leave, shaking your head in disbelief. Is this how your sister ended up? With relief, you head to your room and slip into bed, but the important question is whether you have a Drudenstein or not. If you do, turn to **161**, but if you are still lacking a stone with a hole in it, turn to **20**.

187

You're not really sure what you're doing, but it can't be that difficult. There's a pleasant sizzle as you pour one, two, three ladles of water over the rocks — that should do it — but then you see not a charcoal lump, but a smooth, round stone with a hole in the middle. Using the edge of your towel, you lift it out.

Once you've sweated a bit more, you leave and have a cold shower, taking the holey stone with you. It seems odd for it to be in the sauna, so you place it in your locker for safekeeping. You may not be aware of the significance of this find, but suffice to say, you have acquired a **Drudenstein** and can now head to the relaxation room (turn to **27**).

188

The man is now happily paddling along, pointing out burrows and a wasp nest, so you edge your kayak closer to the grey-haired woman and ask, 'Is there something underneath the lake? I thought I saw a spire poking up through the surface.'

She nods and explains that the region was flooded a few decades ago and the old village submerged. When the water level sinks, the old church spire can be seen. She leans closer and says quietly, 'And that's not the only thing down there. People disappear. Something takes them. Takes them under the lake.'

'What?' You look directly at her, but her expression tells you to ask no more. However, after a few seconds, she relents and whispers, 'You look just like your sister, and I know why you're here. The Grey Women will help and protect you, and we're not only at the Retreat, we're behind the wall too.' She then cups her hand around her mouth and whispers into your ear.

'W-w-what?' you stammer, but at that moment, the man flips his kayak over, so the woman paddles swiftly over to retrieve him from the lake. Tick the codeword **GREY WOMAN** and **subtract 1** from your METAMORPHOSIS score. That seems to end the session, so you head silently back to the shore thinking about what she said. Although it makes no sense to you now, you have just received some very good advice.

If you ever find yourself in a situation where **"your life appears to be in imminent danger"**, you must **add 50** to the current section number and turn immediately to the new section.

The grey woman has her hands full with the guest, who is still spluttering, so you return to the Retreat. You have enough time for another activity before lunch. Reflexology is off the cards today — there's no way someone is waggling your swollen ankle around, so what do you fancy?

A facial	Turn to **6**
A massage	Turn to **198**
Acupuncture	Turn to **90**

Quite what you were thinking when you decided to shift the cauldron across the hearth, we will never know — a moment of madness, perhaps. With a hefty shove, the cauldron lurches towards the back of the fireplace, but to your disappointment, you hear no accompanying click of a gateway opening. There is no time for you to dwell on that though. The sudden movement has disturbed the black chalice's occupant — the Spider Guardian — a huge, tarantula-like creature that scurries at a lightning speed up your arm and sinks its thick fangs into your neck. The venom is fast acting and paralysing. You are aware that the Metamorphosis staff carry you out of the relaxation room, but there is nothing you can do to stop them as they toss your body into the lake. Your rescue mission has most certainly failed.

'It's OK, thanks,' you shout and he nods benevolently, saying, 'You'll know when you're ready.' Which is a bit pushy and creepy, in your opinion, but you think it's probably best to keep that to yourself for now. You can see a few of the others giving you dirty looks for refusing the towel, but the instructor doesn't seem offended and simply gets back on his bike to begin the warm-down.

'You are transforming your lives!' he bellows, leaning back on his saddle to punch both fists triumphantly in the air and in doing so, his vest rises up showing a perfectly toned stomach and a blue butterfly tattoo. However, at this stage, you're simply relieved that you survived. With dangerously wobbly legs, you wipe down the bike, watching as the others put their golden towels into individual plastic cylinders which are sent off via a pneumatic tube system. Is that a fast track to the laundry, you wonder, before giving a final grimace-like smile to the instructor, then staggering out. The next available activities are all thankfully much less strenuous than that, but what would you like to have now?

A facial	Turn to **6**
A massage	Turn to **198**
Reflexology	Turn to **67**
Acupuncture	Turn to **90**

You twist around, so that you are facing the child-sized, aquatic creature who is trying to drown you, and mouth the words that the grey woman told you. Instantly, its squashed green face frowns and then it snarls showing tiny, piranha-like teeth, before letting go and diving back down to the depths. Your life jacket quickly takes you back to the surface and once you've spluttered and gasped for a bit, you get into your kayak and head back as if nothing untoward has just happened. But you have definitely learnt something useful: Not only is the sunken village defended by who-knows-what, but you saw the 5-windowed submerged house from the dining room mural. You're not exactly sure what it means but it must mean something! **Subtract 1** from your METAMORPHOSIS score.

You have to carry on as normal, so what would you like to have for the next activity?

A facial	Turn to **175**
A massage	Turn to **113**
Reflexology	Turn to **37**
Acupuncture	Turn to **85**

192

It's not easy to sprint in a forest, but adrenalin makes you faster than you could ever have believed. Unfortunately though, it's just not good enough. There is a frantic scramble behind you as the beast charges, and then its immense bulk hits you. You are knocked clean off your feet and land crumpled and stunned against a tree trunk. In that split-second, you close your eyes and know that there is nothing now you can do to save yourself. Turn to **150**.

193

Although you don't speak a word about the real reason you're here, you talk on and on about your fears for the future and regrets about your past. It's like the sluice gates have opened and there's nothing you can do to stem the outpouring of emotion. By the end, you are actually crying *and* laughing and the others are patting you on the shoulder. What *are* you doing? You feel like you've found your family, although deep down you are cursing yourself and wishing you could just shut up! Thankfully, the session is then over. **Add 3** to your METAMORPHOSIS score then head to your room. Before you fall asleep though, there is one crucial question: Did you acquire a Drudenstein today? If you have at least one in your pocket, turn to **124**, but if you don't have any, turn to **59**.

As he unlocks your door, the night porter mumbles, 'Runestones are important here. Make sure you collect as many as you can.' You stare dumbfounded, but he starts to explain how the air conditioning works and generally acts like he hadn't said anything bizarre at all. Finally, he leaves and you close the door. You actually made it!

The room is cream with warm oak, so it has a comforting yet virtuously minimal mood to it. Yes, perfect styling for a spa retreat, and naturally, there is no television. That, and the fact you had to give up your phone at the check-in desk, is no surprise though. You knew about the mandatory digital detox rule when you signed up. "It is the most important part of your metamorphosis", the blurb had claimed. You give a slight shake of the head then continue your exploration, finding a mini bar with mineral water, smoothies and yoghurt, and a bowl of fresh fruit. You opt for a strawberry smoothie and a bag of mixed fruit and nuts, then go to bed.

It is a disturbed night though. You keep waking up to the sound of a creaking door, a moving shadow and a low, cruel laugh, but every time you switch the light on and look panickily around the room, you are alone. It's just a dream. So you lie down and eventually fall back asleep, only for the same thing to happen again. And again. **Add 1** to your METAMORPHOSIS score.

In the morning, you awake feeling exhausted but decide to cheer yourself up by flinging open the curtains to see your lake view. It is indeed an impressive stretch of glittering, blue water. You stare for a while, feeling soothed by the scenery, when you notice something strange in the middle of the lake. It looks like the tip of a spire jutting up from the lake surface. How curious! Still, you can't stay here all day, so you get dressed and head down to the breakfast room. A young woman with a riot of tiny cerise butterflies tattooed around her ankle smiles and asks for your room number. Once she's made a note on her clipboard, she asks, 'Have you decided to opt for the juicing detox for the duration of your stay at Metamorphosis?' Well, that leaves you lost for words, but this was on the website too, so you've had plenty of time to mull it over! What do you eventually reply?

'Yes, I'm doing the juice detox diet.'   Turn to **138**
'No, I want the normal diet please.'   Turn to **43**

195

Ah, the juice diet. Such dedication to playing the part of a spa guest and to think you suspected that they were putting poison or drugs into the juices. How cynical and how wrong! No, they were just normal juices; normal, low calorie, non-filling juices. The juices that left you hungry and angry — oh yes, you were the personification of 'hangry', weren't you? That aggressive tetchiness protected you from the more subtle tactics of the cult and allows you to **subtract 3** from your METAMORPHOSIS score. However, if you sneakily bought a bag (or two!) of chilli-flavoured nachos from the shop, you can only **subtract 2** — be honest! Now tally up your final score and turn to **106**.

196

The guest is happily tucking into her meal and smiles at you as you sit down.

'I'm Frankie Morris. Nice to meet you.' She seems friendly enough, so you tell her your name, where you're from and what you do for a living. She then tells you that she is a paranormal investigator — 'Just had a case at a field studies centre cancelled, then a weird one at a hospital!' — she says with a grin, and you wonder if you can trust her with a bit more than your cover story. If you want to confide in Morris, turn to **47** but if you'd rather keep it secret for now, turn to **157**.

197

You remember the buildings you saw from your room this morning. They were only about a mile or two away, so maybe you could wander off and explore this afternoon. If you want to do that, turn to **99**. However, if you'd prefer to stay at the Retreat, then you have a choice of yoga (turn to **5**), hypnotherapy (turn to **151**) or hiking (turn to **57**).

You undress and settle yourself face down on the massage table. With a gentle knock, the masseur enters the room, introduces herself then exposes your back to begin. Now and then Belinda asks, 'Do you have any current health problems or injuries?' and 'Is this pressure OK?' but otherwise it is soothing nature sounds over the speakers. Halfway through though, you realise that she is making noises too — a suppressed pained sound.

'Are you OK?' you ask. There is a sigh, then Belinda says, 'I'm sorry. I'm just disappointed. I've learnt that I can't go through the entrance yet. I've not done enough to transform.'

It seems like she wants a friendly ear to unburden her woes on, so what should you ask now?

'What happens now then?'	Turn to **155**
'Where is the entrance?'	Turn to **19**

You spot the woman from the sauna, sit down and immediately ask, 'Right, what's so important about a yew tree?'

The woman nods decisively and introduces herself. She's called Flora Demdike and is a nurse who normally works in the operating theatres but had a strange experience — '…that's where I got the spiral brand on my back but it's a story for another time…' — and now whenever Hecate needs her, she has to be there.

'Hecate…' you ask hesitantly, trying to recall any useful facts. Flora interjects impatiently.

'Yes, yes, Hecate the God of Witches. Trust me, I know how it sounds. The yew tree is her favourite. This Mother Amber is trying to get the witches to work for her. Hecate said no and now I have to monitor the situation. I can't say much but it's not looking good!'

'Can't Hecate banish Mother Amber or just kill her?'

Flora smiles at your naivety, then says, 'No, that's not the way it works with Gods or demons. You can't kill them. I forced one to eat herself out of existence, but I'm sure Mother Amber will need a different tactic. You really should leave while you can.'

'No, I can't. I'm here to find my sister,' you confide, 'She was here.' Flora nods but does not look confident in your chances. Just as she's about to speak, a waiter arrives and you must answer the crucial question: Are you on the juice detox (turn to **123**) or the normal diet (turn to **159**)?

200

Holding your breath, you cross the threshold and disappear into the narrow tunnel beyond. The door closes behind you, and the hook automatically lowers the cauldron back down to its original place — the fireplace now shows no sign of your unofficial entry. It's dark and cold in the tunnel but there is light ahead, and seeing as there's no going back, you might as well go forward and discover what lies behind the Wall. Turn to Part 2: **201**.

PART TWO: BEHIND THE WALL

201

You arrive at a junction — the wide corridor stretches from left to right and is cold and utilitarian with unforgivingly bright, white industrial lighting. Along the walls and over your head are air ducts, wires and miles of pipes and tubing. You look both ways, but there is no clue about what lies in either direction. No signs, no familiar landmarks and no identifiable sounds, just the constant drone of electrical humming. However, just ahead of you, there are some strange, small markings scratched onto the wall. You're not sure if they are 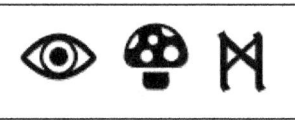 important, but you make a concerted effort to remember them — just in case!

Otherwise, you're just going to have to take potluck as to where you go next, so do you head left (turn to **289**) or right (turn to **246**)?

202

Grabbing the 'B' key, you run back to the corridor alongside the multipurpose room and unlock the hidden door at the back of the wardrobe. A smell of sickly-sweet decay rolls out, and you see the skeletal remnants of countless rodents on the floor. But the main thing that catches your eye is the huge, feathered coat hanging there. No, that's not right, you think, examining it closer. It's not a coat made of feathers; it's a hollowed out, dead bird hanging on the rail. The glazed, beady black eyes stare at you from the limply draped head. You don't have anything to destroy it with, but you do have some runestones and the night porter did say they would be very useful. Gather your stones together and think about their English letters. This type of bird has a 6-lettered name and the runestones should spell it out. Maybe you don't have all the letters. Maybe you have some extra runes whose letters aren't used in the bird's name. But maybe you've got enough to make an intelligent guess... So, what kind of bird is hanging in the wardrobe?

Just as you did with the key, convert the 1st letter of the bird type to a number, **add that to 300**, then turn to that section. For example, if you think it is a **PUFFIN**, you would turn to 316 (P = 16). If the section you turn to makes no sense, then you must have picked the wrong letter and should now turn to **264** to decide upon your next plan of action.

203

You enter the small break room with a smile, but that freezes as you notice yet another mural of the submerged house. The crowd of blurred people have gone from the window, and now there is a grey, hulking creature peering out from the doorway and a huge amber eye in a window. You gulp, then try to act nonchalant. There are two other people here, but as you try to decide who to sit with, you freeze again. How come you didn't notice *that* before? One of the people actually has an Aufhocker on her shoulders! If you want to talk to her, turn to **267**, but if not, there is a grey-haired woman who you could sit with (turn to **312**). Of course, if you'd rather avoid both, you could simply head next door to the changing room (turn to **281**).

The cabinets are just full of the usual, boring stuff —
spare envelopes, boxes of paperclips and file upon file
of instruction manuals. You pick up a folder at random
and flick through the pages. One in particular piques
your interest. It's a weird set of symbols and numbers
— is this some sort of coded instructions for data
protection? Are you supposed to decode what the
symbols represent? Turn to **250** to study this page in
more detail, but remember **this** section number, so you
can return when you've finished.

If you've already seen a switch in the Control Room
which uses these symbols, you can now punch in the
numbers and turn to the section with the same number.
If not, carry on reading.

A perfunctory look through the other folders doesn't
reveal anything exciting, and you start to worry that
you're running out of time. Before you get a chance to
resume your snooping though, you hear footsteps
nearby and dart out of the Control Room (turn to **314**).

205

The creatures start to shuffle towards you, muttering and pointing threateningly. You can't hear what they're saying, but if you had to guess, you reckon that they haven't fallen for your fake infection story. Now they're getting closer, you can see how strong their sinewy arms are — they could really hurt you and from their current mood, that seems to be exactly what they're planning to do. Your life seems to be in imminent danger unless you have a cunning plan up your sleeve.

Well, it would appear that you haven't. Fortunately, these creatures only pin you down, strip off the bandage and wait until real Metamorphosis members collect you. You are unceremoniously turfed into a taxi and sent home. Your rescue mission has failed, but you're still alive and you should be very grateful for that — you have no idea how close you came to having your throat ripped out!

206

The grey-haired woman frowns, then shrugs and says pragmatically, 'Well, there's nothing we can do about that now. You must continue to be vigilant and raise no suspicions about your true intentions. I hope it's enough, but it might not be. The Aufhockers are dedicated and tenacious. If you can find another way to thwart them, all the better.' Your heart sinks at this, but someone else enters the staffroom, so she leaves without saying another word. You nod at the newcomer but decide that you've had enough here. Do you go to the changing room now (turn to **281**) or leave the staff area by the other door in the far wall, even though you have no idea where it leads to (turn to **323**)?

The wardrobe has been a mystery from day 1, so now it's time to face whatever is inside it. However, the wardrobe is locked and whilst there is a key cupboard in the Control Room, you really don't have time to try each key. But maybe during your time behind the walls, you've discovered which letter the wardrobe key is labelled. Using the code A = 1, B = 2, C = 3, etc, **add the number of the key to 200**, then turn to that section. For example, if the key to the wardrobe was labelled 'X', x = 24, so you would turn to 224.

If you haven't received that information, you'll have to do something else. Do you want to deal with the Aufhockers (turn to **278**), fetch the scuba gear (turn to **316**), kill the Neckars that live in the lake (turn to **266**) or have you achieved all that you can and are now ready to head to the submerged house (turn to **225**)?

208

Although you can't see any of the pipe's disgusting contents — there are no lumps of excrement or random body parts floating around — you can definitely see the aftermath of the pollution. There are strange green-skinned, child-sized creatures dead and bobbing about in the water. The Neckars' faces are twisted into agonised death-masks, which you presume is the end-result of the toxic effluent pouring into the lake. Despite their sharp, piranha-like teeth, you almost feel guilty for this massacre, but as you swim past them and get closer to the submerged house, you notice more bodies in the lake. Human bodies which have been tied up and fettered with plant tendrils. Is that what these green Neckars did? Would they have done the same to you? Before you can dwell on that question though, you swim near enough to see the fettered people's faces. If you have noted the names of any of these people: Mishka, João, Phillip, Belinda or Kasper, turn to **269**, but if not, turn to **248**.

209

The next room you see into through the clear glass is where the colonic irrigation takes place. You see a middle-aged man wincing slightly as the staff member presses his belly, then points at the tube. She gives a 'thumbs up' — presumably, something exciting has just floated along the tube — and the man gives a half-smile, half-grimace in response. The tube heads directly to the wall where you are stood and when you look down, you see a wide diameter pipe exiting and running along the length of the corridor. Is this heading to the sewers? But then you realise that this outlet pipe is fed into from *all* the rooms. So what's in the pipe and where is this disgusting concoction heading to?

You approach the door and see the keypad with three symbols at the top. If you know the code, you should turn to the section with the same number **now**.

If you don't know, you attempt a few combinations, but it is pointless. You can now either investigate the 'Offerings Room' if you haven't been there yet (turn to **233**) or go straight ahead along the windowless corridor (turn to **285**).

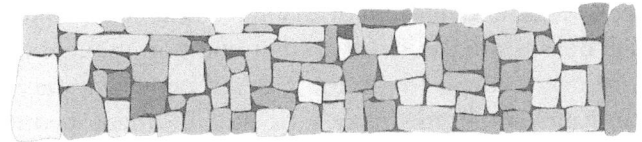

210

With the briefest squint through your tightly closed eyelids, you catch sight of the chair in the centre of the room. A chair with leather straps on the arms and legs. So, people are trapped in here until... what? It reminds you of the scene in 'A Clockwork Orange' and you presume it has the same purpose of extreme brainwashing. The incessantly flashing light penetrates your eyelids, and you are precariously close to suffering the same fate as those strapped in the chair. If you have ticked the codeword STROBE, turn to **240**. If not, turn to **324**.

211

You press against the wall, heart thumping, and know that if anything comes this way, you will be caught. The scratching shuffle isn't getting closer though, so maybe your luck is in, but then you hear a deep croaky voice.

'That was a good one. I hid under the bed and every time they nodded off, I grabbed their ankle.'

'Nice! I went for the old sitting-on-the-chest tactic. You should have heard the scream!'

'Oh, I just tugged at the sheet. Enough to give them a really disturbed nightmare. It was delicious.'

You hear lots of laughter and back patting, then a different door opens and closes, and there is silence. There's no way you're going to follow whatever that was, so you can either investigate the door that the shuffling things came from (turn to **283**), leave that area well alone and continue along *this* corridor (turn to **300**) or you could just go back to where you started and take the right-hand corridor this time (turn to **246**).

212

There's no flashing lights or warning sirens, so you have no idea if that reset was correct or not. In fact, the disgusting contents of the pipe — blood, fat, excrement and vomit, to name a few components — are now flowing with gusto out of the kitchen taps! Whoops! That's not what you had in mind, but it's too late to change it, as you realise that someone is watching you intently. A worker with a silver butterfly tattoo. Damn, you thought they'd all gone to lunch! If you want to approach the worker, although you're not sure what to say or do, turn to **325**, but if you'd prefer to get out of here as quick as you can, turn to **293**.

Plainly, the grey-haired woman isn't going to say anything while the black thing is listening, so you sit silently in a meditative pose. Your patience is rewarded when the poor woman staggers to her feet. She stumbles out under the weight of her Aufhocker, and the grey-haired woman leans forwards and whispers, 'Well done. The last thing you want is to incur the wrath of the acolytes. Having an Aufhocker on your shoulders usually ends in your death, but they are put off by toxins. Obviously, there are none behind the wall, but if you have brought your own, take them.'

Regardless of whether you have brought only one or all of these things — cigarettes from the shop, a small bottle of vodka or whisky, or a bottle of fizzy energy drink — you must turn to **231**, but if you have none of them, turn to **206**.

So you think the last letter is N. Now then, which bird has a 6-letter name which starts with F and ends with N…? Suddenly, the runes whose letters make up the bird's name grow searingly hot. You toss them into the wardrobe and the coat bursts into flames. A few seconds later, all that remains is rancid smoke and a blackened beak amongst the charred falcon feathers. Cross out the runestones that you have now lost, as they are buried beneath the hot ash. Well, that was unexpected, but you feel it has to be a positive step!

Tick the codeword **BURNT FEATHERS**, then decide on your next move. Turn to **264**.

215

What do you want to do now? Face whatever is in the wardrobe (turn to **207**), deal with the Aufhockers (turn to **278**), kill the Neckars that live in the lake (turn to **266**) or have you achieved all that you can and are now ready to head to the submerged house (turn to **225**)?

216

But before you can take another step, you hear a voice shouting. Shouting at you and pointing away from the foyer!

'Oi! Clear off out of here. This whole area is out of bounds today. We need to finish this segment,' the construction worker tells you, pointing vaguely at the wall.

'Oh, was it falling down?' Not the cleverest thing you've ever said, but it doesn't make sense to tear the bricks down only to rebuild them. And there is that smell again! You hold a hand to your face and retch, but the workers plainly don't want to talk to you about this. They turn their backs, and the apparent leader tells the others to put some sawdust over the sudden ooze of yellowy green slime. It seems to be coming from within the wall — have they torn the bricks out to get to the source of the smell? You start to move on as instructed, but as you do, kick something with your foot. It's a small yellow teddy bear. Without thinking, you quickly bend, pick it up and tuck it into your bag. Maybe you can find out later why a child's toy is there. Tick the codeword **TEDDY BEAR**. Once round the corner, you peek back and watch them. After a while, you realise that they're actually putting something behind the wall and bricking it in, but you can't see what it is! Well, going back to the foyer and the stairs is off the table, so you continue along the corridor and soon reach a door which claims to be the Construction Store. If you want to check it out, turn to **310**, but there is another door further on and if you'd prefer to go there, turn to **277**.

217

The Control Room is exactly what you'd expect it to look like with monitors, metal cabinets, switches and dials, but with one exception: there is another mural of the submerged house painted on one wall. This one has a blue cat sprawled in the doorway and a group of indistinct people clustered around one of the windows. You scrutinise them — that one really looks like your sister — but the faces are blurred and you can't be sure. What's more useful is the small cupboard you almost missed. It's painted the same colour as the submerged house's roof and is almost perfectly disguised but at the last second, you see the tiny handle. The cupboard contains row upon row of small keys, labelled A-Z, which means nothing to you now but could be handy in the future.

You do a quick circuit of the room but at the end, still have no idea what the room is controlling. Maybe you need a more thorough search, but you'll have to be quick. Someone must work here and they're bound to arrive soon! Do you want to look at the switches and dials (turn to **303**), the monitors (turn to **226**) or the metal cabinets (turn to **299**)?

You jump into the water, hold your breath and descend about 5 metres before having to return to the surface. You're nothing if not tenacious, so you try again. And again. On the sixth time that you emerge from the lake, gasping and spluttering, you are met by a large contingent of Metamorphosis staff in kayaks. They drag you through the water back to dry land, then hand over your suitcase. For a few seconds, you stare dumbfounded — they're letting you go?

'Just leave. We're grateful you got rid of the Aufhocker, but you can't stay here. Just go!'

So, one good turn deserves another, but you are escorted from Bad Brocken and will not get another opportunity to rescue your sister from Mother Amber.

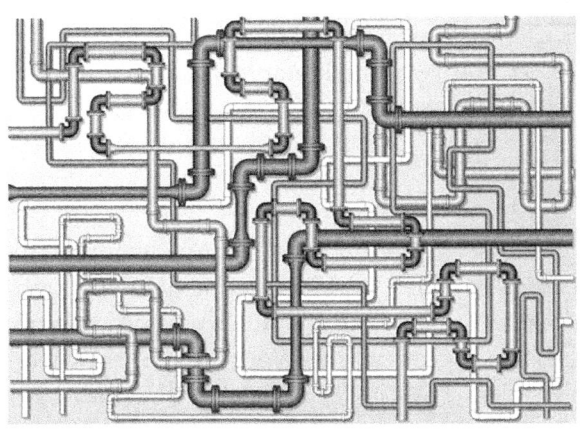

219

You pass by more blackened windows but other than a noise that you're sure sounded like a squeal of pain, you have no idea what is happening behind them. Meanwhile, the pneumatic tubes seem to be getting busier with whoosh after whoosh of cylinders zooming along. You finally approach the door and see the  keypad with three symbols at the top. If you know the code, you should turn to the section with the same number **now**. If you don't know, you attempt a few combinations, but it is pointless. You head off in the opposite direction and soon arrive at the staffroom (turn to **279**).

220

You approach the first door and immediately smell the pungent odour — not like the ever-present stench of decomposition — but an earthier, more animal-like smell. If you want to enter the room despite this, turn to **275**. If not, you should carry on until you reach the next door (turn to **322**).

221

You turn the corner and see the reason for the noise. Two men are busy working on the air duct, with one standing on a ladder and the other passing tools up, but both have their back to you, which is where the problem lies. They haven't seen you, so they carry on their conversation regardless.

'You know these UV air purification bulbs would protect against you-know-who.'

'Sshh, do you want to get us in trouble? You mustn't speak like that.'

'Have you seen the huge duct? The UV bulb in that would be enough to destroy all of 'em!'

'Stop! You're just jealous because Mother hasn't invited you yet.'

'You don't still believe that do you? She only ever takes the pregnant ones. Never the men! We have to stay here and do all the dirty work.'

'That's not true! We all have a chance to be with Mother. At least, we would have if you hadn't…'

But exactly what the worker did, you'll never know, because at that moment, you accidently kick a spanner, and they whip around startled to look at you.

'Oh gosh. You scared us. We thought you were… Anyhow, you look new. Are you new? You should be cleaning up the Disposal Room.' And following that nervous waffle, they start muttering about the UV air purification systems and pretend to be busy with the air duct. With nowhere else to go, you turn and head in the opposite direction, but before you go, tick the codeword **ULTRAVIOLET** if you haven't done so yet. Now you can turn to **298**.

222

You've only gone a few steps when the lights abruptly turn off, plunging you into darkness. You let out a terrified whimper and reach out but touching the slimy wall doesn't make it better. Besides, now the shock is subsiding, you realise that it isn't actually pitch-black — there's red strip lighting all along the ceiling — but then you hear the sound of a door opening and a strange scuffling, scratching sound. Do you want to dart back to the junction and hide out of sight (turn to **211**) or face whatever it is that has emerged from beyond that door (turn to **321**)?

223

You walk around the bed, and she gives a sympathetic pat on the man's shoulder, then joins you.

'I know what it looks like, but I have to keep up appearances. Anyhow, don't forget there is an accessible air duct in the Disposal Room — that might come in handy. Oh, and your sister was moved to the submerged house to be with Mother Amber, but before you head to the lake, remember to destroy the coat in the wardrobe. If you don't, she can escape and the last thing we want is for her to evade justice.'

'What?' you reply, 'But how?'

'Well, first you must...' but just at that crucial moment, the man squirms around pleading, 'Please finish. I must give Mother more, but I can't hang on much longer!' The grey-haired woman tuts and shoves you to the door, saying 'There's never enough time!' You leave and continue until you reach the end of the foyer and another set of stairs leading up — time to investigate what's up there now. Turn to **216**.

224

To your great relief, this is just a staff locker room. And like any other — it's full of lockers! You haven't really got any time to waste, but this is a golden opportunity to have a nose about. However, there are only three lockers unsecured, so which one do you look in first?

> 1M   Turn to **252**
> 3Q   Turn to **309**
> 5G   Turn to **271**

225

With a deep intake of breath to steady your sudden nerves, you set off to the exit that leads to the lake. There will, however, be many obstacles on this path, and you must face the first one almost immediately. If you have ticked the codeword SOOT, turn to **262** but if you haven't, turn to **301**.

226

The screens are standard security monitors with feed coming in from all over the Retreat. You spot the reception foyer, group therapy room and even the relaxation room! You gulp as you realise how lucky you were to get through the Gateway without being noticed. But then another view gets your attention. It's a large tree in a forest with a narrow crack in its trunk. As you watch, a badger wanders into the shot. It has a cub in its mouth, and to your horror, gives a sudden, violent shake which breaks the baby's neck, then drops the dead cub in front of the opening. Once the badger has gone, a huge, grey boar steps out into the clearing and using its snout, pushes both the sacrificed baby and a pile of branches into the tree.

'What the…' you mutter as the boar follows, squeezing into the trunk and inexplicably disappearing. You try to come up with a logical explanation for that but fail. A more productive use of your time would be spent on searching the room, so do you now want to look inside the metal cabinets (turn to **204**) or peruse the switches and dials (turn to **276**)?

227

So what do you want to do now? Face whatever is in the wardrobe (turn to **207**), fetch the scuba gear (turn to **316**), kill the Neckars that live in the lake (turn to **266**) or have you achieved all that you can and are now ready to head to the submerged house (turn to **225**)?

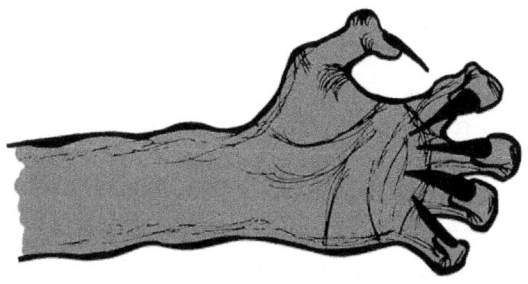

At the far end, a solitary person is testing the hoses for any leaks. At first you think she's simply engrossed in the job, but as you get closer, realise that she is crying.

'Oh, are you OK?' you ask. She raises her head and shakes her tear-stained face. Although you feel uncomfortable with prying, you wonder if she can give you any help — after all, she's presumably not happy here, so maybe she can divulge a few tips… However, when she opens her mouth to answer, gobs of thick blood fall out of her mouth onto the table.

'Ny eef are nissin,' she says, gesturing to her face, and you manage to translate: Her teeth are missing! She tries to reassure you with a pained smile and eventually, you get the truncated story of how she was coerced to give Mother Amber her teeth as a sacrifice and show of loyalty, but now she's seen the light and just wants to leave. She tells you to find the locker room as another disheartened one plotted to sabotage the entire cult. Apparently, he left instructions there which were essential if you wanted to kill the acolytes in the lake, but she doesn't know which locker as he mysteriously and abruptly disappeared without saying…

She waves you away then — 'got to act normal' — so you could either head into the storage section if you haven't been there yet (turn to **302**) or simply leave but if you do, remember the number **236**, so if you need to, you can return to the Diving Room in the future.

Once you've exited, you are back in the corridor. If you earlier activated the 'Glass clear' switch, turn to **265**. If the windows are still blackened, turn to **317**.

You back out into the corridor just as you hear someone enter the Control Room. That was close! But then your attention is taken by the sight in front of you. The blackened glass has indeed cleared and now you see beyond into the spinning class. It's presumably one-way glass because no one is paying any notice to you gawping at them, or maybe they're just exhausted from this early morning work-out. At first, you think your eyes are playing up or that the glass is defected and casting odd shadows, but finally you realise there is *something* on the instructor's shoulders. It looks like a child-sized charred skeleton is being given a piggyback, but the clawed talons stroking the poor woman's throat are not child's play. Even from this distance, you can see the malevolent glee in its black eyes, as the thing hitches itself up and wraps a leg securely under her armpit. She looks slumped from carrying this weight but clearly, there's no way she can get it off. You look around at the other windows — what can you see through those now, you wonder — but before you can make a move, the person emerges from the Control Room. Turn to **291**.

230

You mutter, 'Oh no, no, not me,' as you start to back out, and the young man shouts desperately, 'At least get your overalls! You won't survive without them!' Without even replying, you reach the door and notice an air duct in the far corner of the room. It's wide enough to let a person crawl in and do any maintenance, and although it would be a disgusting job, this could be useful information. Note that the **disposal room** has an accessible air duct.

Now you can either return to the junction and go up the new passageway (turn to **263**) or just go back to where you started and take the left-hand corridor this time (turn to **289**).

231

Well, it's for your own good, you tell yourself, as you either smoke a cigarette, swig the vodka, whisky or energy drink, or, indeed, do it all. If you haven't done so yet, you can now tick the codeword **TOXINS**, then discretely hide any evidence. The grey-haired woman watches this with satisfaction but then worryingly adds, 'I hope it's enough, but it might not be. The Aufhocker are dedicated and tenacious. If you can find another way to thwart them, all the better.' Your heart sinks at this, but a different Favoured Few enters the staffroom, so she leaves without saying anything else. You nod at the newcomer but decide you've had enough. Do you go to the changing room now (turn to **281**) or leave the staff area by the other door in the far wall, even though you have no idea where it leads to (turn to **323**)?

At first, you think it's some strange kind of fish, but then it gets closer. With its green skin and humanoid, child-sized form, you realise that it must be another of Mother Amber's acolytes! And when it grins, you spot the row of tiny, sharp piranha-like teeth. Oh, that's just great! Because it is plainly at home in the water and you are not, it easily grabs your ankles and starts to descend, dragging you with it. Once at the bottom, it nimbly secures you with knotted plant tendrils, then bobs about nearby to watch as you try to release yourself. You're not too worried to start with — after all, you have 40 minutes of air left in the tank and the knots are tricky but not impossible to untie. However, every time you undo one, the Neckar darts forwards and secures you with a new tether. The clock is ticking, and your air is most certainly running out. In fact, it's beginning to dawn on you that your life appears to be in imminent danger, unless you can come up with something fantastic. If not, it's time to think about a plan B…

You might just stand a chance if you have a certain protective runestone, and of course, you brought your bag with you on this diving expedition.

So, if you do have an Algiz runestone, turn to **256**, but if not, turn to **274**.

The 'Offerings Room' is dimly lit and decorated in a most unimaginative way. Thick candles flicker in their ornate holdings, the walls are draped in burgundy velvet and there are framed photographs of butterflies with motivational quotes. The room is obviously where the Favoured Few come to think about their 'gifts' to Mother Amber, although it's not clear whether that is completely voluntary or not… On the nearby cabinet, there is a thick ledger and the open page displays a variety of names with their proposed offerings. Apparently, Mother will soon receive 1 litre of bone marrow, an ear and all twenty nails, but what makes your blood run cold is the final entry, which states that the person is having their 8th session of in-vitro fertilisation, "so that Mother can have the blessed child". You turn around with a deep sigh and clenched fists, and then notice another room through a chink in the velvet. What on Earth is going on in there? All you can see is seizure-inducing flashing lights! Despite that, if you want to go in, turn to **210**, but if you've had enough, you should leave now (turn to **284**).

Once the final number is entered, a nearby light comes on, and you presume that 'Glass clear' has been activated. You are about to resume your snooping but before you get a chance, you hear footsteps nearby and dart out of the Control Room via the door you entered. But which one was that? Well, when you earlier touched a blackened window, if you felt heat and smelled pine, turn to **273**. If, on the other hand, you felt pounding music, turn to **229**.

235

Although it sounds a little insensitive, you ask, 'Why are you having this procedure without any anaesthesia?'

He groans and looks on the verge of passing out but eventually says, 'The greater the sacrifice, the greater the gift to Mother Amber. I have to prove my worth.'

You cynically raise one eyebrow, but although his pale, clammy face looks like cheese left out on a warm day, there's no denying his sincerity. And now you realise that he's absolutely covered in these bruised puncture marks. How much fat has been sucked out? Your expression must have given you away because the grey-haired woman says, 'I know and I've told him that enough is enough, that Mother Amber only invites the pregnant ones but will he listen?' Without waiting for an answer, she starts shunting the metal tubing back and forth under his skin. Blobs of blood-stained yellow fat appear in the tube, and he suppresses a cry of agony.

'They never listen,' you hear her mutter, as you leave and reach the end of the foyer. There is another set of stairs leading up — time to investigate what's on the upper storey now. Turn to **216**.

236

Luckily, you have a rudimentary grasp on scuba diving, so you pick up the air tank, regulator set, wet suit, mask and fins. One last look around and you give a nod of satisfaction — that should do it! Tick the codeword **SCUBA GEAR**, then turn to **215** to think about your next step.

237

You look down at your arm and realise that it's pointing at your fake butterfly. You're desperately thinking of excuses when the leader nods and snorts.

'Yes, another new one. Mother Amber is getting through them quickly these days. They don't seem to be as devoted as they used to be.' The others are plainly bored and start to shuffle impatiently, so the leader points down towards the junction and says slowly and patronisingly, 'You need to go to the Control Room, do you understand?' You nod and the group crawls away. Soon, another door opens and closes, then there is silence. There's no way you're going to follow the creatures — it would be foolhardy to annoy them again! However, you can either investigate where they came from (turn to **283**) or head towards the Control Room (turn to **300**). And if neither of these options appeal, then you could just go back to where you started and take the right-hand corridor this time (turn to **246**).

238

There's no flashing lights or warning sirens, so you have no idea if that reset was correct or not. In fact, the disgusting contents of the pipe — blood, fat, excrement and vomit, to name a few components — are now flowing with gusto out of the showers! Whoops! That's not what you had in mind, but it's too late to change it, as you realise that someone is watching you intently. A worker with a silver butterfly tattoo. Damn, you thought they'd all gone to lunch! If you want to approach the worker, although you're not sure what to say or do, turn to **325**, but if you'd prefer to get out of here as quick as you can, turn to **293**.

239

You find the runestone and present it, very much in the style of an exorcist thrusting a crucifix at a demon. Amazingly though, it works! The Aufhocker frowns, its charred forehead furrowing up, then it snorts and flounces away. You give a massive sigh and are about to replace the rune back in the bag when you realise that the marking has been erased! It is now a plain, smooth and completely useless stone. Note that you have **lost** one Algiz runestone.

When your legs stop wobbling, you leave the room and carry on along the corridor until you reach the other door (turn to **277**).

240

Groping around in your overalls, you find the special glasses and push them onto your face. The relief is immediate — you can almost feel your sizzling brain start to calm down. That was close! Now you can actually see properly, you notice a small tunnel leading off from this room. It looks a tight squeeze, but if you decide to explore it, turn to **247**. If you'd rather get away from the strobing lights and exit the Offerings Room via the main door, turn to **284**.

241

Really? The mice room? Why on Earth did you think you could oust the Aufhockers here? You take a moment and watch the white rodents scamper around, happily unaware of their fate, then think about the next more rational thing you can do. Turn to **227**.

You pass by another window and hear a squeal of pain — it's an old woman having a reflexology session. You wince in sympathy as her feet are manhandled but see how the therapist is being coerced to press harder and harder by the thing on his shoulders. It is grinning as it hooks an unfeasibly long and sharp nail into his mouth and pulls. The flesh stretches until it must surely rip... and then it sees you! You dart away, heart beating furiously and continue walking. Finally, you approach the door and see the keypad with three symbols at the top. If you know the code, you should turn to the section with the same number **now**.

If you don't know, you attempt a few combinations, but it is pointless. You head off in the opposite direction and soon arrive at the staffroom (turn to **203**).

You turn the corner and see the reason for the noise. Two men have blocked the corridor and are busy working on the air duct with one standing on a ladder and the other passing tools up. But both have their back to you, which is where the problem lies. They haven't seen you or your companion, and so they carry on their conversation regardless.

'You know these UV air purification bulbs would protect against you-know-who.'

'Sshh, do you want to get us in trouble? You mustn't speak like that.'

'Have you seen the huge duct? The UV bulb in that would be enough to destroy all of 'em!'

'Stop! You're just jealous because Mother hasn't invited you yet.'

'You don't still believe that do you? She only ever takes the pregnant ones. Never the men! We have to stay here and do all the dirty work.'

'That's not true! We all have a chance to be with Mother. At least, we would have if you hadn't…'

But exactly what the worker did, you'll never know, because at that moment, the Aufhocker launches itself off your shoulders and onto the disloyal worker. It is sheer carnage. A flailing of arms, a shredding of flesh and screams of pure agony. It lasts only 10 seconds and when it's over, the Aufhocker sidles over to the other one and climbs up — you have had a lucky reprieve! You leave the surviving worker weeping with the Aufhocker licking the tears off and head alone in the other direction, but before you go, tick the codeword **ULTRAVIOLET** if you haven't done so yet. Now you can turn to **298**.

You pass by more blackened windows but other than noises which sound like shrieks of fear, you have no idea what's happening beyond the glass. Meanwhile, the pneumatic tubes seem to be getting busier with whoosh after whoosh of cylinders zooming along. You finally approach the door and see the keypad with three symbols at the top. If you know the code, you should turn to the section with the same number **now**.

If you don't know, you attempt a few combinations, but it is pointless. You can now either investigate the 'Offerings Room' if you haven't been there yet (turn to **233**) or go straight ahead along the windowless corridor (turn to **285**).

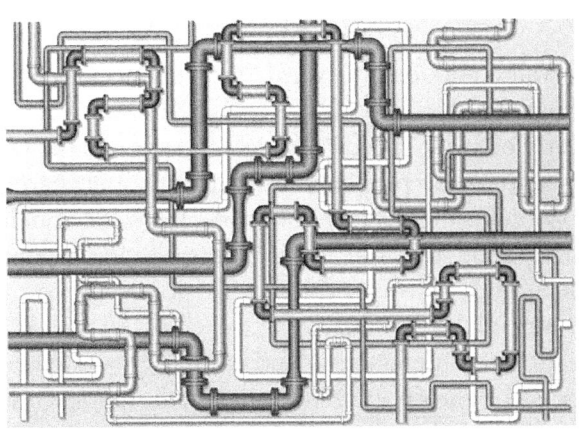

245

Now you've explored what there is behind the walls, you're ready to head off to the submerged house. After all, if you are going to stand any chance of rescuing your sister, you need to find *and* face Mother Amber. Besides if you stay here much longer, your cover will be blown — they must already be wondering why the Disposal Room clean up hasn't been finished yet! But what should you do?

If you think there is something important to tackle in the big, wooden wardrobe, turn to **207**. If you'd prefer to deal first with the Aufhockers, turn to **278**. If you'd rather fetch the scuba gear for your dive under the lake, turn to **316**, but if you have a way of killing the Neckars that live in the lake and want to do that, turn to **266**.

However, if you have done all you can, you should set off for the exit — your time behind the weeping and oozing walls is over. Turn to **225**.

246

You walk cautiously forward, footsteps echoing along the concrete. Every now and then, there is a whoosh as a plastic cylinder speeds through the pneumatic tubing. They seem to be purposefully heading somewhere, and you toy with the idea of following them. So much for 'going behind the wall to find your sister' — you are clueless and the way things are going, if you find anything, it'll be a miracle.

You soon reach a junction and can either go straight on in the same direction as the pneumatic tubing (turn to **318**) or head left (turn to **263**).

You crawl through and thankfully find that it soon widens into a normal passageway. The only trouble is that's all it is — an empty passageway! Just when you're wondering about the wisdom of this, you pass a painting on the wall. An icy landscape of rugged, snow-topped mountains, and it is signed with the initials GW. GW? You sigh with barely concealed frustration but try to commit the icy landscape to memory. You have no idea how that is going to be useful, but you never know. You carry on and soon pass a door. It is slightly ajar, and although the light is on, you can't tell what's in the room beyond. It is silent, but is that a good thing or not? If you want to peek in, turn to **270**. If you'd prefer to creep past, continue reading.

Soon you reach the end of the passageway, open the exit and find yourself in a wide foyer with some closed doors along its length, and at the other side there is a staircase leading up. To what, you can't tell, but if you'd like to investigate the upper storey, turn to **292**. On the other hand, if you'd prefer to stay on this level and snoop around these rooms, turn to **220**.

248

It is with a heavy heart that you study the pale, shocked faces and the butterfly tattoos vividly coloured on the grey skin. Only the other day, they were working at the Retreat but now, judging by the ripped throats, they succumbed to the Aufhocker's talons. After being dumped in the Disposal Room, their corpses were finally brought here to be fettered in front of the submerged house. As what? A trophy? A warning? You are filled with a deep sadness but also a growing anger. Maybe this will be useful though as you approach the submerged house. Turn to **Part 3: 326**.

249

He almost weeps with relief and quickly thrusts the mop at you.

'Thank you. Thank you so much. Look, you'll get to know the place, but I warn you — stay away from the Offerings Room. It's dangerous enough, but there's another room within it and that has flashing lights and is lethal unless you have the right protective gear. That said, a grey-haired woman did tell me there was a tunnel leading from it and she'd left something helpful in there. I don't know what she meant by helpful; she spoke in riddles!' You nod thoughtfully, half-heartedly swiping the mop over the floor, and before you can change your mind, the young man darts for the door. You wait for ten seconds, then hurl the mop into the corner and follow him out.

Now you can either return to the junction and go up the new passageway (turn to **263**) or just go back to where you started and take the left-hand corridor this time (turn to **289**).

The title is 'Keypad Codes', which definitely sounds useful. Now, if only you could decipher it...

butterfly	spider	butterfly	spider	**16**
tree	mushroom	bird	spider	**10**
butterfly	mushroom	mushroom	tree	**9**
tree	bird	bird	tree	**12**
14	**9**	**14**	**10**	

Below the table, it says, "There are 5 symbols: tree, bird, mushroom, butterfly and spider. Each symbol has a different value: 1, 2, 3, 4, 5. Each row and column **add up** to the number at the end, so can you match up the symbol with its value?"

It's probably handy if you make a note of each symbol and its numerical value in the table at the front of the book. Now return to the last section you were at.

The Engineering Room is loud — a relentless cacophony of spinning cogs, thudding pistons and the continuous whoosh of pneumatic tubes — and the air is heavy with a mixture of metal, grease and a more unpleasant, noxious odour. There are workers all around, wearing overalls and thick gloves, and most are emptying plastic cylinders into a vat. You see used cotton wool, acupuncture needles and even toenail clippings going in! However, one worker is operating what looks like a huge salad spinner, only it is full of golden towels instead of lettuce. Is it using centrifugal force to get every last drop of sweat out? Why not just wash them…? And does the sweat go in the vat too?

The workers haven't noticed you, so you follow the vat's exit pipe to see where this disgusting concoction ends up. At one side of the Engineering Room, you find a collection of switches and levers that control when and where the pipe's contents go, but as you extend a tentative finger, you hear a panic-filled shout. One of the workers runs over and practically shoves you off your feet.

'Get away. If you discharge that pipe into the lake you'd hurt the poor Neckar! And what would Mother say if you wasted her elixir?! Who are you and where should you be?'

You go through the routine of explaining that you're new. and he simply tuts then says, 'Typical! Get out and don't come back until you've learnt how to serve Mother properly. Carry on like that and you'll have an Aufhocker on your back before the day is done!'

He stands on guard, protecting his precious pipe, until you reach the exit. Remember the number **311** — it will be useful if you want to return to the Engineering Room in the future.

You leave now and arrive back at the junction. You can now either investigate the 'Offerings Room' if you haven't been there yet (turn to **233**) or go straight ahead along the windowless corridor (turn to **285**).

252

There is a spare shirt and a deodorant stick, but otherwise there seems to be nothing useful here. At the last second, you spot a small piece of paper folded up in the corner. You pick it up and read these instructions:

Turn the lever 90 degrees clockwise

The switches should be ON, OFF, ON

Set the pressure to 400 psi

You have no idea what that means, but there's no harm in keeping this scrap of paper for future reference. You're about to have a snoop in another locker when the door opens, and someone walks in. They look slightly startled, then say, 'Oh, are you the newbie? You're meant to be cleaning out the Disposal Room, aren't you?' You nod in what you hope is a joyful way, then step away from the lockers and exit the room. You soon reach the stairs heading back down to the other side of the foyer — time to investigate what's here now. Turn to **216**.

253

There's no flashing lights or warning sirens, but you can rest assured that the disgusting contents of the pipe — blood, fat, excrement and vomit, to name a few components — are now flowing with gusto into the lake. Just as you wanted! Tick the codeword **POLLUTION**. You allow yourself a little mental pat on the back and smile with satisfaction, then realise that someone is watching you intently. A worker with a silver butterfly tattoo. One of the Favoured Few! Damn, you thought they'd all gone to lunch! If you want to approach the worker, although you're not sure what to say or do, turn to **325**, but if you'd prefer to get out of here as quick as you can, turn to **293**.

254

The Aufhocker leers, licks its lips in anticipation and starts to draw itself up, as it prepares to clamber onto your shoulders. Your life appears to be in imminent danger — are there any forgotten strategies to combat this thing? Maybe a runestone could help? If you can quickly find an Algiz runestone in your bag, turn to **239**, but if not, turn to **297**.

You almost forget the grey-haired woman's words, but in the nick of time, you point dramatically at the lead creature and say them. There is a collective intake of breath, followed by looks of shock and outrage at each other, then the group turns and shuffles away. The leader is the last one to go, and you hear it mutter, almost to itself, 'I can't believe it…' then it is gone. You hear a different door open and close, but there's no way that you're going to follow the creatures into wherever they've gone — it would be foolhardy to annoy them again! However, you can either investigate where they came from (turn to **283**) or go back to the other corridor (turn to **300**). And if neither of these options appeal, then you could just go back to where you started and take the right-hand corridor this time (turn to **246**).

After a desperate search in the soggy bag, you pull out the rune and thrust it at the little green face. The Neckar looks disgusted, then furious and dives off to sulk somewhere in the depths of the lake. Before you can bask in this success though, an eel darts out, grabs the stone from your hand and swallows it before swimming away. Note that you have **lost** one Algiz runestone. On the plus side, you can now untie yourself and swim closer to the submerged house. As you get closer, you realise that the aquatic acolyte had been busy, for there are many bodies tied up and fettered with plant tendrils. If you have noted the names of any of these people: Mishka, João, Phillip, Belinda or Kasper, turn to **269**, but if not, turn to **248**.

It's the large multipurpose room, and a yoga class is currently in session. The instructor, a grey-haired woman, looks up, then stares directly at you. With a jolt, you jerk away from the window feeling guilty at your voyeurism. You thought it was one-way glass! None of the others seem to see you though, so you wait while the grey-haired woman makes her way meanderingly but deliberately towards you. She reaches the window then rests her hand on the large wardrobe. You can hear her say to the group, 'You must use the runes to open up and destroy what is bad within!' Her words are designed to sound like typical Metamorphosis speech, but you see her give a distinct and unmistakable nod to the wardrobe. You frown — what is in the wardrobe that needs to be destroyed? And how do you use the runes to do that? But there's no way you can ask her and in any case, she quickly leans forward, breathes onto the glass then writes 'B' in the condensation. She swiftly turns back to the class and continues with the asanas. B? Is that supposed to help with the wardrobe? And then you facepalm as you see the edge of a small doorway. There's a back entrance to the wardrobe! It's almost invisible with no frame or handle, but there is a tiny keyhole and you remember the Control Room and the labelled keys — maybe that's what she means by B! You'll sneak back there soon, but while you're here, you might as well get the lay of the land! You go forwards and arrive at a junction. To your left is another clammy, reeking but windowless corridor (turn to **285**), straight ahead is the 'Offerings Room' (turn to **233**) and if you go right, you'll reach an unmarked, locked door (turn to **209**).

258

You start down the stairs, and the Aufhocker immediately wriggles around to shift its weight to the back. In doing so, it braces its feet against your left arm. Which codeword did you tick? CHRYSALIS (turn to **319**) or BANDAGE (turn to **280**)?

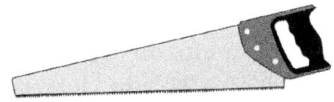

259

The screens seem to be standard security monitors with feed coming in from all over the Retreat. You spot the reception foyer, group therapy room and even the relaxation room! You give a gulp as you realise how lucky you were to get through the Gateway without being noticed. But then another view gets your attention. It's a large tree in a forest with a narrow crack in its trunk. As you watch, a badger wanders into the shot. It has a cub in its mouth, and to your horror, gives a sudden, violent shake which breaks the baby's neck, then drops the dead cub in front of the opening. Once the badger has gone, a huge, grey boar steps out into the clearing and using its snout, pushes both the sacrificed baby and a pile of branches into the tree.

'What the…' you mutter as the boar follows, squeezing into the trunk and inexplicably disappearing. You try to come up with a logical explanation for that but fail. Finally, you decide to resume your snooping, but before you get that chance, you hear footsteps nearby and dart out of the Control Room, turn to **314**.

260

With more luck than skill, you inject the morphine into a vein and watch with relief as her face relaxes and her agonised breathing calms and slows. And gets even slower. And stops. Wait, what?! You try to resuscitate her but shouting 'Wake up!' is not going to work here. You have killed her, although it could be argued that it was a mercy killing. Nevertheless, there is nothing else you can do, so in a state of mild shock, you leave and soon reach a junction. To the left there are stairs heading down (turn to **298**) and to the right, you can hear voices and occasional clattering and banging (turn to **221**). Where do you go?

261

The stench of decay hits you like a sledgehammer, and you gag instantly. After a few seconds, the retching eases and your streaming eyes take in the dark and dismal room. It's like a slaughterhouse and you can see drying puddles of blood and the solitary corpse, its throat ripped so savagely that it's almost been decapitated.

'It's not what I expected either,' says a small voice from the shadows. You shriek, then feel foolish when you see the young man step forward with a crimson-stained mop. He looks defeated and is about sixteen years old. You nod and he continues.

'I wanted so much to get behind the wall. I was told how beautiful it would be to get closer to Mother, but this is it. I've not seen her yet. She never comes here. She stays in the submerged house and we, well, we just have to make sure that the stuff gets to her. It's disgusting. I don't know why she wants it. Every day, it's horrible work and then there's the threat of...'

'Of what?' you prompt, but he shakes his head. 'It's not like what I thought, but I don't know how to get out,' is all he says before asking hopefully, 'Are you new here? Are you taking over from me?'

Well, that's a disturbing prospect, but what's your reply? If you tell him that you're not, turn to **230**, but if you confirm that you are his replacement, turn to **249**.

262

You scurry along the now-familiar corridors, but they are littered with black flakes and claws — the remnants of the Aufhockers — and soot patches have been blasted over the walls. Although you exposed only one to the UV rays in the air duct, they seem to be networked, and the effect spread to each and every Aufhocker. You make it safely to the exit door, run out into the sunshine and head swiftly to the lake. There's no time to enjoy the weather though. Just because you've destroyed one of Mother Amber's acolytes, it doesn't mean that the others won't come after you. The best course of action is to get to the submerged house, but that's easier said than done! You steal a kayak, then paddle out to where the church spire juts up from the lake surface. Well, it's as close as you can get, now all you have to do is dive down.

Have you ticked the codeword SCUBA GEAR? If you have, turn to **290**, but if not, turn to **218**.

263

You turn the corner and instantly notice that this section has some blackened windows in the wall. You go up to one and press your nose against the glass, but it is impossible to see through. You head to another and when you place your hand on the window, you feel a pulsing beat through your fingers. Music? At this time of the morning? You listen a little longer but realise that this is not getting you anywhere. A little further ahead though, you spot a short passageway leading to the Control Room, so decide to go there (turn to **217**).

264

What do you want to do now? Deal with the Aufhockers (turn to **278**), fetch the scuba gear (turn to **316**), kill the Neckar that live in the lake (turn to **266**) or have you achieved all that you can and are now ready to head to the submerged house (turn to **225**)?

265

You are staggered at what can now be seen as you walk down this corridor. There is no privacy here at the Retreat. Your every move could've been watched, if not by the Metamorphosis staff, then by these charred leeches. Through the next cleared glass, you see one squatting on the shoulders of a masseur. It strokes its unfeasibly long claws over the man's cheek, before leaning in to salaciously lick his neck. You watch as the man flicks his hand in irritation, as if he's sensed a fly on his skin and realise he has no idea of what he's carrying. In another room, a staff member puts the used acupuncture needles into a cylinder before depositing it into the pneumatic tube. Seconds later, it whooshes past your head. This is much bigger than you originally thought. You almost laugh — not so long ago, you reckoned that you'd find your sister in a couple of days, then go home. You thought that the only problem might be persuading her to leave the Cult. Never in your worst nightmares, did you think it would turn out like this with these creatures! Feeling more dread than you ever thought possible, you approach the staffroom (turn to **203**).

266

In order to carry out your plan though, you need to get to the Engineering Room. If you have already been in this particular place, you were told of a number that would help you to return. Well, now's your chance to use it, so turn to the section with that same number.

If you've forgotten it or you don't know where the Engineering Room is, you haven't got the time to search for it. You'll just have to try to avoid the lake-dwelling acolytes and instead decide on your next move. Turn to **293**.

267

The Aufhocker seems to smile as you sit down and leans forward with its face crinkling up — is it smelling you? After a few good sniffs, it rubs its charred face against the woman's, then settles back. She looks terrified but still manages to nod a greeting to you.

'You're newly transformed, aren't you?' You nod, still staring at the thing, which is now repetitively clicking two talons together. 'I know this looks frightening, but it's for my own good. I showed weakness, so Mother Amber is helping me to remember the true path.'

'How long will it stay with you for?' You eventually ask, nerves making your voice crack.

'Until I prove my worth again. I worked so hard to get behind the wall, and I won't fail Mother now. I'm determined to join her.' The Aufhocker smirks at this, and a black flake falls off its mouth then drifts down onto the table. You are about to ask her if there is any coffee when she rises, albeit with some difficulty given the weight on her shoulders, and heads for the exit. Once she's gone, the grey-haired woman frowns at you, then says, 'I know what you were about to do, but you have to be more careful. Think before you talk about such things like coffee! You are supposed to believe in Metamorphosis, so act like it!' And before you can ask her anything, she marches furiously from the room. It's not a lot, but it's all you're going to get from her. So, seeing as a brew is off the cards, what will you do next? Go next door to the changing room (turn to **281**) or leave by the other door in the far wall, although you have no idea where it leads to (turn to **323**)?

'I knew you weren't really transformed,' he whispers nervously. 'I saw you before. When you saw it. I saw your face. And you're right to be scared. They are vicious monsters and if they are Mother's acolytes, what does that make her? I don't want to go under the lake to Mother anymore, but I can't leave!'

His fear is unsettling, and you feel a queasy weight in your stomach but finally ask, 'Why can't you leave?' The young man half-gasps, half-laughs hysterically.

'Leave? No one leaves. Those shoulder-sitters would slit your throat if you tried to leave after being behind the wall. They're like vampires, but where's the sunshine back here?'

It takes you a little while to catch his meaning.

'Oh, so sunlight kills them. Would sun beds have the same effect?' He shakes his head and says, 'There are no solariums here. Everything is too natural and pure for that! But there are UV bulbs used for air purification in the ducts.' This is useful information, so tick the codeword **ULTRAVIOLET**, although if you can't access the source of UV rays, it will be pointless. The man rushes out before you can quiz him about his bruised limbs, leaving you with no option but to head back into the staff room and exit by the other door (turn to **323**).

269

With a heavy heart you recognise a pale, shocked face. Yesterday, they were working at the Retreat but now, judging by the ripped throats, they succumbed to the Aufhocker's talons. After being dumped in the Disposal Room, their corpses were finally brought here to be fettered in front of the submerged house. As what? A trophy? A warning? You are scared by this but angry too, and maybe this will be useful as you approach the submerged house. Turn to **Part 3: 326**.

270

With a hesitant push you open the door wider and wait. Nothing, so you poke your head inside and see that it's just a storeroom with hacksaws, wire saws, blades, specimen buckets, scalpels… Hang on! This isn't for building repairs, is it? You remember the offerings written in the ledger and realise that this is where the Favoured Few fetch the surgical instruments they need. Urgh! You can even see dried, crusty blood on the teeth of the saws. Just then you notice what looks like a body behind a shelf. You dart around and see that it's actually a wet suit, regulator and air tank. Why has that been dumped there? There's no answer to that, but the equipment may come in use, so tick the codeword **SCUBA GEAR**. You now head back into the passageway and at the end, open the exit. You find yourself in a wide foyer with some closed doors along its length, and at the other side there is a staircase leading up. To what, you can't tell, but if you'd like to investigate the upper storey, turn to **292**. On the other hand, if you'd prefer to stay on this level and snoop around these rooms, turn to **220**.

At first glance it looks empty, but then you spot a tatty paperback tucked away at the back. You flick through the pages hoping for a hidden clue or message, but 'The Cluster of Echoes and the Octopus' is about molluscs and billiards, so isn't very useful! You're about to snoop in another locker when the door opens, and someone walks in. They look slightly startled, then say, 'Oh, are you the newbie? You're meant to be cleaning out the Disposal Room, aren't you?' You nod in what you hope is a joyful way, then step away from the lockers and exit the room. You soon reach the stairs heading back down to the other side of the foyer — time to investigate what's here now. Turn to **216**.

Your breath is taken away by the stench of decay from the puddles of blood in the Disposal Room. You resist the urge to vomit and make your way to the access flap in the large air duct. Once you've crawled in, you can see the bulbs for the UV air purification systems — that'll do the job, you hope. With no real conviction that you're doing the right thing, you shout, 'I faked my butterfly tattoo!' and expose your unblemished skin. For a few seconds, you think you need to come up with a plan B, but then with a slither, an Aufhocker suddenly appears and leaps onto your back.

You time it almost perfectly. It draws a claw over your neck, but at the same moment, you lurch towards the bulb and the UV rays hit it straight in the eyes.

You're expecting screams or writhing agonies, but instead the Aufhocker merely gives a gasp of surprise, then disappears leaving a small pile of soot behind. Tick the codeword **SOOT** then clamber back out of the air duct. The scratch on your throat is sore and bleeding a little, but it should scab over fairly quickly. You leave the reeking Disposal Room and weigh up your next move. Turn to **227**.

273

You back out into the corridor just as you hear someone enter the Control Room. That was close! But then your attention is taken by the sight in front of you. The blackened glass has indeed cleared and now you see beyond into the sauna. It's presumably one-way glass because no one is paying any notice to you gawping at them, or maybe they're just enjoying the heat. Just then, a Metamorphosis staff member enters to pour scented water over the coals and at first, you think your eyes are playing up or that the glass is defected and casting odd shadows, but finally you realise there is something on his shoulders. It looks like a child-sized charred skeleton is being given a piggyback, but the clawed talons stroking the poor man's throat are definitely not child's play. Even from this distance, you can see the malevolent glee in its black eyes as the thing hitches itself up and wraps a leg securely under the man's armpit. He looks slumped from carrying this weight, but clearly there's no way he can get it off. You look around at the other windows — what can you see through those now, you wonder — but before you can make a move, the person emerges from the Control Room. Turn to **291**.

274

You never give up trying to unknot the plant tendrils, but inevitably, your air does run out. You are luckily only semi-conscious when you rip out the useless regulator and take in a huge breath. The lake water fills your lungs and then it is over. Maybe your sister will look out from the submerged house and see your fettered corpse drifting back and forth in the slight currents, and she'll know that you did try to save her.

275

You're not quite sure what you were expecting but hundreds of cages containing hundreds of mice wasn't high on your list of potential guesses. Still, that explains the earthy smell. They are squeaking incessantly but look well cared for, so why are they here? They're obviously not pets, but not laboratory specimens either. However, with a casual nose about, you soon find a vat which puts paid to your hopes that these mice weren't being ill-treated here — the vat is connected to a carbon dioxide tank! That still doesn't make sense though — why raise mice just to kill them? What's the point? Even more nonsensical is the half-filled in crossword puzzle, which is tucked behind the vat.

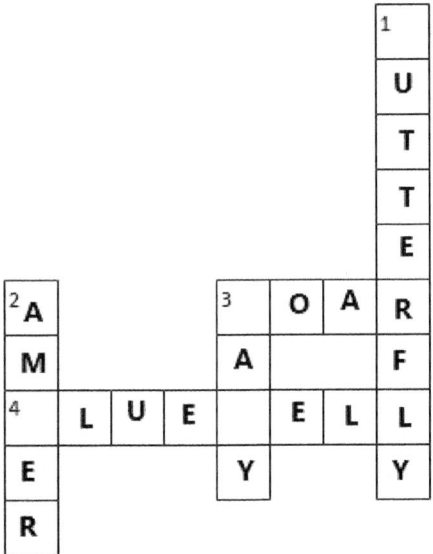

There are no clues but it's not rocket science what the words are! But why are there blank squares? Oh, there are just too many questions, and you're not going to find the answers stuck in here surrounded by death row rodents! You leave and head to the next room — this time cautiously listening at the door before you enter. Turn to **322**.

276

When you examine the switches and dials in more detail, you can see that they are labelled, but unfortunately, names like 'Tube G16 (psi)', 'Output pH' and 'Duct 2 Dobson units' don't enlighten you at all. However, you spot one with the label 'Glass Clear' and wonder if that's got anything to do with the blackened windows. It's not going to be that easy to find out though. Instead of a simple switch, it has a keypad with three symbols on it. Are they a code for the numbers needed?

If you already know what the symbols represent, you can punch in the numbers and turn to the section with the same number **now**.

If not, you wonder whether the answer is somewhere in this room, but before you get a chance to resume your snooping, you hear footsteps nearby and dart out of the Control Room (turn to **314**).

277

However, as you approach, you hear an ominous drip-drip-drip from within the room. Well, you suppose it could be spilt herbal tea, but given what you've seen so far, that seems unlikely.

You brace yourself and enter the room, only to be met by a scene of unspeakable horror. A woman smiles weakly at you from the bed but cannot even lift her head from the pillow. She is pale, which makes sense seeing as most of her blood is pooling on the floor and her left foot is in the middle of the room.

'I couldn't get pregnant, so they made me make a bigger offering,' she whispers.

'And that was your foot?' And, although that is a rather obvious question, she nods, then says, 'I had to do most of it myself, but it was unbearable and I couldn't quite finish. Could you help me, please?'

Well, of course you can, but exactly how will you help her? If you want to first administer morphine to relieve her pain, turn to **260**, but if you'd rather just bandage the stump to stop the haemorrhage, turn to **313**.

278

This is going to be the trickiest task of all. The Aufhockers will not go down without a fight and their claws look impressively lethal — you better have found out their weaknesses if you're going to stand a chance! If you have ticked the codeword ULTRAVIOLET, turn to **307**, if not, turn to **227**.

279

You enter with a smile, but that freezes as you notice yet another mural of the submerged house. The crowd of blurred people have gone from the window and now there is a grey, hulking creature peering out from the doorway and a huge amber eye in a window. You gulp, then try to act nonchalant. There are two other people in the break area, but as you try to decide who to sit with, you freeze again. How come you didn't notice that before? One of the people has a thing on her shoulders! A blackened, sinewy, child-sized thing clinging to her back. Its arms and legs are wrapped around her torso and hooked over her shoulders. It's stroking her neck with dagger-like talons and gives a curious look at you. For some long, drawn-out seconds, you watch each other, then the woman gives a small cough and says quietly but urgently, 'It's my Aufhocker. Don't stare! You're new, aren't you? Shouldn't you be cleaning the Disposal Room?' If you still want to talk to her, turn to **267**, but if not, there is a grey-haired woman who you could sit with (turn to **312**). Of course, if you'd rather avoid both, you could simply head next door into the changing room (turn to **281**).

A thin, leathery foot scrapes over your arm as the Aufhocker hitches itself up. Inevitably, it's where your fake bandage is, so the fabric simply falls off revealing your unblemished skin underneath. If you weren't in such dire straits you might have laughed at the Aufhocker's expression — a comical mix of outrage, disgust and shock — but you wouldn't have had time to do that anyway. It thrusts a bony clawed hand into your mouth and in one swift move, wrenches your tongue out. Once it has thrown the slab of muscle against the wall with a wet slap, it pushes your chin up so the cascade of blood flows back into your airways. You will eventually drown, but that will be a welcome relief from the white-hot pain and fear you are currently enveloped in.

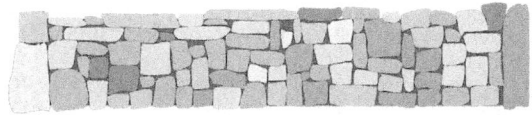

Obviously, all the money was spent on the Retreat side of the building, you think as you go into the dilapidated changing room. You don't actually have a plan, other than putting off the Disposal Room job for a bit longer! Just then, a young man emerges from one of the cubicles. He has a haunted look in his eyes, is thin and gaunt and has bruising all over his arms and legs. He doesn't look as if he's thriving behind the wall, so if you want to ask him for any help or advice, turn to **268**. If you think it's wiser to keep playing the part of a Favoured Few and ask for some overalls, turn to **305**.

282

You take the regulator out, then mouth the words the grey-haired woman told you. The green-skinned creature looks stunned for a few seconds, then positively affronted and swims off to sulk somewhere in the depths of the lake. Without its hindrance, you can now untie yourself and swim closer to the submerged house. As you get closer, you realise that the aquatic acolyte had been busy, for there are many bodies tied up and fettered with plant tendrils. If you have noted these names: Mishka, João, Phillip, Belinda or Kasper, turn to **269**, but if not, turn to **248**.

283

As silently as you can over hard concrete, you creep towards the door, then inch it open. It's a narrow staircase leading up. Once you've checked that the door doesn't automatically lock, you head up and arrive at an exit. Peeking out, you are shocked to see a familiar passageway — these are the Retreat bedrooms! The scratchy, shuffling things were in the guest bedrooms! While this might be useful to know, now that you've got behind the wall, there's no way you're going back, so you close the door. As you creep back down the staircase, you notice something that you'd missed on the way up. A **small bottle of whisky** tucked into the corner of one of the treads! Did one of those creatures drop it? You can't imagine that but decide to keep it anyway — some Dutch courage may be useful in the future! You head back to the junction and can now either see what's down the other corridor (turn to **300**) or you could just go back to where you started and take the right-hand corridor this time (turn to **246**).

284

Unfortunately, that is the last mistake you will ever make. Did you really think the Aufhockers would let you leave the Offerings Room without promising any kind of gift for Mother Amber? It sidles up to you like a wisp of smoke, but the claw that slices through the skin of your neck is quite substantial. There is a sudden burn and then the feeling of release as blood cascades down your chest. You drop to your knees in shock and try to stem the flow, but the Aufhocker grabs both wrists and holds them until you pass out. This isn't new or shocking. In fact, it's a commonplace occurrence behind the wall, so someone will soon drag your corpse to the Disposal Room, then mop up. Business as usual at Metamorphosis!

285

You walk down the chilly corridor until you arrive at a wide foyer with some closed doors along its length, but to the side there is a staircase leading up. To what, you can't tell, but if you'd like to investigate the upper storey, turn to **292**. On the other hand, if you'd prefer to stay on this level and snoop around these rooms, turn to **220**.

'Excuse me,' you say politely. The grey-haired woman looks up, then smiles.

'Good that you found this place. You need diving equipment to stand any chance of finding your sister. Beware though, the lake is filled with Neckar!'

'What? Did you say 'nectar'? Why should I be worried about that!?'

'The Neckar are more of Mother Amber's acolytes,' she explains patiently. 'They protect the submerged house and dispose of those who displease the Aufhockers. The Favoured Few have to take the corpses down to the Neckar, where they get… *arranged* down in the lake.' She pauses and you probably should use this opportunity to ask some pertinent questions, but where do you start? She carries on regardless.

'If you go down without a corpse, they'll drown you. Even if you have an air tank on, they'll just fetter you to the lake floor until it runs out. You must destroy them first and the only way to do that is to pollute the lake. All her acolytes cannot stand toxins.'

'Yes, but how do I do that?'

It is a sensible question, but like so many times before, your timing is distinctly off. Another staff member walks in at that moment. He looks grim and simply points at a wetsuit. The grey-haired woman mouths the words 'disposal time', then waves you away.

Remember the number **236** as it will be useful if you want to return to the Diving Room in the future. If you haven't done so already, you could now head into the maintenance area (turn to **228**), but if you're ready to leave, you will find yourself back in the corridor. If you earlier activated the 'Glass clear' switch, turn to **265**, however, if the windows are still blackened, turn to **317**.

Instead of heading to the stairway that connects to the Retreat's guest bedrooms, you go in the opposite direction and arrive at a door. When you enter, you are almost asphyxiated by a heavy, musty odour, but soon realise that you are surrounded by a herd of heaving, sleeping, snoring creatures. Stunned by the sight, you simply stand and stare but then hear a slight shuffling nearby. It seems the light from the open door is disturbing their beauty sleep.

'Oh, for Heaven's sake, do shut the door. The light is giving me a migraine!' The gravelly voice sighs, then tuts, so you leave as silently as possible. It's the sensible thing to do, besides, the chink of light had already shown you that there were no air ducts anyway in that room. Pity! It would've benefitted from a bit of air purification! With no other option, you give up your Aufhocker homicide plan and think about your next move. Turn to **227**.

However, as you approach, you hear an ominous drip-drip-drip from within the room. Well, you suppose it could be spilt herbal tea, but given what you've seen so far, that seems unlikely.

You poke your head round the door, but the Aufhocker squeals in annoyance and gives the door such a shove that it hits the wall, bounces back and almost smacks you in the face. Presumably, it wants to see this scene of unspeakable horror. The woman gives a weak sob when she sees the Aufhocker but cannot even lift her head from the pillow. She is pale, which makes sense seeing as most of her blood is pooling on the floor and her left foot is in the middle of the room.

'I think I'll finally be invited to go under the lake now. I just needed to make a bigger offering, seeing as I couldn't get pregnant,' she whispers.

'And that was your foot?' And, although that is a rather obvious question, she nods, then says, 'I did most of it myself, but couldn't quite finish. Could you wrap the stump up, please?'

That is the absolute last thing you want to do, but you can't refuse. However, when you reach out for the bandage, a clawed index finger instantly appears in front of your face, wagging back and forth. You freeze and look sideways at the Aufhocker, who juts its chin in a challenging way, then grins as you lower your hand. Obviously, it wants the poor woman to bleed out and who are you to argue? The Aufhocker sniggers next to your ear — its hot breath making your flesh crawl — and the woman simply stares with tears in her eyes as she realises the fate that the Aufhocker has condemned her to. There is nothing else you can do for her, so you mouth 'Sorry' and stumble out to the corridor, the Aufhocker urging you on, like a burnt and skeletal jockey, until you reach a junction. To the left there are stairs heading down (turn to **258**) and to the right, you can hear voices and occasional clattering and banging (turn to **243**). Where do you go?

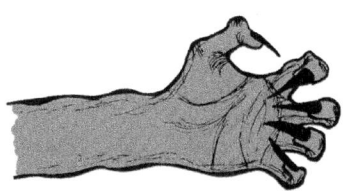

You stride quickly down the corridor. There's nowhere to hide, so you're keen to get to wherever it leads to. However, you can't help but notice the black-speckled patches of mould over the walls and in a few spots, there's even a green slime oozing from cracks in the concrete. Although it's disgusting, you examine it closer. It looks like they kept adding new layers to the wall, maybe in an attempt to block out the rot. Unsuccessfully, that much is clear! Suddenly, you stop as a glint of bright yellow catches your eye. There's something trapped near the ceiling between the pipes. You peer up, teetering on tiptoes and see a baby's plastic dummy. It's harmless in itself but there's something deeply unsettling about the fact that it's here. You feel a cold shiver, but know you have to plough on, so you do and eventually reach a junction. You can either continue straight on (turn to **222**) or head right (turn to **300**).

290

It's not easy to get a wetsuit on quickly whilst balancing on a kayak, but in an impressively short time, you insert the mouthpiece, dive in and start to descend. Soon, you can make out the shapes of the submerged buildings — you're nearly there! But hang on… What's that?

Did you tick the codeword POLLUTION? If you did, turn to **208**, and if not, turn to **232**.

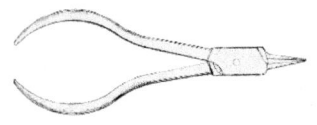

'The Drudes have been back from the nightshift for ages. Why didn't you lock the connecting door? We don't want guests wandering behind the walls, do we?' The Metamorphosis staff member waits impatiently for your response, but you stand there, mouth gaping like a goldfish. Drudes? What can you say? Luckily, you're saved from answering, as she gives a tut and a world-weary shake of the head before stating, 'You're new, aren't you? They really should do some onboarding or at least explain what the Aufhockers are, so we don't have this shock every time.'

'Aufhockers?'

'The black things on the shoulders. They're one of Mother Amber's acolytes. Now you're behind the wall, you're privileged enough to see them. They protect Mother by making sure nobody is disloyal.'

You gather your wits and remember your new disguise as a Favoured Few, so reply, 'Of course. Mother deserves absolute loyalty.' She nods, satisfied with your answer, then becomes business-like again.

'Right then, go to the staff room and ask someone to show you where the overalls are kept. I like to throw new recruits in at the deep end, so your first job can be cleaning out the Disposal Room.' Well, that doesn't sound great, but your only option is to plaster a smile on your face and say, 'Happy to do it.' However, once you reach the next junction, where do you actually go? To the staff room as she instructed (turn to **265**) or head left towards the unmarked, locked door (turn to **242**)?

292

You climb the stairs yet the foul odour still hangs in the air — it smells like someone unplugged a refrigerator but forgot to empty it — and the thick green ooze is becoming a familiar sight as it dribbles down the wall. Soon, you pass by a room and seeing as the door is ajar, you peek inside.

The young woman cries out and reaches for you, but the other person bats her arm down, hissing, 'Stay strong, Ruby. For every great destiny, there must be a great sacrifice. You will go to the submerged house and join Mother. She will reward you for this!'

You stay there, awkwardly stood in the doorway, wincing as the pliers are inserted into Ruby's already-bloody mouth. Next, you hear the distinct sound of a tooth being wrenched out, followed by a heart-rending scream. There is nothing you can do but as the door closes, leaving Ruby to her fate, she sobs, 'I want to go home.' You go on, feeling shaken by that encounter. Is that what your sister has endured? Are you about to see her being tortured in a room or has she already gone under the lake? Maybe that question will be answered sooner rather than later — you have reached the next door. Turn to **224**.

293

What do you want to do now? Face whatever is in the wardrobe (turn to **207**), deal with the Aufhockers (turn to **278**), fetch the scuba gear (turn to **316**) or have you achieved all that you can and are now ready to head to the submerged house (turn to **225**)?

294

You go forwards and arrive at a junction. To your left is another clammy, reeking, windowless corridor (turn to **285**), straight ahead is a door leading to the 'Offerings Room' (turn to **233**) and if you go right, you'll end up at an unmarked, locked door (turn to **244**).

295

You look down at the bandage, adopt an innocent expression, then say, 'My tattoo got infected.' There is a protracted pause, in which the creatures shake their heads and mutter amongst themselves. You can't tell what they're saying but it doesn't look like they're convinced. If you're carrying a Drudenstein, turn to **308**, but if not, turn to **205**.

296

There's no flashing lights or warning sirens, so you have no idea if that reset was correct or not. In fact, the disgusting contents of the pipe — blood, fat, excrement and vomit, to name a few components — are now flowing with gusto into the flotation tank! Whoops! That's not what you had in mind, but it's too late to change it, as you realise that someone is watching you intently. A worker with a silver butterfly tattoo. Damn, you thought they'd all gone to lunch! If you want to approach the worker, although you're not sure what to say or do, turn to **325**, but if you'd prefer to get out of here as quick as you can, turn to **293**.

297

With nothing to stop it, the Aufhocker climbs onto you. Of course, you try to push it off and drag its arm from around your neck but you just cannot. You stand there for a few stunned seconds, breathing heavily from the exertion, while it squirms about, trying to get comfy. It settles with one leg hooked over your shoulder and the other wrapped around your rib cage, before reaching down and plucking the teddy bear from your bag. It tuts and grates its teeth over your chin, leaving a thin trail of black mucus behind, then throws the cuddly toy far into the corner. Cross out the codeword TEDDY BEAR! You leave now and carry on along the corridor until you reach the other door (turn to **288**).

298

You pass by a corridor that is signposted as being to the lake. Well, that's useful to know, but you're not ready to go there just yet, so you carry on and head down the stairs. It's warm and humid and there are no windows to give you an idea of where you are. However, you soon hear an argument going on behind the wall, so press your ear against the plaster and strain to listen.

'What do you mean, there's no spell? I did one!'

'Gods are different from demons. You had to *force* a demon out of existence; a god has to be *persuaded* to not exist.'

'How is anyone supposed to do that, Hecate?'

'Hypocrisy is usually the way. But Freyja must be stopped — this nonsense with the babies is just going too far.'

'Nonsense?!' The voice sounds incredulous. 'It's an atrocity!'

'I know, I know. It's a God/sacrifice thing, you wouldn't understand. Come on.'

And with that, the voices disappear. You try to sift through all that you've just heard — Freyja? Who's that? Is it another name for Mother Amber? Maybe these mysterious voices know her from before she became a cult leader... Oh, so many questions but not a single answer. You continue along this muggy dark corridor until a thin but steep set of stairs take you up towards a trapdoor. There is only silence on the other side and when the trapdoor is raised, you are back in the Control Room. Turn to **245**.

299

The cabinets don't fill you with any hope of insightful revelations. They are just full of the usual stuff — spare envelopes, boxes of paperclips and file upon file of instruction manuals. You pick up a folder at random and flick through the pages. One in particular piques your interest. It's a weird set of symbols and numbers — is this some sort of coded instructions for data protection? Are you supposed to decode what the symbols represent? Turn to **250** to study this page in more detail, but remember **this** section number, so you can return when you've finished.

You close the cabinets and start to worry that you're running out of time to find anything useful. So, what do you want to look at next? The switches and dials (turn to **276**) or the monitors (turn to **259**)?

300

Well, that's curious. Along this section, there are many blackened windows in the wall. You go up to one and press your nose against the glass, but it's impossible to see through. You head to another and when you place your hand on the window, you feel the heat warming your palm. After a while longer, you realise there is a smell of pine too, but this isn't getting you anywhere. A little further ahead though, you spot a short passageway leading to the Control Room, so decide to go there (turn to **217**).

301

It's not the greatest plan, but it's the only one you've got: Run as fast as possible to the exit you saw earlier. It starts well — you make it around the first corner — but then you hear a slithering sound from behind. However, when you take a panicked look back, the corridor is empty. Are you imagining things…?

Two Aufhockers drop down from the ceiling and instantly attach themselves to your body with their piercing talons. This myriad of puncture wounds would be painful enough but with a strength you cannot believe these desiccated, charred creatures have, they then rip off these portions of flesh. You are alive to see them devour these delicacies but that won't last long.

You walk past racks of air cylinders, fins and wet suits until you reach the far end. There is a grey-haired woman crouched down here and she is busy sorting through a tangled pile of regulators, so hasn't noticed you yet. If you have ticked the codeword GREY WOMAN, turn immediately to **286**. If not, continue reading.

You decide not to bother her and simply peruse the equipment. There's everything here for both scuba diving and snorkelling, but it's weird that neither of those activities were on the itinerary. Still, all of this is *behind* the wall, so it's not like guests could just stroll in and pick up their gear. Which means it's only the Favoured Few who need to go diving in the lake… Well, you're not getting any answers here, but it's handy to know where all this stuff is. Just in case…

Remember the number **236** as it will be useful if you want to return to the Diving Room in the future. If you haven't done so already, you could now head into the maintenance area (turn to **228**), but if you're ready to leave, you will find yourself back in the corridor. If you earlier activated the 'Glass clear' switch, turn to **265**, however, if the windows are still blackened, turn to **317**.

303

When you examine the switches and dials, you see they are labelled, but unfortunately, names like 'Tube G16 (psi)', 'Output pH' and 'Duct 2 Dobson units' don't enlighten you at all. However, you spot one with the label 'Glass Clear' and wonder if that's anything to do with the blackened windows. It's not going to be that easy to find out though — instead of a simple switch, it

 has a standard keypad with three symbols on it. Are they a code for the numbers needed? You make a quick note of them,

but until you know what the symbols represent, this keypad is useless. You should continue your search around the Control Room now.

What do you want to look at next? The metal cabinet (turn to **204**) or the monitors (turn to **259**)?

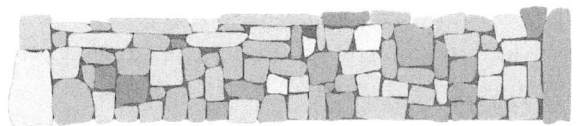

304

You stare in an intimidating fashion, then repeat the grey woman's words. The Aufhocker curls its dried, charred lip in a sneer, but you can tell that these words have hit home. It actually looks like it might cry. Instead though, it merely turns its back on you and flounces away. You give a massive sigh and when your legs stop wobbling, you leave and carry on along the corridor until you reach the other door (turn to **277**).

305

The man reaches into a cupboard, fetches some overalls and remarks, 'But the locker room is up the stairs.' That's weird, you think, but the man rushes out before you can quiz him about it. You pull the overalls on — they are unattractive but fit vaguely and might help you stay in disguise — then reach into a pocket and find a pair of industrial looking glasses. Tick the codeword **STROBE**, then head back into the staff room and exit by the other door (turn to **323**).

306

So, you think that the 1st letter of the bird is F. Interesting, but that could've been a lucky guess. Maybe the only runestone you had was Fehu… To deal with the coat, once and for all, you need to really know what type of bird it is, so this time take the last or 6th letter, convert it to a number and **add it to 200**, then turn to that section. For example, if you think that the bird is a BUDGIE, you would turn to 205 (E = 5). If the section doesn't make sense, you must have been wrong and should turn to **264** in order to plan your next move.

307

Well, that's a step in the right direction. At least you know that UV rays, like those in the air purification bulbs, kill the Aufhockers, but the question now is: where can you find an accessible air duct? If you know of such a place, you should go there now, but is it the Drudes' daytime sanctuary (turn to **287**), the mice room (turn to **241**) or the Disposal Room (turn to **272**)?

308

With nervous beads of sweat trickling down your spine, you frantically think of strategies to get out of this situation, but the creatures suddenly give a strange and unified gesture. It's as if they've detected something in the air, and then they nudge and push each other away down the corridor without another word. You hear a different door open and close, then there is silence. There's no way that you're going to follow the creatures into wherever they've gone — it would be foolhardy to annoy them again! However, you can either investigate where they came from (turn to **283**) or go back to the other corridor (turn to **300**). And if neither of these options appeal, then you could just go back to where you started and take the right-hand corridor this time (turn to **246**).

309

At first glance it looks empty, but then you spot some graffiti at the back.

die Birke ist so besonders, so zeigt Hagalaz seine Liebe

Well, if you spoke German that might be useful, but... You're about to snoop in another locker when the door opens, and someone walks in. They look slightly startled, then say, 'Oh, are you the newbie? You're meant to be cleaning out the Disposal Room, aren't you?'

You nod in what you hope is a joyful way, then step away from the lockers and exit the room. You soon reach the stairs heading back down to the other side of the foyer — time to investigate what's here now.

Turn to **216**.

310

The air is thick with cement dust and when you flick a switch on, you can see that it is, indeed, full of construction equipment. This is a place that apparently has to do a lot of bricklaying! What's that all about? Suddenly, you hear a noise — a slight, soft sound like silk being dragged over the floor — and spin around to see an Aufhocker stood right behind you. Emitting a strangled gasp, you back up against the wall, but it follows, leaning towards you, scrutinising, smelling and even casting a thin, black tongue out to lick your arm. If you have ticked the codeword TOXINS, you should turn to **320**. If not, turn to **254**.

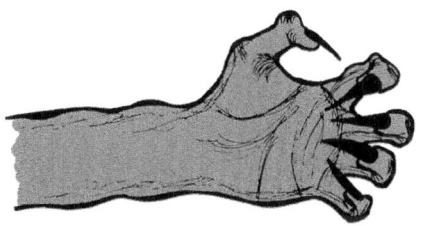

311

You arrive slightly out of breath back at the Engineering Room, unlock the door and sneak in. Maybe it's already lunchtime because the place looks deserted. Perfect! You head over to the switches, levers and dials that you saw earlier, remembering how panicked the man was about discharging toxins into the lake. You rub your hands together in anticipation — this will wipe the smiles from their faces!

The pipe in question has these controls: a lever pointing to the right, the switches are ON, ON, OFF, and the gauge is reading 200 psi. That's all well and good, but how do you reset the controls, so that the poisonous pipe contents are discharged into the lake?

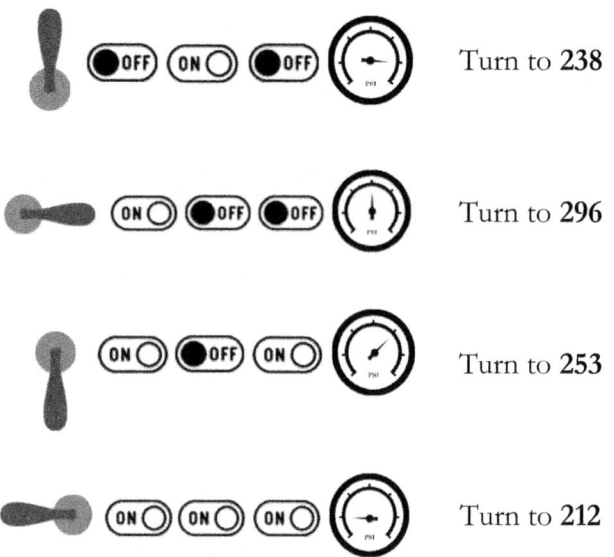

Turn to **238**

Turn to **296**

Turn to **253**

Turn to **212**

312

You smile encouragingly at the grey-haired woman, but she stares resolutely ahead. It could have something to do with the leering black thing, who has swung itself around the poor woman's head and is now coiled underneath her chin, so it can look at you. If you have ticked the codeword GREY WOMAN, immediately turn to **213**. If not, continue reading.

After a tense few minutes, in which it is clear that there is no coffee, you quell your disappointment and stand up, saying, 'Well, I'm looking forward to my first day.' The woman with her Aufhocker and the grey-haired woman stand too, remarking, 'Keep a pure heart,' and 'Be worthy of Mother's love,' then leave. Now that you're alone, you decide to head next door to the changing room (turn to **281**).

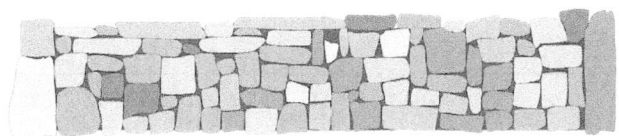

313

Touching the raw stump is absolutely the last thing you want to do, but you can't leave her like that, and whilst it's not exactly a professional dressing, at least it's tight enough to slow down the bleeding. You then ask if she needs anything else.

'All I want is to go home before I lose any more parts of my body. I used to think this was the answer. A beautiful place that accepted me and loved me, but I was a fool and realised too late. A grey-haired woman handed me this page from a magazine. She said it would be useful if I got to the submerged house, but I didn't understand. Does it make sense to you?'

You stare dumbfounded at the page. It appears to be a blueprint of a house with one room circled. It's labelled Schlafen and from the symbols, you guess it's the master bedroom. Why does a master bedroom have the word 'key' written on it? Eventually, you shake your head. Nothing here makes sense. She pats your hand and says, 'You can keep it. I don't think I'll be doing any diving now,' then falls asleep. There is nothing else you can do for her, so tick the codeword **BLUEPRINT,** note that the '**Master bedroom**' was circled, then leave. You soon reach a junction and to the left there are stairs heading down (turn to **298**); to the right, you can hear voices and occasional clattering and banging (turn to **221**). Where do you go?

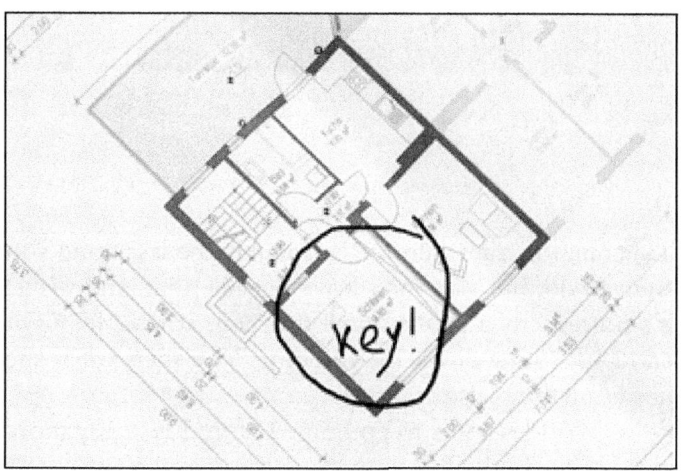

314

Well, that was close, and you can hear whoever it is pushing switches and opening up drawers, so figure that you have enough time to get away. You head further up the corridor and reach another junction. The right-hand way is signposted — it leads to the staff room and if you want to go there, turn to **279**, but if you'd rather head left towards an unmarked, locked door, turn to **219**.

315

To your surprise, you enter into a huge warehouse-like space dedicated to scuba gear. There is the equipment store on your right and if you want to check this out, turn to **302**, but if you'd rather head left to the cleaning and maintenance area, turn to **228**.

316

If you were fortunate to find a dumped set of diving equipment, you've already ticked the codeword SCUBA GEAR and don't need to worry about that anymore (turn to **215**).

If not, then you need to get back to the diving room to fetch it. If you've already been there, you were told of a number that would help you to return. Well, now's the time to use it, so turn to the section with that same number.

If you've forgotten or you don't know where the Diving Room is, you'll have to hope you can hold your breath for long enough and decide on your next move instead. Turn to **215**.

317

You walk down the corridor, hearing more agonised cries and dry cackles behind the black glass. A barrage of cylinders suddenly zooms one after the other through the pneumatic tubing, and you head into the staff room (turn to **279**).

318

The corridor is gradually sloping downwards and it could be your imagination, but you're sure the air is getting thicker and colder. Halfway along, you notice that the tubes have taken a left turn, burrowing into the wall and going who-knows-where. So much for following that clue! You reach out to the concrete, then recoil as your fingers touch a slimy moisture. Is that just condensation or is it oozing out from the wall itself? A few steps further and then you can smell it. A rotten stench, which is faint at first but cloying by the time you're at the door, and you can't tell whether it's coming from within this room or the slimy ooze. A wave of nausea washes over you, but you read the sign and realise that you've reached the 'Disposal Room'. It's not clear what is being disposed of and you're not sure that you *want* to find out right now, but the door is unlocked so if you want to enter, turn to **261**. If you'd rather not, you can either return to the junction and go along the other, less smelly route (turn to **263**) or just go back to where you started and take the left-hand corridor this time (turn to **289**).

319

A thin, leathery foot scrapes over your arm as the Aufhocker hitches itself up. Inevitably, it's where your fake butterfly tattoo is, so the colours are smudged over your skin. If you weren't in such dire straits you might have laughed at the Aufhocker's expression — a comical mix of outrage, disgust and shock — but you wouldn't have had time to do that anyway. It thrusts a bony clawed hand into your mouth and in one swift move, wrenches your tongue out. Once it has thrown the slab of muscle against the wall with a wet slap, it pushes your chin up so the cascade of blood flows back into your airways. You will eventually drown, but that will be a welcome relief from the white-hot pain and fear you are currently enveloped in.

320

Its face abruptly transforms into the most disgusted grimace that the charred leather can make. You feel slightly offended — do you really taste that bad? — but then remind yourself that this is a good thing. Finally, the Aufhocker wipes its tongue on its arm, then flounces away. You give a massive sigh and when your legs stop wobbling, leave and carry on along the corridor until you reach the other door (turn to **277**).

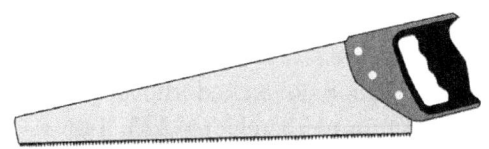

321

The plan was to act confident, but instead you feel a desperate urge to scream and wet yourself, possibly at the same time. You're not sure what you were expecting but it wasn't that! Five creatures emerge from the doorway and crawl laboriously across the floor. They seem to have long legs but these are bent up, so they're waddling on their haunches. Thick claws scrape the concrete and matted, bristly fur drags along. Fur? Well, it looks like fur over its belly and rump but draped from its shoulders are greasy, black feathers. What is it?

Suddenly, the first creature seems to notice you and stops suddenly. The others bump into it then look across at you, as the leader points with a long, wiry arm and says, 'You! Are you new here?' You stand there, mute with fear and total indecision, but then, one of the others gestures to your upper arm. Which codeword have you ticked? CHRYSALIS (turn to **237**) or BANDAGE (turn to **295**)?

322

There is a persistent slurping noise coming from within. It sounds like a vacuum cleaner sucking up sludge and who knows — maybe that's exactly what it is. You enter and instantly realise that it isn't. A grey-haired woman is performing liposuction on an already thin man, who is whimpering through clenched teeth. You hear him say, 'A bit more. She needs it more than I do,' and the woman looks at you with a 'What can I do?' expression. If you have ticked the codeword GREY WOMAN, turn immediately to **223**, but if not, you could try to talk to the man (turn to **235**).

323

It's just another grey corridor with grey walls oozing malodorous slime, and you pass another window. Did you activate the 'Glass clear' switch in the Control Room? If you did, turn to **257**, but if not, turn to **294**.

324

You try to get to the door but have no coordination over your body anymore. You collapse on the floor and although your eyelids begin to open, it's almost like you can't see the lights at all. You can feel your mind fraying and coming apart, and you might, no doubt, be disappointed to find yourself in the near future with a hacksaw in one hand and your amputated leg in the other. However, you will be incapable of forming a single, coherent thought, so probably not.

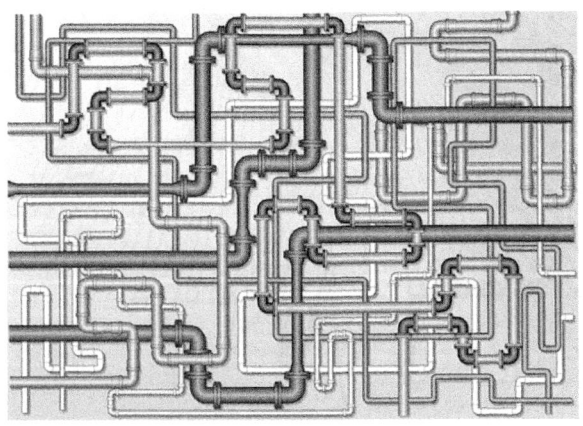

You feel slightly queasy as the worker faces you fully and looks ready for a fight. What do you really think you're going to do here? Kill him to guarantee his silence? However desperate things get — that's not you!

'You're not a real Favoured Few,' he announces, and you swallow nervously. Maybe begging or offering money would be a reasonable alternative, you think, but he continues, 'I want to leave too. This place isn't what I thought it was. Mother Amber isn't who I thought she was! I know you're going to the submerged house, but how are you going to get everyone out?'

There is an embarrassed pause before you admit that you hadn't actually thought about that. Not to worry though, the worker isn't concerned about your poorly concocted plans. He has waited a long time to bring the entire Metamorphosis cult down, and he wants to share all that he knows.

'There is a secret passageway from the house, which the boar uses. It connects to the tree, Yggdrasil, and you know you're in the right place because there is a tree root in the house.'

This is, indeed, useful information and when you are in the right location *and* ready to escape from the house, you can open up the passageway by **adding 20** to the section you are currently at. For now though, you both have to pretend that it's business as usual. The worker goes back to maintaining the smooth running of the pneumatic tubes and you leave. Turn to **293**.

PART THREE: THE SUBMERGED HOUSE

326

There isn't any sign of life in the submerged house — no blue cats or amber eyes — but that's where you head to. After you open the door and swim into the hallway, there is the strangest sensation as all the pressure is instantly removed from your body. You had become accustomed to the weight of the lake, but now, nothing. You blink, sag against the nearby wall, then slowly realise that the water has indeed gone. You are stood in a dry, air-filled hallway... At the bottom of a lake! Now, you feel more confident that you're in the right place and it's time to finish this.

You peel the wet suit off and leave the diving gear in a pile by the door then look around. The hallway stretches out far ahead of you — almost the full length of the house — and is lit only by a single, naked lightbulb. The wallpaper is old and peeling, the carpet threadbare. It's not a welcoming home, that's for sure. There are numerous doors leading off the hall but all of them are closed, so there's no way of knowing who or what is behind each one. The first one on your right sounds deserted and if you want to go into that room, turn to **377**. However, if you'd rather go a little further and open the door on your left, turn to **341**.

The apparent leader of this cluster — a strange, featureless, shifting, black shape — steps forward and gives a nervous cough, but before it can say anything, Freyja starts chanting weird words and making ornate gestures with her hands. Is she summoning someone? Everyone pauses and looks around expectantly. Is something going to happen?

Suddenly, the front door slams open and you are horror-struck by the prospect of the lake flooding in, like blood from the lifts in 'The Shining', but instead, a huge bird-coat hybrid bursts into the house. The falcon-feathered garment swoops down the hallway, wraps itself around a smug and relieved Freyja before taking off again in a frenzy of flapping.

You cower with your arms protectively covering your head, but as quick as it came, the bird-coat has gone, and Freyja has escaped with it.

The shape seems to be totally unprepared for that and looks back at the other two figures for guidance. One steps forward, nods his head and says, 'I'm Al-Kutbay, this is Cai-shen and this…' gesturing to the shape, '…is The Machinator. We are The Cluster. Normally, we don't meet… people. This is a bit awkward.' That's the understatement of the day, you think, as a long silence follows. Only when Hagalaz sniffs, does The Machinator speak up.

'Exactly,' it says, although whether it's agreeing with the boar or its own thoughts, is unclear. 'Freyja was undertaking an experiment, but she had rather overstepped the mark in many ways, so we felt we needed to step in.'

Cai-shen nods and repeats 'Step in,' which puts The Machinator off its stride, but it also looks grateful for the support and continues, 'We didn't think that she'd go off like that. It's a bit inconvenient, to be honest. It's taken us an age to track her down.'

The three figures start muttering with each other and you can hear fragments of the conversation — 'retrieve any useful data', 'repeat using the same variable' and 'that's two we've lost!' — but then without warning or any goodbyes, they simply vanish.

You whisper, 'Where have they gone?' but there is only a stunned silence. Tick the codeword **WUNJO**. Suddenly, you hear the sound of footsteps clattering up the cellar steps and realise that, with Freyja's departure, the cell doors have automatically opened up.

Turn to **348**.

328

Seeing as you are no art expert, studying the painting takes all of five seconds, then you shrug your shoulders and say, 'I could've painted that,' even though you plainly couldn't. However, before you turn away, you notice a slight irregularity. Not in the painting itself but in the frame. There's a slight gap and when you poke it, the carved wood falls out revealing a hidden microphone and switch. Is the switch for a recording device or perhaps it links to a tannoy system? You have no idea and no way of finding out, but it definitely seems sensible to switch it on. The only trouble is it

 needs a code to be punched in… This should be no trouble though if you've seen these symbols before.

When you've worked out what the switch code is, turn to the section with the same number **now**.

However, if you don't know it, then you could search the cabinet if you haven't done that already (turn to **344**) or go back into the hallway (turn to **383**).

329

Next, you pass by another door on the left and can hear someone talking inside the room. If you want to see who it is, turn to **416**, but if you simply want to reach the end of the hall, turn to **381**.

'You unleashed the snails!' she accuses. You almost laugh — unleash would not be the word you'd use to describe the snails' recent break-out — but you nod in agreement, then ask, 'Why? What did they do?'

She points to the window in the living room, out of which there are now no corpses. It takes a second or two for you to realise what has happened.

'They chewed through the tendrils? They unfettered the corpses?'

Freyja nods, her mouth so tightly screwed together that her lips have gone white.

'I saw through the mural. The corpses washed up on the lake shore and all the guests have left. The Retreat staff are furious and dismayed. Their faith has gone and it's all your fault! Where will my life-sustaining elixir come from now?'

You wonder again why anyone would consider that putrid concoction to be 'life-sustaining' but each to their own, you guess! However, you've no time for any further musings because Freyja's temper is showing no signs of abating. Maybe you should attack her? You dismiss that idea instantly — she is plainly strong and would probably snap you in half. However, if you've found a necklace in the submerged house, perhaps you could use that to de-escalate the situation. If you have a necklace, turn to **423** but if you don't, you'll have to look for an alternative weapon (turn to **384**).

It's not a totally unsuccessful hunt. Whilst there weren't any knives, you did find an old-fashioned knife-sharpener — a weighty **steel rod** that will make a good cudgel — and a few **tins of cat food**. Make a note that you have acquired these items, then you can either look at the tanks if you haven't done so already (turn to **422**) or go down to the cellar (turn to **397**).

'Now you will wish that you never came here. No one insults a God! Do your worst, Hagalaz!' she cries with a triumphant punch in the air. You take a deep breath in and wait, wide-eyed and frozen with fear, for the boar to charge. Only it doesn't. Hagalaz doesn't move a muscle, except to blink and give the occasional snort.

'Hagalaz, what are you doing? You disobey me?' Freyja is plainly losing her temper again and she yells, 'Are you a traitor? Are you not worthy of my love?' A painful silence follows, but eventually the boar says, 'You broke them! I brought all that birch for your cribs. So much love went into that collection, but you smashed them to bits and threw them to one side as if they were nothing more than rubbish. All that love and you never cared…' It would be an Oscar winning performance, except for the fact that the boar is not acting. There are genuine tears rolling down the coarse, grey cheeks — Hagalaz is truly heartbroken. Freyja looks wounded, almost distraught by this, but as you watch, you see her expression harden, until with a sneer, she finally shouts, 'Of course, I broke the cribs. The babies died, what was I supposed to do? If you'd made good cribs; if you'd have picked the best birch, they would have lived. It's all your fault! I only kept you on here because I felt sorry for you, and this is what I get in return!'

At this point, Freyja has reached a crescendo of rabid aggression, and there is no way that you can diffuse this. All you can do is get out of the way, while she erupts.

However, before you duck and cower from Freyja's almighty fury, we really must factor in whether you ticked the codeword FREEDOM. If you did, turn to **421**. If not, turn to **391**.

333

You stand on tiptoes again and peer into the cell. It is another pregnant woman, who smiles and says, 'Has Mother blessed you? Does she want you here too? All she needs is love — love, devotion and sacrifice — and the rewards will be bountiful for the Favoured Few.'

You pause, then state the obvious: 'But she's locked you in a cell!' The woman merely shakes an indulgent head at you.

'This is how she helps us to fully transform. If you were ready, you'd understand.' She looks as if she's about to continue this preaching but abruptly stops and stares upwards. After a couple of seconds of tense listening, she turns back to you enraptured and announces, 'She's here!' Despite having no plan of action, you vault for the stairs — you're not letting Mother bloody Amber get away now! Turn to **362**.

334

With a twist of the lever, there is a muted gurgle and the shrimps are now freely roaming the lake. A quick peek out of the window reveals a red dot here and there, which you presume are the shrimps! Oh well, that didn't achieve anything too exciting, but hopefully the shrimp are happy with their new-found freedom. Seeing as you don't want a mass slaughter of aquatic creatures on your conscience, you decide to obey the instruction and release no more, then head over to see if the pantry has anything interesting to offer. Turn to **395**.

335

Apart from a mouldy handkerchief and a mussel shell, the drawers appear to be empty, but then you open the bottom one. With a screech and a hiss, a ball of blue fur erupts out of the drawer. Every claw on each foot is primed for attack, and it rakes your arms in a frenzy, then retreats to the far side of the room, where you could swear it says, 'The root is the root.' Or was it 'the root is the route'? Or maybe, 'the route is the root'? At this point, you realise you're debating what a cat has just said and let's be honest — that is not normal!

Once the shock subsides, the pain takes over. OK, so they're only scratches and not what you'd call life threatening, but they are bleeding a bit and there are *lots* of them! You pull your sleeves down before turning to the cat. It is grooming its paws and looking quite unphased by the whole experience.

'Oh, that's right. Clean my blood from your claws, why don't you?' However, the cat studiously ignores your sarcasm and begins to lick its blue fur. It doesn't look like it's going to either speak or attack you again, so if you haven't done so already and want to risk disturbing what could be lurking in the dressing table, turn to **402**. If you've seen all you want to see in this room, you should leave now and continue along the hallway (turn to **369**).

336

You type in 336 — well, the maths wasn't difficult, just a simple multiplication then addition —and from somewhere below your feet, you hear a deep thud as all the cell doors unlock. Tick the codeword **FREEDOM**. But before you go to fetch your sister, there is a different noise from the hall. With a sinking feeling in your stomach, you know that you have to deal with this first, and you are not looking forward to it. Turn to **370**.

337

You peer into the house, half-expecting there to be a tiny version of you in the playroom, but all you see is a snail crawling through the kitchen. Suddenly, there is a hissing shriek and the blue cat launches itself off the rocking horse and onto your back, before jumping onto the roof of the doll's house. It obviously doesn't want you to poke around it anymore... If you haven't already done so and you want to risk the cat's wrath by taking a look at the Lego, turn to **413.**

If you're ready to leave the playroom, you could go back towards the entrance and enter the first room on the right if you haven't been there yet (turn to **377**). Alternatively, you could either continue along the corridor and go through the second door on the right-hand side (turn to **352**) or ignore that and head towards the end of the hallway (turn to **329**).

338

This is plainly the dining room with an impressively large table, although it is less than impressively covered with dust. It could seat ten people and there is a cabinet full of expensive plates and crystal glasses at one end. At the other end, there is simply an oil painting of a bland icy landscape. If you want to look through the cabinet, turn to **344** but if you'd rather study the artwork, turn to **328**. Alternatively, you could simply go back into the hallway to try another door (turn to **383**).

339

You never really believed that people could actually foam from the mouth with anger — you thought it was just an exaggeration — but now you know it's true. Freyja marches up and down the hall, spraying white flecks of saliva as she rages at the boar and stops every now and then to punch a hole through the wall.

In the midst of this volcanic tantrum, there is a shadowy shimmer in the hallway and a cluster of figures materialises. From Freyja's expression, you guess she knows who they are and is not pleased to see them. However, the introductions must wait for now, because if you've ticked the codeword BURNT FEATHERS, you should turn to **358**. If not, turn to **327**.

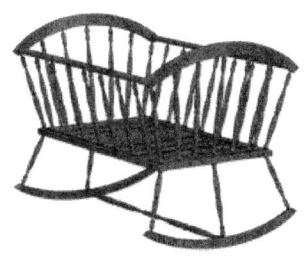

340

You stand on tiptoes again and peer into the cell. This woman looks drawn and distinctly unpregnant, and she says urgently, 'If you're getting your sister out, can you get me out too?' But before you can answer, the woman peeks down into your bag. Have you ticked the codeword TEDDY BEAR? If you have, turn to **379**, but if not, turn to **393**.

Although the teddy bear wallpaper is faded, it's clear that this was a playroom. The toys are still strewn around with a set of tin soldiers posed in mid-battle and a majestic rocking horse at the far end. However, the blue cat, who is currently curled up on the horse's saddle, and a pile of broken birch twigs are clear signs that all is not right in this room. You approach the rocking horse cautiously, not wanting to upset the cat or anything that might be nesting amongst the birch and see that the twigs had been tied together. That makes you pause and look closer. It's not just a pile of branches — obviously, the birch had been used to make something, which was then broken and destroyed. Almost as if somebody lost their temper and gave it a good stomping…

'She does that every time,' a voice drawls and you realise that the blue cat has spoken. 'Every time one of them dies, she goes berserk and stomps all over the cribs. Poor Hagalaz.' With this, the cat pauses and gives a massive yawn.

'Why "poor Hagalaz"?' you ask. The cat flexes its claws against the saddle then says, 'Well, that boar must be run ragged trying to bring her a never-ending supply of birch for the cribs. I wonder if he knows what Freyja does with his lovingly crafted cots…'

The cat gives you a slow, deliberate blink before wrapping a paw over its head and resuming its nap. Your conversation appears to be over, so you look around the rest of the room. There is a familiar-looking doll's house in one corner and a half-built pile of Lego in the other. If you want to examine the doll's house first, turn to **349**, but if the Lego is tempting you more, turn to **413**.

She agrees to go with you into the dining room and sits at the head of the table. You are wondering how to broach this, but there's no need to worry — Mother Amber is more than happy to talk.

'I suppose the Grey Women helped you, didn't they? I like them even if they do speak in riddles. You know, I asked Hecate to support me. I told her all about what The Cluster did with the prion and the babies and the zombie disease, but would she help me?' This is obviously a rhetorical question, because she doesn't even look at you, never mind wait for a response. 'No, she doesn't! Says that the witches will never be party to such atrocities. Atrocities, I ask you! People have always sacrificed their most beloved to their gods. How else can they prove their devotion? But when I do it, suddenly it's an atrocity!'

At this point, you interject with, 'But the babies are given to you healthy, aren't they? So why do they die?'

Mother Amber slams her fist down on the table.

'Exactly! And that's where the problem is. I accept the gift and put them into the birch cribs that Hagalaz makes, but then they die! Why do they die?'

You quickly mull over the possibilities, then ask, 'Do you feed them?'

Mother Amber looks genuinely confused at this question, but finally replies, 'Why should I do that? I'm the God of love. Surely being accepted by a god is all they need. Maybe the mother's sacrifice is not given to me willingly and with a full heart...' She stares into space, apparently missing the point that babies actually need milk. Although you're worried about pushing your luck, you have to know the truth about the green, stinking ooze that weeps from behind the Walls in the

Retreat, so say, 'And when they die, you brick the bodies up, don't you?'

She looks at you with astonishment, then says, 'But of course! How else can you make a building more impenetrable, more able to withstand an attack? It has to be fortified with the blood of the innocents!' It's on the tip of your tongue to say 'reinforced steel girders', but the moment has passed. Mother Amber suddenly leaps to her feet, states, 'Hagalaz calls me!', then leaves. For someone as tall and well-built as she is, Mother Amber moves remarkably swiftly and silently, and you have no idea where she has gone to, just that she has gone. Not to worry though — your plan worked a treat! Her words have been painfully relayed via the microphone to the speakers in the cells. Tick the codeword **REVELATIONS**, then head back into the kitchen. Turn to **376**.

343

The runestone Wunjo represents celebration, a restoration of harmony and above all, triumph! You emerge from a crack in the trunk of a great tree, accidentally kick over one of the 8 mushrooms and inhale the sweet fresh air in the forest. As the others join you, there are smiles and tears, and you hug your sister with relief at being finally free from Freyja's grasp. Free to go home, but although Mother Amber and Metamorphosis are no more, Freyja is out there somewhere and what if she returns in a new guise with new followers? With a nervous glance over your shoulder, you bid farewell to the Retreat and head to the airport. But before you go, why not turn to **426**, so you can discover what The Cluster will do now...

There's no way you're going to get all this crockery out, but you shift the plates and bowls to one side and look behind them. Even though it isn't a thorough search, it does pay dividend, as you find a bright red, plastic baby's dummy and a cheap watch. The dummy is curious enough, but the watch is of particular interest! There must have been thousands of them sold, but it really does look identical to one that your sister had before she left… At this point, there is an almighty crash as the lopsided weight of the crockery causes the shelf to collapse, which in turn shakes the painting off the wall. The splintered pieces of frame mingle with the shards of porcelain, and all you can do is sweep the debris underneath the table — out of sight, out of mind! Once finished, you quickly sneak back into the hallway (turn to **383**).

The boar slowly shuffles back into the hall, its huge grey bulk once again filling the narrow space. The amber eyes stare at Freyja but it's unclear what to read into that look — is it adoration or hate?

However, the most important question is: did you tick the codeword BETRAYAL? If you did, turn to **412**, but if not, turn to **361**.

346

Well, unless a submarine magically arrives, there's only one solution. You wade down the hallway towards the front door and pick up the scuba gear that you discarded earlier.

'It's the only way,' you say to your sister, 'I came here to rescue you and that's what I'll do. The others can't do it with the babies, but you're not so big that you can't fit in the wet suit. You have to do it. For me, please and once you're out, you can get help for us.' At that moment, you both look around at the rapidly rising water and know that there will be no time for another rescue mission. The mathematics are undeniable — two people will be saved instead of one — so you bite your tongue and tell your sister that it's what Mother Amber would want. She considers your words then reluctantly pulls on the wet suit and heads out to safety. If you earlier ticked the codeword TYR, turn to **408**. However, if you ticked WUNJO, turn to **378**.

347

'Did you tamper with the tanks!' she shouts accusingly, but before you can explain or deny, she continues her rant. 'How dare you! You were trying to undermine me, to turn my followers against me!'
You have no idea why the tanks are so important, but there's no way to find out — Freyja is beside herself with rage. You try to calm things down saying, 'I didn't do anything to the tanks. Maybe it was one of the others.' It's a risky ruse, but you think that these megalomaniacs are all paranoid and insecure, so maybe you can use that to deflect her. It works!

'I will find them and rip their heart out! But despite their ploy, my flock still adore me. They will still give me their love and the life-sustaining elixir!'

You wonder again why anyone would consider that foul concoction to be 'life-sustaining' but each to their own, you guess! However, you have no time for any further musings, because even though her murderous intentions are directed elsewhere, Freyja's temper is showing no signs of abating. Maybe you should attack her? You dismiss that idea instantly — she is plainly strong and would probably snap you in half. However, if you've found a necklace in the submerged house, perhaps you could use that to de-escalate the situation. If you have a necklace, turn to **380** but if you don't, turn to **414**.

Hagalaz slopes off, obviously feeling bereft by the loss of his mistress, but the hall is still quite crowded. There is someone who's rambling on about molluscs, the mothers now reunited with their babies, the pregnant women including your own sister and even the blue cats are here. Only the grief-stricken women are missing — they have chosen to remain in the cellar for now. Everyone is looking expectantly at you, as if they've nominated you as their *de facto* leader. And someone does have to take charge because now that Freyja has left, the lake is starting to trickle back in. You're not sure how long you have, but soon it really will be a submerged house. You need to get these people out! However, that may not be as easy as you'd think. They've been indoctrinated to be loyal to Mother Amber, and whilst the truth about Freyja is beginning to come out, old habits die hard. What might help is whether you've ticked the codeword REVELATIONS? If you have, turn to **360**, and if not, turn to **365**.

Although you haven't yet explored much of the submerged house, you're absolutely convinced that this doll's house is its replica. It even has the same tatty wallpaper in the hall. If you ticked the codeword BLUEPRINT, maybe you're starting to have a brainwave. Could the magazine page be referring to a room in this doll's house rather than the actual house? Well, it's worth a try, isn't it? But only if you can recall which room was circled on the blueprint…

From the floor plan at the start of the book, you will see there is a number associated with each room — choose the room, then **add** that number to this section and turn to the new section.

For example, if the magazine page had the *kitchen* circled, you would turn to 380, as the kitchen's special number is 31 (349 + 31 = 380).

No worries though, if you haven't ticked the codeword BLUEPRINT — you can still have a closer look at the doll's house (turn to **337**).

'I try so hard to please Freyja,' says Hagalaz, 'But it's worth it when she puts a hand on my head or tells me that she's pleased with the offerings I bring. It's only right that a God is shown devotion, isn't it?'

To be honest, you feel like you're losing the plot but still manage to give a weak nod of encouragement.

'That's the way it's always been,' the boar continues, 'Gods are given offerings or even sacrifices.'

'And what does Mother... I mean Freyja, give back to the people?'

Your question seems to stump Hagalaz, who chews thoughtfully before saying, 'Well, the knowledge that she's happy, I suppose. That's enough, isn't it?'

You can't help but raise an eyebrow at this, and Hagalaz looks slightly unconvinced too. You decide to press on with this advantage.

'Does she even appreciate what you bring her?'

'Oh yes, she puts the babies in my precious birch cribs. My work is very important!'

If you have discovered some evidence to the contrary — a room which would show Hagalaz that Freyja doesn't actually cherish the birch cribs he lovingly crafts for her, now would be a good time to send the boar there to find out the truth.

From the floor plan at the start of the book, you will see that there is a number associated with each room — choose the room, then **add** that number to this section and turn to the new section. For example, if you want to send the boar to the pantry, you would turn to 405 (350 + 55 = 405).

If the section you turn to makes no sense, then you have sent Hagalaz on a pointless wild goose chase and should now turn to **404**.

With all the drama, you'd forgotten about the women imprisoned in the cellar. You did wonder where they'd gone after you unlocked the cells and here is your answer — they'd gone to find their children. The three mothers enter the hall, all cradling their babies, who, now that they've been fed and cuddled, are sleeping contentedly. Freyja points and starts to splutter, 'They are mine...' but one of the women steps forward and spits at Freyja. That is shocking enough, but when she also decisively says, 'You are no mother,' you gasp. Surely, that's a step too far, and Freyja's retaliation will be volcanic.

Well, you'd think so, but her followers in the Retreat still love her and Hagalaz remains utterly devoted. Losing these babies is an insult, but there'll be other sacrifices, and Freyja didn't get to be a God by being so easily defeated! So, instead of taking out her grievances on the mother, Freyja turns to you.

'This is all your fault. You unlocked the cells!' For a second, you're tempted to point out how irrational this argument is. After all, if she hadn't locked the women up in the first place… but you won't get that chance. With an iron grip, she lifts you high up by the throat. The choking is bad enough, but as her temper boils over again, she starts to pound you bodily against the wall. You will be long dead by the time Freyja eventually calms down, and no doubt, your sacrifice will be greatly appreciated by the deity. Plus, it's a useful reminder to the others to stay in line — all in all, a win-win for Freyja.

352

You step into a cosy and inviting study, lit only and inexplicably by flickering flames in the fireplace. Where does the smoke go to, you wonder…? There is a small window opposite and as you step further into the room, you see that the view is not of the lake floor with its macabre decorations, but the control room! There is a worker hunched over the monitors and gesticulating wildly to someone else who is just out of sight. Maybe they're not impressed with the Aufhocker annihilation. How ungrateful — they should give you a medal for that! As tempting as it is to spy on them, you do have more urgent matters to take care of, so you survey the room and decide on your next move. Will you have a root through the desk drawers (turn to **392**) or quickly peruse the bookshelves (turn to **375**)?

353

The boar slowly shuffles back into the hall, its huge grey bulk once again filling the narrow space. The amber eyes stare at Freyja but it's unclear what to read into that look — is it adoration or hate?

However, the most important question is: did you tick the codeword BETRAYAL? If you did, turn to **332**, but if not, turn to **398**.

354

A small green light appears, so you assume that the device has been switched on. Remember the number **342** as it will be handy if you want to return to the dining room — you never know when you might need to use the microphone to record or transmit a conversation. Now you could either check out the cabinet if you haven't done that already (turn to **407**) or go back into the hallway (turn to **383**).

355

The runestone Tyr represents courage, willingness to self-sacrifice and above all, victory! It doesn't feel like a victory though, as you emerge from a crack in the trunk of a great tree, accidentally kick over one of the 8 mushrooms and inhale the sweet fresh air in the forest. It is, in fact, a bitter-sweet moment, as you are alone. With a mutinous and stubborn expression, your sister had refused point-blank to come with you. It was only because the blue cats (of course, it was the blue cats!) invoked some power and stopped the water from coming in, that you eventually decided to leave her. Maybe with some time, she will come to her senses. That's what you hope and at least, you know that she is definitely free from Freyja's grasp, but with a heart full of regret, you bid farewell to the Retreat and head to the airport.

But before you go, why not turn to **426**, so you can discover what The Cluster will do now…

356

The door unlocks with a brisk click, and you enter a large and rustic kitchen. There's no fitted units or modern appliances, so surely no one cooks here, but then you remind yourself that you're at the bottom of a lake — why would there be dinner parties? You have to stay focused, so you appraise the kitchen for clues and weapons. There are some strange looking tanks and a half-open door leading down to the cellar. Talking of weapons though, there surely must be some knives in here…

So, what will you do first? Have a rummage through the cupboards and drawers (turn to **331**), investigate the odd tanks (turn to **422**) or head down to the cellar (turn to **397**)?

357

You whip out the note and study the three numbers scrawled on it. Maybe you've already heard some other information that you now realise could be used with these numbers. If so, you should calculate what the 3-digit number is, then simply head straight to the section with the same number.

If not, you do the obvious thing and add them up, but when you type that in, the keypad buzzes and the little red light stays resolutely red. You swear and threaten acts of violence against the poor, inanimate gadget, but to no avail! Even though you're not quite ready to give up, you suddenly hear a suspicious noise in the hall and know you're going to have to deal with that first.

Turn to **370**.

The apparent leader of this cluster — a strange, featureless, shifting, black shape — steps forward and gives a nervous cough, but before it can say anything, Freyja starts chanting weird words and making ornate gestures with her hands. Is she summoning someone? Everyone pauses and looks around expectantly, but nothing happens. She repeats the whole thing but again, nothing happens. Freyja looks wildly in the air and out of the windows in the nearby rooms, before exploding at the assembled group.

'Where is my coat?' she demands to know. Well, you weren't expecting that! All this over a coat? Hagalaz shuffles reluctantly forward and whispers in her ear. Everyone watches with bated breath, and then the second explosion comes.

'Burnt? BURNT! Who burnt my coat? I'll kill them. I'll rip their lungs out. I'll…'

'Now then, Freyja, enough of this nonsense,' interrupts the shadowy shape, 'We've got a job to do. You *had* a job to do.'

'And I did it,' she screams, 'Look how adored I am. These sheep worship me. I told you love was the best way to keep them under control. I was right!'

The shape seems slightly alarmed by how unhinged she is and looks back at the other two figures for guidance. One steps forward, nods his head and says, 'I'm Al-Kutbay, this is Cai-shen and this…' gesturing to the shape, '…is The Machinator. We are The Cluster. Normally, we don't meet… people. This is a bit awkward.' That's the understatement of the day, you think, as a long silence follows. Only when Hagalaz sniffs, does The Machinator speak up again.

'Exactly,' it says, although whether it's agreeing with the boar or its own thoughts, is unclear. 'Freyja, your experiment here hasn't been a total failure, but you have rather overstepped the mark in many ways and we cannot allow this to continue any longer.'

Cai-shen nods and repeats 'Any longer,' which puts The Machinator off its stride, but it also looks grateful for the support and continues, 'You cannot escape without your coat, so you have no option but to terminate the experiment and return to The Cluster.'

After another protracted pause, Freyja nods resignedly, gathers her strength and pride, then goes to stand with the other three. And in a heartbeat, they all vanish.

You whisper, 'Where have they gone?' but there is simply a stunned silence. Tick the codeword **WUNJO**. Suddenly, you hear the sound of footsteps clattering up the cellar steps and realise that, with Freyja's departure, the cell doors have automatically opened up.

Turn to **348**.

359

With a twist of the lever, there is a muted gurgle and the carp are now freely roaming the lake. A quick peek out of the window reveals a dense shoal of fish, which dart quickly away from the house and are soon out of sight! Oh well, that didn't achieve anything too exciting, but hopefully the carp are happy with their new-found freedom. Seeing as you don't want a mass slaughter of aquatic creatures on your conscience, you decide to obey the instruction and release no more, so now you can either look through the cupboards and drawers if you haven't done so already (turn to **331**) or head down to the cellar (turn to **397**).

360

You announce that it's time to go, and the women nod in agreement. Your sister says, 'We all heard over the speakers what she said about the babies. How she let them die then bricked them...' but she can't continue. After a pause, you opt for practical pragmatism and the tricky matter of getting all these people to dry land before the house fills with lake water and everyone drowns. If you've heard of a secret route out of the house, that would be very useful indeed and all you need to do is remember where it is...

From the floor plan at the start of the book, you will see there is a number associated with each room — choose the room, then **add** that number to this section and turn to the new section. For example, if you think the secret passage is located in the study, you would turn to 406 (360 + 46 = 406). If the section you turn to makes no sense, then you are wasting time and should now turn to **403** to think about a plan B!

361

For a tense few seconds, you think that Hagalaz might defy her. It's difficult to read a boar's emotion, so you can't really tell, but then you hear him say, 'Whatever you wish for, I am your humble servant.' Oh. That does not sound good!

However, by the skin of your teeth, you get a reprieve when there is noise from somewhere else in the house. Before we find out what *that's* all about, we must know whether you've ticked the codeword FREEDOM. If you have, turn to **421**. If not, turn to **391**.

You sprint up the stairs, into the hall and there she is: Mother Amber! Your immediate impression is that she's tall and strong. No, make that tall and *very* strong. You're not sure what she thinks when she sees you, but her lips curl up in a smirk, so it probably isn't very flattering. She's wearing an animal skin coat and looks like she's just come off the battlefield, an image which is enhanced when she raises a drinking horn and downs the contents in one. Once she's tossed the horn to one side, she walks over to you. Regardless of whether you ticked CHRYSALIS or BANDAGE, she rubs a thumb over the unblemished skin on your bicep.

'It's funny how they chose the butterfly, isn't it? I never told them; they came up with that themselves. Silly, how humans put such importance on irrelevant rituals and symbols. Still, it's better that way. After all, it has more meaning for the people than it does for me.'

She suddenly reaches towards you again and touches your nose. When she takes her hand away, you see soot smeared over her fingers.

'You killed the Aufhocker.' It is a statement not a question, but she is impressed rather than angry.

'You are a formidable opponent and it is right that I fight worthy warriors. Should we go somewhere more comfortable to talk before our battle?'

Well, that's interesting. Maybe she'll reveal some truths that could be used against her! And maybe if your sister heard it, she'd see the light… But where is the best place to have such a conversation? If you know of a room that would be perfect for this subterfuge, you also know a number that will help you to return there. Turn now to the section with that same number. If not, then you should head to the living room (turn to **424**).

363

The woman puts up no resistance as you grab her arms, however, you're not ordinarily a violent person, so her frailty stops you in your tracks. You can't hurl her to the floor! Instead you opt for a stern shaking, then ask, 'Who are you? What are you doing here? Why aren't you taking care of these babies?'

In retrospect, asking so many questions at once probably wasn't the wisest thing to do. The woman stares fearfully, then starts howling, 'Yes, they need their mothers. Get their mothers. Look in the pantry!'

And with that, she is lost in her own world. She may well have useful information, but you can't waste any more time trying to find it.

At that moment though, you hear a door creak shut. You're not sure *where* it is, but there is definitely someone else moving around the house. You scurry to the door and sneak out. Everything is silent now, but it sounded like it came from the far end of the hall, so that's where you head to. Turn to **381**.

364

The runestone Wunjo represents celebration, a restoration of harmony and above all, triumph! It doesn't feel like a triumph though, as you emerge from a crack in the trunk of a great tree, accidentally kick over one of the 8 mushrooms and inhale the sweet fresh air in the forest. It is, in fact, a bitter-sweet moment, as you are alone. With a mutinous and stubborn expression, your sister had refused point-blank to come with you. It was only because the blue cats (of course, it was the blue cats!) invoked some power and stopped the water from coming in, that you eventually decided to leave her. Maybe with some time, she will come to her senses. That's what you hope, but although Mother Amber and Metamorphosis are no more, Freyja is out there somewhere, and what if she reappears in a new guise with new followers before you can return and persuade your sister to come home? With a nervous glance over your shoulder, you bid farewell to the Retreat and head to the airport.

But before you go, why not turn to **426**, so you can discover what The Cluster will do now…

365

You announce that it's time to go, but your sister vehemently shakes her head.

'This is just a test,' she states. 'A test of our loyalty and I will not fail Mother.'

It has to be said, you try every strategy you can think of to persuade your sister that Mother does not have her best interests in mind, however, you unequivocally fail.

After a pause, you opt for practical pragmatism — maybe when your sister realises her choices are to either live or drown, it will become an easier decision! So if you have heard of a secret route out of the house, that would be very useful and all you need to do is remember where it is…

From the floor plan at the start of the book, you will see there is a number associated with each room — choose the room, then **add** that number to this section and turn to the new section. For example, if you think the secret passage is located in the kitchen, you would turn to 396 (365 + 31 = 396). If the section you turn to makes no sense, then you are wasting time and should now turn to **346** to think about a plan B!

366

With a twist of the lever, there is a muted gurgle and the snails are now freely roaming the lake. A quick peek out of the window tells you nothing, but then you weren't exactly expecting to see them galloping away! Oh well, that didn't achieve anything too exciting, but you should still tick the codeword **GASTROPOD**. Seeing as you don't want a mass slaughter of aquatic creatures on your conscience, you obey the instruction and release no more, then head over to see if the pantry has anything interesting to offer. Turn to **395**.

367

With all the drama, you'd forgotten about the women imprisoned in the cellar. You did wonder where they had gone after you unlocked the cells and here is your answer — they'd gone to find their children. The three mothers enter the hall, all cradling their babies, who, now that they've been fed and cuddled, are sleeping contentedly. Freyja points and starts to splutter, 'They are mine...' but one of the women steps forward and spits at Freyja. That is shocking enough, but when she also decisively says, 'You are no mother,' there is a collective gasp. Surely, that is a step too far. There's no way that Freyja will tolerate such a condemning insult.

At that precise moment though, there is a shadowy shimmer in the hallway and a cluster of figures materialises before your eyes. From Freyja's expression, you guess she knows who they are and is not pleased to see them. However, the introductions can wait for now, because if you've ticked the codeword BURNT FEATHERS, you must turn to **417**. If not, turn to **373**.

The runestone Tyr represents courage, willingness to self-sacrifice and above all, victory! It doesn't feel like a victory though, as the lake water is now lapping around your chest, but at that moment, there is a hiss from the top of the kitchen cabinets. The blue cats had retreated there for safety; however, the water is getting too close for their liking. You have no idea what power they invoke, but before your eyes, the water begins to drop and soon the house is back to its submerged yet dry self.

'I thought Freyja had ceased to exist?' you ask the felines, and they merely nod in agreement.

'Then, how...?'

With that, they smirk at each other, then stalk towards the study to curl up in front of the fire. It would seem that you're not getting any answers from them!

So, your sister is safe and so are you, although it didn't quite work out as you hoped. Maybe in time, the authorities will investigate your sister's strange tales or more likely, you can convince Hagalaz to eventually share the location of the secret passageway, but until then, you while away the days by watching the Retreat through the mural in the dining room. It's got new management now and Metamorphosis is ancient history. Occasionally, someone spots you and the cats in the mural, but the Drudes are still doing a great job of convincing them that it's the nightmares messing with their minds! And who knows? Maybe one day a different deity will be enticed to take Freyja's place. But before you go, why not turn to **426**, so you can discover what The Cluster will do now...

369

If you haven't been there yet, you could go into the room on your left (turn to **341**). However, a little further along there is another door on the right, and if you'd prefer to go there instead, turn to **352**.

370

You smell it before you see it. A dank but earthy odour that fills the hall and emanates from the huge boar who is stood there. It grunts and snorts through the mouthful of birch twigs, then stares balefully with its amber eyes. Slowly, it raises one front leg and swipes it back in a deliberate warning. Your life appears to be in imminent danger unless you know of some canny trick to get yourself out of this dire situation. If you don't, you'd better turn to **415**.

371

With a twist of the lever, there is a muted gurgle and the shrimps are now freely roaming the lake. A quick peer out of the window reveals a red dot here and there, which you presume are the shrimps! Oh well, that didn't achieve anything too exciting, but hopefully the shrimp are happy with their new-found freedom. Seeing as you don't want a mass slaughter of aquatic creatures on your conscience, you decide to obey the instruction and release no more, so now you can either look through the cupboards and drawers if you haven't done so already (turn to **331**) or head down to the cellar (turn to **397**).

You don't actually want to look out of the window —
the ever-present corpses shifting in the water are
upsetting to see — but you should check that nothing is
swimming towards the house to attack you. Luckily, it's
all clear, but as you sigh with relief, the water shimmers
before your eyes and then the view changes completely.
It's the dining room! The dining room at the Retreat!
You stand there, mouth gaping in surprise and watch as
people glug down their healthy juices with an
expression that says: Why did I sign up for this? I'd give
anything to be on a beach sipping cocktails right now.
Suddenly, one of the guests looks directly at you and
their eyes widen in shock. The mural, you realise!
They're looking at the mural of the submerged house
and now, *you're* in it! You duck down and crawl away
under the window frame, but in doing so, spot the
rather thick, gnarled tree root which is inexplicably
protruding through the wall into the living room. It's
bizarre but so many things are, so you simply crawl
over it and leave. Once back in the hall, you stand up
and decide where to go next. Do you go to the room
that is now straight ahead (turn to **406**) or the one that
is now on your left (turn to **338**)?

The apparent leader of this cluster — a strange, featureless, shifting, black shape — steps forward and gives a nervous cough, but before it can say anything, Freyja starts chanting weird words and making ornate gestures with her hands. Is she summoning someone? Everyone pauses and looks around expectantly. Is something going to happen?

Suddenly, the front door slams open and you are horror-struck by the prospect of the lake flooding in, like blood from the lifts in 'The Shining', but instead a huge bird-coat hybrid bursts into the house. The falcon-feathered garment swoops down the hallway, wraps itself around a smug and relieved Freyja before taking off again in a frenzy of flapping.

You cower, arms protecting your head, but as quick as it came, the bird-coat has gone, and Freyja has escaped with it.

The shape seems to be totally unprepared for that and looks back at the other two figures for guidance. One steps forward, nods his head and says, 'I'm Al-Kutbay, this is Cai-shen and this…' gesturing to the shape, '…is The Machinator. We are The Cluster. Normally, we don't meet… people. This is a bit awkward.' That's the understatement of the day, you think, as a long silence follows. Only when one of the babies gurgles, does The Machinator speak up.

'Exactly,' it says, although whether it's agreeing with the baby or its own thoughts, is unclear. 'Freyja was undertaking an experiment, but she had rather overstepped the mark in many ways, so we felt we needed to step in.'

Cai-shen nods and repeats 'Step in,' which puts The Machinator off its stride, but it also looks grateful for the support and continues, 'We didn't think that she'd go off like that. It's a bit inconvenient, to be honest. It's taken us an age to track her down.'

The three figures start muttering with each other and you can hear fragments of the conversation — 'retrieve any useful data', 'repeat using the same variable' and 'that's two we've lost!' — but without warning or any goodbyes, they simply vanish.

You whisper, 'Where have they gone?' but nobody answers. There is only a stunned silence. Tick the codeword **WUNJO** then turn to **348**.

374

You present the runestone to the root then wait. Little did you know, but Eihwaz represents Yggdrasil — the Tree of Life — and it is indeed a conduit. To your amazement, cracks appear in the plaster and a fissure opens up in the wall revealing a dark, thin passageway. Squeezing into it is a nightmarish prospect, but then so is staying in the submerged house. With no other option, you grit your teeth and try, once more, to persuade your sister into the twisting and claustrophobic tunnel. If you ticked the codeword TYR, turn to **355**. If you ticked WUNJO, turn to **364**.

Strangely, although the books appear to be leather-bound classics, when you flick through a couple, you see they're all filled with blank pages. Even though this search looks like being a lost cause, you persevere and to your amazement, find something tucked away on the top shelf. A small, engraved wooden box. It has delicate, tiny brass fittings and when you give it a tentative shake, there is an intriguing rattle from within. There's just one problem though — it's locked! If you have found a tiny brass key that might fit in the tiny brass lock, you should remind yourself of its serial number. Take the first three numbers and turn to the section with the same number. For example, if the serial number was MA40719, you would turn to 407.

If you haven't found a key, then you could search the desk drawers (turn to **392**) or if you've already done that, you should leave the study and continue towards the end of the hallway (turn to **329**).

You were intending to go back down to the cells, but the moment you arrive in the kitchen, you instantly notice a second door next to the cellar stairs. That can't have been there before, can it? Surely you'd have noticed! It's stood slightly ajar and when you peer cautiously through the tiny gap, you can see it's nothing exciting — it's just the pantry. Still, if you want to do an exhaustive search of its nooks and crannies, turn to **395**. Alternatively, if you haven't yet had a chance to examine the strange tanks, now would be a good opportunity, so turn to **411**.

You enter into what looks like the master bedroom, although you doubt that anyone actually sleeps here. The huge iron and brass bed frame would have made quite an impression in the past, but now it stands quietly rusting without a mattress. The only other furniture is a chest of drawers and a dressing table. There are no ornaments, no pictures and no possessions. Suddenly, you realise that the view through the window isn't quite what you were expecting. Instead of the lake, you can see the staffroom, complete with some of the Favoured Few morosely sipping coconut water. They look shell-shocked and you wonder if they're feeling lost now that they don't have the Aufhockers' victims to dispose of. Still, you can't spend all day watching them, so you could either examine the chest of drawers (turn to **335**) or the dressing table (turn to **402**). However, if you'd prefer to leave and carry on along the hallway, turn to **369**.

378

The runestone Wunjo represents celebration, a restoration of harmony and above all, triumph! It doesn't feel like a triumph though, as the lake water is now lapping around your chest, but at that moment, there is a hiss from the top of the kitchen cabinets. The blue cats had retreated there for safety; however, the water is getting too close for their liking. You have no idea what power they invoke, but before your eyes, the water begins to drop and soon the house is back to its submerged yet dry self.

'I thought Freyja had gone away?' you ask the felines, and they merely nod in agreement.

'Then, how…?'

With that, they smirk at each other, then stalk towards the study to curl up in front of the fire. It would seem that you're not getting any answers from them!

So, your sister is safe and so are you, although it didn't quite work out as you hoped. Your sister doesn't report any of this — she knows that Mother Amber is out there somewhere and waits loyally for her return. Maybe you'll eventually convince Hagalaz to reveal the location of the secret passageway, but until then, you while away the days by watching the Retreat through the mural in the dining room. It's got new management now and Metamorphosis is ancient history. Occasionally, someone spots you and the cats in the mural, but the Drudes are still doing a great job of convincing them that it's the nightmares messing with their minds! It would seem that it's not only your sister who's waiting for Freyja's return.

But before you go, why not turn to **426**, so you can discover what The Cluster will do now…

379

'Where did you get that? That's the teddy bear I gave my son when he was born. What are you doing with it?' You hesitate, not really knowing how to explain that you found it dropped in a corridor, where *something* was being bricked up behind the wall. Your silence speaks volumes though and you hear her sob, then say, 'He's dead, isn't he?'

You don't answer; you don't need to.

'We have to end this. My name's Verity. You need to open up the cells. I think the master lock is in the kitchen, but all I've heard is "Multiply then add" said over and over again. As if someone is trying to memorise a formula. It's no good without the numbers though! I'm sorry that's all I know.'

You're about to ask, 'Who was talking?' when she quietly announces, 'She's here!' and there's no chance to get any more information about the secret lock. Now, you vault for the stairs — you're not letting Mother bloody Amber get away! Turn to **362**.

380

You really haven't thought this through properly; in fact, you only start to wonder what you're going to do with the necklace when you pull it out of the bag. Threaten to smash it? Pretend that you found it? What? Maybe this wasn't such a good idea after all… Your fears are groundless though. Freyja casts a disinterested eye over the gold and amber jewellery and shrugs.

'Oh, you've got Brísingamen. I haven't seen that in a while.' Well, this wasn't the reaction you were hoping for, but at least she seems calmer.

'I used to take Brísingamen everywhere with me,' she reminisces. 'It made me irresistible, made people love me, but I didn't need it here. It was funny. I just told people how special they were to be picked by me and that was that. All the rest, the metamorphosis, healthy eating, mindfulness stuff — they came up with that themselves. The whole thing just snowballed. I put the necklace in a drawer and I haven't used it in ages!'

You think you're in the clear now, but abruptly, her mercurial mood changes again and she remembers that she's furious with you. With eyes like daggers, she glares, then throws her head back and bellows, 'HAGALAZ!' Turn to **353**.

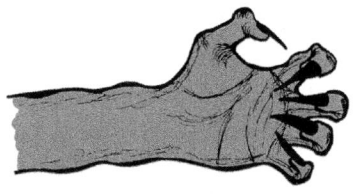

381

At the end of the hall, your attention is instantly caught by the thick, industrial pipe running from floor to ceiling with a small outlet tap halfway up. Does this contain all the foul, collected matter from the Retreat? Probably, unless you diverted it into the lake... Did Mother Amber really drink from that tap? The very idea makes you feel sick, so instead, you focus on the tricky decision ahead. Do you want to investigate the room on the left (turn to **409**), go through the door straight ahead (turn to **338**) or head into the room on your right (turn to **406**)?

With a tiny click, the wooden lid releases and lifts up. The box has a solitary piece of paper in it.

Cell Doors!

54   4   120

This has to be important you think, so fold it up carefully and place it into a pocket. You're feeling pretty pleased with yourself when you look again inside the box and see a handful of bloodied teeth. You give a cry of disgust and rear back. Yes, definitely human teeth and now you know what the rattling noise was! Feeling a weird mixture of both sad and sick, you abandon your search and exit the room, then head towards the end of the hall (turn to **329**).

383

Well, you can either go into the room that's now on your right (turn to **409**) or through the door that is now on your left (turn to **406**).

384

You rummage quickly through your bag, while Freyja looks on bemused. Maybe you have a knife sharpener, which you could bludgeon her over the head with or perhaps you found some tins of cat food that you could throw at her…

'What are you doing?' she asks disdainfully. 'Are you actually going to attack me?'

You gulp — what were you thinking? — it's a preposterous idea! You wonder whether you should fall on your knees and beg for forgiveness, but then Freyja surprises you by bursting into laughter. A huge belly-shaking laugh that doubles her over and even makes her slap her thigh. You feel slightly humiliated by this derogatory assessment of your fighting skills, but otherwise are relieved that she's in a good mood again. This doesn't last long though — she is mercurial, to say the least — and soon she remembers that she's furious with you. With eyes like daggers, she glares, then throws her head back and bellows, 'HAGALAZ!' Turn to **345**.

385

You all troop into the living room and head over to the wall where the thick, gnarled tree root protrudes through. So far, so good and now, you just need to make the passageway open up.

'You do know what to do?' your sister pointedly enquires, which annoys you, but now is not the time for sibling bickering. And anyway, it's a fair question — so, do you know? If somebody told you the instructions, you should do that **right now**.

However, even if no one told you how to activate the conduit, it's still not over! Have a look inside your pockets or bag and see if you acquired the topaz runestone of Eihwaz. If you have it, turn to **418**. If not, you really are running out of options, and you'll just have to turn to **403** and think of something else.

386

You peek cautiously in and see a woman slumped, head bowed, on the cell floor. She is heavily pregnant and missing her left leg. For a few seconds, you stare awkwardly — what can you say?

'You should get out while you can,' the woman says. 'The root is in the living room. Use that instead of facing the Neckar. They'll kill you.'

'I'm not leaving anyone behind. We'll all get out, and your baby can be born safely away from here.'
It is as if you haven't spoken though. She simply stares ahead and says flatly, 'Funny, isn't it? How the matter they collect nourishes Mother but kills her acolytes. I think it's just because she's an egocentric narcissist. She's got to be different because it makes her special. I can't leave. It's too late for me. I had a miscarriage, so they made me amputate my own leg. I was so brainwashed, I actually agreed to it. I actually thought it was a good idea. Turned out that I'd been pregnant with twins and was still carrying one of them, so I ended up here in a cell with only one leg and my baby will be taken as soon as it's born and that's that!'
You're about to plead with her that it's never too late, but she bows her head again and won't speak. Meanwhile, the other voices are still pleading with you. You can't waste any more time here, so do you go to the one whose cell is nearest to the stairs (turn to **333**) or the one whose cell is furthest away (turn to **340**)?

The runestone Wunjo represents celebration, a restoration of harmony and above all, triumph! It doesn't feel like a triumph though, as the lake water is now lapping around your chest, but at that moment, there is a hiss from the top of the kitchen cabinets. The blue cats had retreated there for safety; however, the water is getting too close for their liking. You have no idea what power they invoke, but before your eyes, the water begins to drop and soon the house is back to its submerged yet dry self.

'I thought Freyja had gone away?' you ask the felines, and they merely nod in agreement.

'Then, how…?'

With that, they smirk at each other, then stalk towards the study to curl up in front of the fire. It would seem that you're not getting any answers from them!

So, your sister is safe and so are you, although it didn't quite work out as you hoped. Maybe in time, the authorities will investigate your sister's strange tales, but it's more likely that they'll simply dismiss her bizarre and surreal ramblings. As for Hagalaz? Well, he might reveal the location of the secret passageway, but until then, you while away the days by watching the Retreat through the mural in the dining room. It's got new management now and Metamorphosis is ancient history. Occasionally, someone spots you and the cats in the mural, but the Drudes are still doing a great job of convincing them that it's the nightmares messing with their minds! And who knows? Maybe one day they'll be rewarded by Freyja's triumphant return.

But before you go, why not turn to **426**, so you can discover what The Cluster will do now…

388

You stay in the hallway but listen intently as Hagalaz bustles into the playroom. There is a very protracted silence, then a gut-wrenching mixture of porcine squeal, roar and wail fills the house. The boar sounds utterly heartbroken, and you feel a slight twinge of guilt at being the one to bring such bad tidings.

Nevertheless, Hagalaz now realises that Mother Amber or Freyja or whoever she is, smashes the cribs to bits in a petulant tantrum and that's how little she values Hagalaz and his birch offerings. Tick the codeword **BETRAYAL**, then turn to **404**.

389

With a twist of the lever, there is a muted gurgle and the snails are now freely roaming the lake. A quick peek out of the window tells you nothing, but then you weren't exactly expecting to see them galloping away! Oh well, that didn't achieve anything too exciting, but you should still tick the codeword **GASTROPOD**. Seeing as you don't want a mass slaughter of aquatic creatures on your conscience, you decide to obey the instruction and release no more, so now you can either look through the cupboards and drawers if you haven't done so already (turn to **331**) or head down to the cellar (turn to **397**).

You troop into the living room and head over to the wall where the thick, gnarled tree root protrudes through. So far, so good and now, you just need to make the passageway open up.

'It doesn't matter what you do. I'm not coming with you. Mother Amber will test our commitment and I will not fail her!' your sister insists again, which annoys you, but this is not the time for sibling bickering. The water has now reached your hips, so if somebody told you the instructions, you should do that **immediately**. However, even if no one told you how to activate the conduit, it's still not over! Have a look inside your pockets or bag and see if you acquired the topaz runestone of Eihwaz. If you have it, turn to **374**. If not, you really are running out of options, and you'll just have to turn to **346** and think of something else.

391

You, Hagalaz and Freyja freeze and listen, heads all tilted to one side. The noise occurs again and this time it's clear — it's just the boiler! Freyja turns to you and smiles. It is a self-satisfied smirk and so it should be. You have neither convinced the God of the error of her ways nor rescued your sister. Your well-intentioned heroics have actually been a resounding failure, but there's no time to dwell on that.

Freyja strides forward and picks you up by the throat. The choking is bad enough, but as her temper boils over again, she starts to pound you bodily against the wall. You will be long dead by the time Freyja eventually calms down, but no doubt, your sacrifice will be greatly appreciated by this deity.

392

The heavy wooden drawers slide open with juddering squeaks and you find an array of bizarre items: garden secateurs, a dried, pressed bluebell, a walkie talkie and an ornate but weirdly shaped helmet. You examine this with interest, but the only thing you can conclude is that the helmet would not fit any *human* head. You throw it back into the drawer and stand up. Now what? You could peruse the bookshelves (turn to **375**) but if you've already done that, you leave the study and continue towards the end of the hallway (turn to **329**).

393

She drops back down again, unable to hold herself up at the bars for any longer, but you hear her say, 'Please don't forget about me. I had my baby a month ago, but I haven't seen him. She keeps me here. I want to find my baby and go back to Phillip. I have to get out!' It sounds like she's about to say more but abruptly stops. After a few tense seconds, she quietly announces, 'She's here!' Despite having no plan of action, you vault for the stairs — you're not letting Mother bloody Amber get away now! Turn to **362**.

The apparent leader of this cluster — a strange, featureless, shifting, black shape — steps forward and gives a nervous cough, but before it can say anything, Freyja starts chanting weird words and making ornate gestures with her hands. Is she summoning someone? Everyone pauses and looks around expectantly, but nothing happens. She repeats the whole thing but again, nothing happens. Freyja looks wildly around before exploding at the assembled group.

'Where is my coat?' she demands to know. Well, you weren't expecting that! All this over a coat? Hagalaz shuffles reluctantly forward and whispers in her ear. Everyone watches with bated breath and then the second explosion comes.

'Burnt? BURNT! Who burnt my coat? I'll kill them. I'll rip their lungs out. I'll…'

'Now then, Freyja, enough of this nonsense,' interrupts the shadowy shape, 'We've got a job to do. You had a job to do.'

'And I did it,' she screams, 'Look how adored I am. These sheep worship me. I told you love was the best way to keep them under control. I was right!'

The shape seems slightly alarmed by how unhinged she is and looks back at the other two figures for guidance. One steps forward, nods his head and says, 'I'm Al-Kutbay, this is Cai-shen and this…' gesturing to the shape, '…is The Machinator. We are The Cluster. Normally, we don't meet… people. This is a bit awkward.' That's the understatement of the day, you think, as a long silence follows. Only when one of the babies gurgles, does The Machinator speak up again.

'Exactly,' it says, although whether it's agreeing with the baby or its own thoughts, is unclear. 'Freyja, your experiment here hasn't been a total failure, but you have rather overstepped the mark in many ways, and we cannot allow this to continue any longer.'

Cai-shen nods and repeats 'Any longer,' which puts The Machinator off its stride, but it also looks grateful for the support and continues, 'You cannot escape without your coat, so you have no option but to terminate the experiment and return to The Cluster.'

After another protracted pause, Freyja nods resignedly, gathers her strength and pride, then goes to stand with the other three. And in a heartbeat they all vanish.

You whisper, 'Where have they gone?' but nobody answers. There is simply a stunned silence. Tick the codeword **WUNJO** then turn to **348**.

395

Well, well, well. Contrary to your pessimistic prediction, there is something very interesting lurking behind an old cereal box. A keypad with a yellowed and tatty label — 'Cell Doors' — taped above it and judging from the screen, you have to input a 3-digit number. If your maths is correct, there are 1000 different combinations, but you don't have time to waste in trial and error. Have you found a note in the submerged house that you think could be useful here? If so, turn now to **357**, but if not, continue reading.

Not willing to give up so easily, you keep pushing random buttons, before eventually accepting that today is not going to be your day. With a mini-tantrum and a curse, you slam the pantry door shut and stomp back into the hall. Turn to **370**.

You approach the window and look out into the murky depths of the lake. Just as you dreaded, the woman is pointing at the array of fettered corpses swaying back and forth in a gentle current. Did you miss her? Is your sister tied up in the plants with her throat sliced open? You scrutinise each face but it's not easy. Some have plainly been down here for a long time… After a while, you give up and are about to ask her which one your sister is, but then notice the tears running down her face and realisation hits you.

'Oh, *your* sister!'

She nods and sniffs, so you give your condolences, then wonder how you can sensitively turn this conversation around to the half-dead babies in here. After all, that seems to be more important given the circumstances.

'Need to free her. Free them all,' she mutters.

'Well yes, but are these your babies?'

Not exactly subtle, but sometimes the direct approach is the best. Not here though. Judging by her matted hair and dirty, worn clothes, she's been here a while and is beyond anyone's reach. Instead of answering, she rocks back and forth and, in a singsong, child-like voice, says:

'It has no legs but has a foot

And tentacles but has no arms

They can be cooked but die with salt

And man can't carry what they can.'

And with that, the woman is lost in her own world. If you know the answer to the riddle, that may come in handy later, but you can't waste any more time here. Suddenly, you freeze. What was that noise? You wait and… there it is again! It sounds like it's coming from the far end of the hall, so you tiptoe to the door, sneak out and head there to investigate. Turn to **381**.

You've watched enough horror films to know that cellars are the worst place to go, and this is no different. You reach the bottom of the narrow staircase and see the first row of cell doors ahead. Actual cell doors with bars and there are many rows down here! Without having any plan in mind, you opt for the easiest thing and just shout out your sister's name. You're not expecting anything to come of this, so it's a total shock when she replies, 'Is it you? What are you doing here?' You rush over and pull on the cell door but of course, it is locked.

'I can't believe I've found you,' you say. 'Don't worry, I'll get you out.'

'Get out? I'm not leaving! Mother Amber is my family now. And I've only got three months to go.' This statement, said with a calm and sincere voice, shakes you to the core. Although you knew she'd been influenced by the cult, you weren't expecting such devotion. She's in a cell, after all! And then, the other words filter into your brain. Three months to go! You grab the bars and pull yourself up, so that you can see through the small opening. It's just a glimpse but it's enough to see that she is, indeed, pregnant. You swear under your breath and are so engrossed with trying to factor this into your plan, that you barely register the small speaker in the corner of her cell. Finally though, you point to it and ask, 'Why is that there?' Your sister smiles beatifically and replies, 'So Mother can bestow us with her blessings.' Just then, she gasps and points at your neck.

If you have a rather valuable piece of jewellery there, you must immediately turn to **425**. Otherwise, your sister has merely spotted the long scratch from the

Aufhocker, but before you can explain yourself, you hear two other voices from their cells, both beseeching you to come to them. Do you approach the one whose cell is nearest to the stairs (turn to **333**) or the one whose cell is furthest away (turn to **340**)? There is, however, a third, silent cell in this row and if you want to investigate, turn to **386**.

398

For a tense few seconds, you think that Hagalaz might defy her. It's difficult to read a boar's emotion, so you can't really tell, but then you hear, 'Whatever you wish for, I am your humble servant.' Oh. That does not sound good!

However, by the skin of your teeth, you get a reprieve when there is noise from somewhere else in the house. Before we find out what *that's* all about, we must know whether you've ticked the codeword FREEDOM. If you have, turn to **351**. If not, turn to **391**.

399

You give a cursory flick through the magazines because you never know what you'll find. Unfortunately, on this occasion, your instincts are correct. They're a mixture of genres — 'Trends in Bio-engineering', 'Nordic Hair' and 'The Douglas Herald' — but none are interesting. Articles about genius schoolgirls who reach the final in the great Golden Hare treasure hunt do not sound useful in situations like this! You continue to the door and once back in the hall, decide where to go next. You can go to the room that is now straight ahead (turn to **406**) or the one that is now on your left (turn to **338**).

400

The runestone Tyr represents courage, willingness to self-sacrifice and above all, victory! You emerge from a crack in the trunk of a great tree, accidentally kick over one of the 8 mushrooms and inhale the sweet fresh air in the forest. As the others join you, there are smiles and tears, and you hug your sister with relief at being finally free from Freyja's grasp. Free to go home and safe in the knowledge that Mother Amber and Metamorphosis are no more. With barely a backward glance, you bid farewell to the Retreat and head to the airport.

But before you go, why not turn to **426**, so you can discover what The Cluster will do now…

401

With a twist of the lever, there is a muted gurgle and the carp are now freely roaming the lake. A quick peek out of the window reveals a dense shoal of fish, which dart quickly away from the house and are soon out of sight! Oh well, that didn't achieve anything too exciting, but hopefully the carp are happy with their new-found freedom. Seeing as you don't want a mass slaughter of aquatic creatures on your conscience, you decide to obey the instruction and release no more, then head over to see if the pantry has anything interesting to offer. Turn to **395**.

The dressing table used to have a trio of mirrors but the frames are empty now, save for a few jutting shards of glass. It also has three slim drawers, which don't look like they can contain much, but to your surprise, you find a beautiful **gold and amber necklace**. Although it must be incredibly valuable, stealing precious jewellery is probably not the best way to win Mother Amber over. Nevertheless, if you decide to take it, slip it around your neck and make a note of your theft, then if you haven't done so already, you could check out the chest of drawers (turn to **335**). If you've seen all you want to see in this room, you should leave now and continue along the hallway (turn to **369**).

403

Well, unless a submarine magically arrives, there's only one solution. You wade down the hall towards the door and pick up the scuba gear you discarded earlier.

'It's the only way,' you say to your sister, 'I came here to rescue you and that's what I'll do. The others can't do it with the babies, but you're not so big that you can't fit in the wet suit. You have to do it. For me, please and once you're out, you can get help for us.' At that moment, you both look around at the rapidly rising water and know that there will be no time for another rescue mission. The mathematics are undeniable — two people will be saved instead of one — so your sister reluctantly pulls on the wet suit and heads out to safety. If you earlier ticked the codeword TYR, turn to **368**. However, if you ticked WUNJO, turn to **387**.

404

You know you can't stand in the hallway for ever, but before you can go anywhere or do anything, you hear the sound of stomping feet. Abruptly, Mother Amber reappears in front of you and she looks furious.

'What did you do, weak one?' Although you are undeniably scared, she is starting to get on your nerves, so in response, you snap, 'What now, Freyja? Am I not worshipping you enough?' She gives a worrying snarl at your impunity and the casual use of her true name — she's used to more adoration than that! However, she also looks unsure, which has to be good for you. By the way, did you tick the codeword GASTROPOD? If you have, turn to **330**. If not, turn to **347**.

405

You touch the tree root and say, 'Yggdrasil'. To your amazement — you didn't think it would actually work — cracks appear in the plaster and a fissure opens up in the wall revealing a dark, thin passageway. Squeezing into it is a nightmarish prospect, but then so is staying in the submerged house. With no other option, you grit your teeth and lead everyone into the twisting and claustrophobic tunnel. If you ticked the codeword TYR, turn to **400**. If you ticked WUNJO, turn to **343**.

406

This door is locked, and if someone has gone to so much trouble, they must have something pretty important in there. You're convinced that it must be the way to go, but do you want to check out the other two rooms before you tackle this one? If you do, you turn around and can either go to the door that's now straight ahead (turn to **409**) or into the room that's now on your right (turn to **338**).

If you do want to enter this mysterious room, you must unlock it first. But that should be easy — someone has scrawled a clue in a Metamorphosis-type rhyme on the door, and there are 5 scribbled out letters.

TO ENTER THE KI CHEN, PAY REYJA THE PR CE

GIFT HER YOUR BAB , SUPREME SACRI ICE

Once you've identified the 5 missing letters, rearrange the anagram to spell a number, then **subtract** that from this section and turn to the new section. For example, if the missing letters were G, E, H, I, T, you might think that they spell EIGHT and you would then turn to 398 (406 – 8 = 398). If this is all too difficult, then you can have a look around the house again, but deep down, you know that you have failed in your rescue mission and may even pay with your life.

407

One look tells you this is a fool's errand. There's no way you can search the cabinet with all this crockery in the way, but a quick peek does pay a small dividend — there's a bright red, plastic baby's dummy tucked between the plates and bowls. This discovery is both curious and unsettling, but you've got bigger fish to fry, so you head back into the hallway (turn to **383**).

408

The runestone Tyr represents leadership, willingness to self-sacrifice and above all, victory! It doesn't feel like a victory though, as the lake water now laps around your chest, but at that moment, there's a hiss from the top of the kitchen cabinets. The blue cats had retreated there for safety; however, the water is getting too close for their liking. You have no idea what power they invoke, but before your eyes, the water begins to drop and soon the house is back to its submerged yet dry self.

'I thought Freyja had ceased to exist?' you ask the felines, and they merely nod in agreement.

'Then, how…?'

With that, they smirk at each other, then stalk towards the study to curl up in front of the fire. It would seem that you're not getting any answers from them!

So, your sister is safe and so are you, although it didn't quite work out as you hoped. Your sister doesn't report any of this — she simply refuses to accept that Freyja has truly gone and instead waits loyally for her resurrection. Maybe you'll eventually convince Hagalaz to reveal the location of the secret passageway, but until then, you while away the days by watching the Retreat through the mural in the dining room. It's got new management now and Metamorphosis is ancient history. Occasionally, someone spots you and the cats in the mural, but the Drudes are still doing a great job of convincing them that it's the nightmares messing with their minds! It would seem that it's not only your sister who's waiting for Freyja's return.

And before you go, why not turn to **426**, so you can discover what The Cluster will do now…

409

It's a fairly well-kept living room, although there's not a lot of furniture — just a magazine rack and a sofa facing the television. Wait! What? A television? If only to satisfy your curiosity as to whether it actually works, you switch it on, then sit down. With a burst of static, the screen clears and the TV comes to life. Judging from the fashions, it appears to be an eighties quiz show and the host shows a die to the camera, then says to the earnest but dim contestants:

'… so the item brought in by Parsimony was the die and the clue was: "Sister, sister, heed our call; strength in numbers or else you'll fall; chasing ghosts or chasing hares; was once a folly but now  he cares; all your wits you'll need to muster; to pass the test set by The Cluster." Well, that's not easy, is it, Clive and Barbara? Do you have any ideas what it could be?'

The couple look poleaxed, then Clive says, 'I think it could be the bin, Ted.'

Unfortunately, you'll never know if Clive was right, because at that point, the television promptly dies, leaving only the white spot from the cathode ray on the screen. You decide to leave now, but when you get up from the sofa, do you go to the left, which takes you past the window (turn to **372**) or to the right where the magazine rack is (turn to **399**)?

410

You touch the tree root and say, 'Yggdrasil'. To your amazement — you didn't think it would actually work — cracks appear in the plaster and a fissure opens up in the wall revealing a dark, thin passageway. Squeezing into it is a nightmarish prospect, but then so is staying in the submerged house. With no other option, you grit your teeth and try, once more, to persuade your sister into the twisting and claustrophobic tunnel. If you ticked the codeword TYR, turn to **355**. If you ticked WUNJO, turn to **364**.

411

There are three of them — industrial, thick metal tanks with tubes and pipes going in and out. Through a tiny gap at the top, you can just about make out ripples of aerated water but certainly not what is in them. Not that you need to, because each tank is labelled and apparently contain 'Grass Carp', 'Pond snails' and 'Red cherry shrimp'. At the back of the tanks is a small, hand-written sign instructing whoever that "only one should ever be released. They should never be released into the lake together!!" Would they eat each other, you wonder? Have a huge battle to the death? As you mull over this you notice that there is, indeed, a release valve at the back of each tank, so if you want to free the creatures from one of the tanks you can. Maybe it is potluck or maybe you have an inkling of which one you should release, even if you don't know why…

So, do you release the carp (turn to **401**), the snails (turn to **366**) or the shrimp (turn to **334**)?

412

'Now you will wish that you never came here. No one insults a God! Do your worst, Hagalaz!' she cries with a triumphant punch in the air. You take a deep breath and wait, wide-eyed and frozen with fear, for the boar to charge. Only it doesn't. Hagalaz doesn't move, except to blink and give the occasional snort.

'Hagalaz, what are you doing? You disobey me?' Freyja is plainly losing her temper again and she yells, 'Are you a traitor? Are you not worthy of my love?'

A painful silence follows, but eventually the boar says, 'You broke them! I brought all that birch for your cribs. So much love went into that collection, but you smashed them to bits and threw them to one side as if they were nothing more than rubbish. All that love and you never cared...' It would be an Oscar winning performance, except for the fact that the boar is not acting. There are genuine tears rolling down the coarse, grey cheeks. Hagalaz is truly heartbroken. Freyja looks wounded, almost distraught by this, but then you see her expression harden and with a sneer, she shouts, 'Of course, I broke the cribs. The babies died, what was I supposed to do? If you'd made good cribs; if you'd have picked the best birch, they would have lived. It's all your fault! I only kept you on here because I felt sorry for you and this is what I get in return!'

At this point, Freyja has reached a crescendo of rabid aggression and there's no way to diffuse this. All you can do is get safely out of the way, while she erupts.

However, before you duck and cower from Freyja's almighty fury, we really must factor in whether you ticked the codeword FREEDOM. If you did, turn to **367**. If not, turn to **339**.

413

It's difficult to tell what the multicoloured brick building was meant to be. It has plenty of windows, doors and rooms, and even a set of rudimentary stairs, but now you come to mention it, there is something strange about it — every wall has a double layer of bricks, like exterior walls have, so that insulation foam can go in between, only this doesn't have foam… You wrinkle your nose in disgust at the piece of blackened, dried flesh wedged between the bricks. Once you find a long, thin yellow Lego brick, you poke it in and nimbly flick the object out, only to instantly wish you hadn't. It's a piece of umbilical cord. The part that stays with the baby for a few days until it drops off naturally. It still has the plastic clamp on one end! What is it doing between the walls in a Lego building? With a 'Urgh', you stand up, feeling both confused and disgusted. If you haven't already done so and want to risk searching the doll's house, you should turn to **349**.

If you're ready to leave the playroom, you could go back towards the entrance and enter the first room on the right if you haven't been there yet (turn to **377**). Alternatively, you could either continue along the corridor and go through the second door on the right-hand side (turn to **352**) or ignore that and head towards the end of the hallway (turn to **329**).

414

You rummage quickly through your bag, while Freyja looks on bemused. Maybe you have a knife sharpener which you could bludgeon her over the head with or perhaps you found some tins of cat food that you could throw at her…

'What are you doing?' she asks disdainfully. 'Are you actually going to attack me?'

You gulp — what were you thinking? — it's a preposterous idea. You wonder whether you should fall on your knees and beg for forgiveness, but then Freyja surprises you by bursting into laughter. A huge belly-shaking laugh that doubles her over and even makes her slap her thigh. You feel slightly humiliated by this derogatory assessment of your fighting skills, but otherwise are relieved that she's in a good mood again. This doesn't last long though — she is mercurial, to say the least — and soon she remembers that she's furious with you. With eyes like daggers, she glares, then throws her head back and bellows: 'HAGALAZ!' Turn to **353**.

415

You brace yourself, but the boar puts the trotter back down, lowers its head to delicately drop the twigs on the carpet and says, 'I'd rather not attack you if I don't have to. I mean, I don't want to damage the precious birch. Are you here to cause trouble for Freyja?'

Your jaw drops. It's a talking pig! But before you manage to inadvertently insult anyone, you shake your head and say earnestly, 'I'm not here to hurt anyone. I just want to rescue my sister.' The boar frowns at this.

'I, Hagalaz, bring offerings and birch for the cribs. Your sister will bring a baby to show her love for Freyja. Why should she need rescuing? It is an honour!' There is an awkward pause, then you say, 'I don't understand. Where I come from, babies are the most important thing in a family. When they cry, they get fed. When they want to be held, someone picks them up. The world revolves around them.'

Hagalaz simply looks confused at this notion but tries to explain how it is. Turn to **350**.

416

It's dark inside but when you reach towards the light switch, a voice hisses, 'Don't! It upsets them.'

You gulp and peer around the room. You can see odd shapes in the middle and a person moving towards the far wall. The woman switches on a small lamp, then walks back to her chair, but you are more stunned by the furniture in here. The room has three cots in it — strange and uncomfortable cribs made entirely of birch twigs bound together — and all are occupied. You edge closer and see babies lying in them. At first, you have the sickening thought that they are all dead, but then one makes a tiny squirm and another whimpers. They are alive but only just! Is this woman supposed to be caring for them? Before you can interrogate her though, she gasps, points to something outside the window, then whispers, 'Sister!'

Sister? Does she mean your sister? Outside in the lake? Or is this a trick, a distraction? If you want to look at what she's pointing at, (turn to **396**) but if you'd rather grab her, pin her to the floor and demand that she answers your questions, (turn to **363**).

The apparent leader of this cluster — a strange, featureless, shifting, black shape — steps forward and gives a nervous cough, but before it can say anything, Freyja starts chanting weird words and making ornate gestures with her hands. Is she summoning someone? Everyone pauses and looks around expectantly, but nothing happens. She repeats the whole thing but again, nothing happens. Freyja looks wildly around before exploding at the assembled group.

'Where is my coat?' she demands to know. Well, you weren't expecting that! All this over a coat? At this point, Hagalaz shuffles reluctantly forward and whispers in her ear. Everyone watches with bated breath and then the second explosion comes.

'Burnt? BURNT! Who burnt my coat? I'll kill them. I'll rip their lungs out. I'll…'

'Now then, Freyja, enough of this nonsense,' interrupts the shadowy shape, 'We've got a job to do. You *had* a job to do.'

'And I did it,' she screams, 'Look how adored I am. These sheep worship me. I told you love was the best way to keep them under control. I was right!'

The shape seems slightly alarmed by how unhinged she is and looks back at the other two figures for guidance. One steps forward, nods his head and says, 'I'm Al-Kutbay, this is Cai-shen and this…' gesturing to the shape, '…is The Machinator. We are The Cluster. Normally, we don't meet… people. This is a bit awkward.' That's the understatement of the day, you think, as a long silence follows. Only when one of the babies gurgles, does The Machinator speak up again.

'Exactly,' it says, although whether it's agreeing with the baby or its own thoughts, is unclear. 'Freyja, your experiment here has failed. You were right to reprimand Al-Kutbay on his somewhat cavalier approach to the babies in The Crucible, but what you have done here is much worse.'

Cai-shen nods and repeats 'Much worse,' which puts The Machinator off its stride, but it also looks grateful for the support and continues, 'You cannot escape without your coat, so as a God faced with their own hypocrisy there is only one path forward for you now. You know what you must do, Freyja.'

After another long pause, Freyja nods sadly, gathers her strength and pride, then stands tall and… is gone.

One of the women whispers, 'What's just happened?' and The Machinator replies solemnly, 'She has ceased to exist,' as if that explains everything, before blustering on: 'Now then, all well and good, time for us to go too, very busy, oh yes, nice to meet you' and suddenly, The Cluster has vanished as well, leaving you, Hagalaz, the women and their babies in stunned silence. Tick the codeword **TYR** then turn to **348**.

418

You present the runestone to the root then wait. Little did you know, but Eihwaz represents Yggdrasil — the Tree of Life — and it is indeed a conduit. To your amazement, cracks appear in the plaster and a fissure opens up in the wall revealing a dark, thin passageway. Squeezing into it is a nightmarish prospect, but then so is staying in the submerged house. With no other option, you grit your teeth and lead everyone into the twisting and claustrophobic tunnel. If you ticked the codeword TYR, turn to **400**. If you ticked WUNJO, turn to **343**.

You peer into the doll-sized master bedroom and see a rusting bed frame, a broken dressing table and a chest of drawers. You're about to give up the search when you spot some loose sticky tape — something has been secured to the ceiling of the tiny room! It's a bit fiddly, but eventually you rip the rest of the tape off and retrieve the tiny object. It's a brass key. You look for any markings or clues to what it opens, however, it just has the serial number **CE38214** etched on. Nevertheless, it may prove useful, so you tuck it into a pocket for safekeeping. Note that you have a **tiny, brass key**, and then if you haven't already done so, you could check out the Lego building, turn to **413.**

If you're ready to leave the playroom, you could go back towards the entrance and enter the first room on the right if you haven't been there yet (turn to **377**). Alternatively, you could either continue along the corridor and go through the second door on the right-hand side (turn to **352**) or ignore that and head towards the end of the hallway (turn to **329**).

You don't dare get any closer, so instead you shout, 'The cats are Mother Amber's favourite!' The effect is instantaneous. The boar's shoulders slump with abject disappointment and its head tilts to the side, a confused frown crinkling its coarse grey head.

'Really?'

In the stunned silence that follows, you realise that not only has the boar spoken, but it has spoken to you and is waiting for an answer.

'Um, yes,' you eventually reply, but from the far end of the hallway, there is a loud and mocking scoff. With some pushing and shoving, and the occasional 'Move over, Hagalaz!', two blue cats squeeze their way past the boar's bulk, then sit in front of you. One of them blinks and looks haughtily first at you, then the boar, then back at you again.

'Where did you hear that nonsense?' It eventually asks, then without giving you any chance to speak, says to the boar, 'Don't listen to such rubbish, Hagalaz. If Freyja has any favourites, it's herself. It always has been. You know how vain and self-centred she is!' It turns back to you and hisses, 'Well?'

They are very intimidating cats, so you tell them about the grey-haired women. At that, the other one smiles admiringly and says, 'Oh, I like the Grey Women. Very clever, very generous with cooked chicken. Freyja has always tried to get them on her side and a formidable alliance that would be, but they remain loyal to Hecate. No, no, we are not Freyja's favourite. In fact, we're only here for the carp!'

The blue cats then elegantly walk away, and Hagalaz tries to explain how it is. Turn to **350**.

With all the drama, you'd forgotten about the women imprisoned in the cellar. You did wonder where they'd gone after you unlocked the cells and here is your answer — they'd gone to find their children. The three mothers enter the hall, all cradling their babies, who, now that they've been fed and cuddled, are sleeping contentedly. Freyja points and starts to splutter, 'They are mine...' but one of the women steps forward and spits at Freyja. That is shocking enough, but when she also decisively says, 'You are no mother,' there is a collective gasp. Surely, that is a step too far. There's no way that Freyja will tolerate such a condemning insult.

At that precise moment though, there is a shadowy shimmer in the hallway and a cluster of figures materialises. From Freyja's expression, you guess she knows who they are and is not pleased to see them. However, the introductions must wait for now because if you've ticked the codeword BURNT FEATHERS, you should turn to **394**. If not, turn to **373**.

There are three of them — industrial, thick metal tanks with tubes and pipes going in and out. Through a tiny gap at the top, you can just about make out ripples of aerated water but certainly not what is in them. Not that you need to, because each tank is labelled and apparently contain 'Grass Carp', 'Pond snails' and 'Red cherry shrimp'. At the back of the tanks is a small, hand-written sign instructing whoever that "only one should ever be released. They should never be released into the lake together!!" Would they eat each other, you wonder? Have a huge battle to the death? As you mull over this you notice that there is, indeed, a release valve at the back of each tank, so if you want to free the creatures from one of the tanks you can. Maybe it is potluck or maybe you have an inkling of which one you should release, even if you don't know why…

So, do you release the carp (turn to **359**), the snails (turn to **389**) or the shrimp (turn to **371**)?

You really haven't thought this through properly, in fact, you only start to wonder what you're going to do with the necklace as you're pulling it out of your bag. Threaten to smash it? Pretend that you found it? What? Maybe this wasn't such a good idea after all… Your fears are groundless though. Freyja casts a disinterested eye over the gold and amber jewellery and shrugs.

'Oh, you've got Brísingamen. I haven't seen that in a while.' Well, this wasn't the reaction you were hoping for but at least she seems calmer.

'I used to take Brísingamen everywhere with me,' she reminisces. 'It made me irresistible, made people love me, but I didn't need it here. It was funny. I just told people how special they were to be picked by me and that was that. All the rest, the metamorphosis, healthy eating, mindfulness stuff — they came up with that themselves. The whole thing just snowballed. I put the necklace in a drawer and haven't used it in ages!'

You think you're in the clear now, but abruptly, her mercurial mood changes again and she remembers that she's furious with you. With eyes like daggers, she glares, then throws her head back and bellows: 'HAGALAZ!' Turn to **345**.

424

She agrees to go with you into the living room and sits down on the sofa. You're wondering how to broach this but there's no need to worry — Mother Amber is more than happy to talk.

'I suppose the Grey Women helped you, didn't they? You know, I asked Hecate to support me. I told her all about what The Cluster did with the prion and the babies and the zombie disease, but would she help me?' This is obviously a rhetorical question, because she doesn't even look at you, never mind wait for a response. 'No, she doesn't! Says that the witches will never be party to such atrocities. Atrocities, I ask you! People have always sacrificed their most beloved to their gods. How else can they prove their devotion? But when I do it, suddenly it's an atrocity!'

At this point, you interject with, 'But the babies are given to you healthy, aren't they? So why do they die?' Mother Amber slams her fist down on a cushion.

'Exactly! And that's where the problem lies. I accept the gift and put them into the birch cribs that Hagalaz makes, but then they die! Why do they die?'

You quickly mull over the possibilities, then ask, 'Do you feed them?'

Mother Amber looks genuinely confused at this question, but finally replies, 'Why should I do that? I'm the God of love. Surely being accepted by a god is all they need. Maybe the mother's sacrifice is not given to me willingly and with a full heart...' She stares into space, apparently missing the point that babies actually need milk. Although you're worried about pushing your luck, you have to know the truth about the green, stinking ooze that weeps from behind the Walls in the Retreat, so say, 'And when they die, you brick the bodies up, don't you?

She looks at you with astonishment, then says, 'But of course! How else can you make a building more impenetrable, more able to withstand an attack? It has to be fortified with the blood of the innocents!' It's on the tip of your tongue to say 'reinforced steel girders', but the moment has passed. Mother Amber suddenly leaps to her feet, states, 'Hagalaz calls me!', then leaves. For someone as tall and well-built as she is, Mother Amber moves remarkably swiftly and silently, and you have no idea where she has gone to, just that she has gone. You exit the living room too and head back into the kitchen. Turn to **376**.

'What are you doing with Mother's necklace? You're going to ruin everything and I'm so close to full transformation! Give it to me!' With that, she reaches through the bars and tries to grab the jewellery. When

that fails, she rummages in her own pockets and brings out a topaz runestone, saying, 'I'll swap you. Please!' This is said in a desperate tone that rapidly disintegrates into sobbing hysteria. Well,
this is a tricky one. Do you barter or not? What is more important? Keeping the necklace or soothing your distraught sister? Maybe the runestone is more precious than the necklace, but maybe you've already acquired this particular runestone so you could keep them both... Make your decision then record which items you have now placed out of sight in your bag.

However, if you refuse to take her runestone, your sister has a temper tantrum and flings it across the cell, where it happens to roll into a drain and is most definitely gone for good.

It might be a good idea to speak to some of the other prisoners now, so do you go to the cell nearest to the stairs (turn to **333**) or the one which is furthest away (turn to **340**)? However, if you want to investigate the third, silent cell in this row, turn to **386**.

The Cluster — now reduced from five to three — sit around the table in silence. Occasionally, Al-Kutbay sighs and Cai-shen drums his fingers and they muse upon the fourth, failed experiment. Finally, The Machinator stands, gives a brisk clap and says, 'Well, onwards and up! Remember, even when the experiment doesn't go so well, we still glean valuable information from it!'

'Your relentless optimism is getting on my nerves!' snaps Al-Kutbay, 'I don't even know anymore why we're bothering with the humans. Who cares if they can be controlled or not? They'll all be extinct soon enough!'

'Oh, that's just typical! Try to stop the experiments before I get my go! Just because you know that my way will be the best one! You can be so petty,' accuses Cai-shen.

The Cluster are not known for acts of physical violence against each other, so the pair simply sit back, fume and glare at each other.

'Of course, we're not going to stop the experiments,' The Machinator states. 'We have learnt so much about this fascinating species, but there is more to discover, and I'm sure that your methodology, Cai-shen, will highlight some interesting facets of their intellect and emotions. We haven't tested greed yet…'

Silence descends again, until Al-Kutbay suddenly asks, 'What was the name of that boar?'

'Hagalaz, I believe. Why?'

'I thought Freyja's boar was called Hildisvíni.'

'Oh, that was an earlier one. He left her when she lost his helmet but refused to apologise, then claimed he was overreacting and should be grateful that she let him serve her at all, then did some quality gaslighting by insisting that he never had a helmet in the first place!'

'To be honest,' says The Machinator, 'The red flags about Freyja were there all along, weren't they? Still, the next one will work, I'm sure of it! When will you start?'

Cai-shen smiles, then replies, 'Soon. Very soon.'

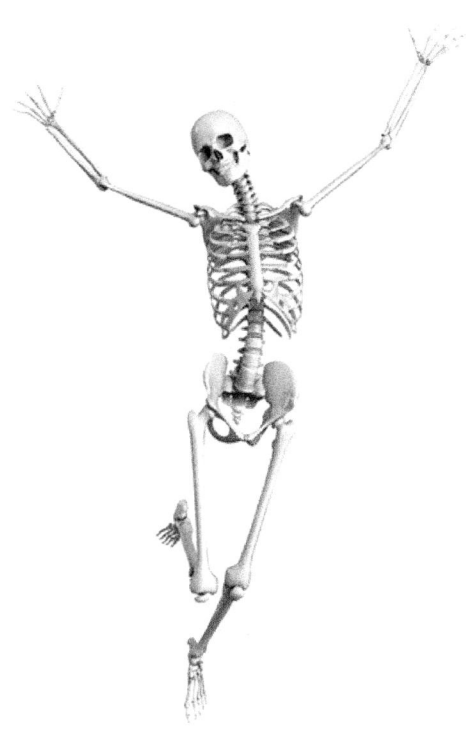

Printed in Great Britain
by Amazon

11633309R00185